IN SEARCH OF NEW BABYLON

A NOVEL BY

DOMINIQUE SCALI

TRANSLATED BY W. DONALD WILSON

TALONBOOKS

Talonbooks
278 East First Avenue, Vancouver, British Columbia, Canada V5T 1A6
www.talonbooks.com

First printing: 2017

Typeset in FF More
Printed and bound in Canada on 100% post-consumer recycled paper

Interior and cover design by Typesmith

Talonbooks acknowledges the financial support of the Canada Council for the Arts, the Government of Canada through the Canada Book Fund, and the Province of British Columbia through the British Columbia Arts Council and the Book Publishing Tax Credit.

This work was originally published in French as *À la recherche de New Babylon* by Éditions La Peuplade of Chicoutimi, Quebec, in 2015. We acknowledge the financial support of the Government of Canada, through the National Translation Program for Book Publishing, an initiative of the *Roadmap for Canada's Official Languages 2013–2018: Education, Immigration, Communities*, for our translation activities.

Library and Archives Canada Cataloguing in Publication

Scali, Dominique
[À la recherche de New Babylon. English]
      In search of New Babylon / by Dominique Scali ; translated by W. Donald Wilson.

Translation of: À la recherche de New Babylon.
Issued in print and electronic formats.
ISBN 978-1-77201-124-1 (softcover).– ISBN 978-1-77201-125-8 (EPUB). –
ISBN 978-1-77201-126-5 (Kindle). – ISBN 978-1-77201-127-2 (PDF)

      I. Wilson, W. Donald, 1938–, translator II. Title.
III. Title: À la recherche de New Babylon. English

PS8637.C25A6613 2017   C843'.6   C2016-907740-3   C2016-907741-1

I knew it would end like this.
With me dying and you looking on.

———◆◇◆———

PROLOGUE

Memoirs of a
Silent Preacher

PARIA, 1881

PARIA

MAY 1881

Three long guns rested on hooks in a place of honour to the left of the chimney piece. The first was a bayonetted musket used by the great-grandfather in the Revolutionary War. The second was a flintlock rifle used by the grandfather in the Mexican War. The third was a breech-loading carbine carried by the father in the Civil War. Though they were displayed like trophies, all were loaded, ready to be used again and again.

In other times and in other places, boys would try to scare their little sisters by telling tales of wild wolves that would come in the middle of the night to gobble them up. But here, north of Vermilion Cliffs, there were no wolves, only Navajos and Mormons. There was no forest in which animals could take cover, only ancient red rock formations that stood like statues. In this harsh landscape, the only possible threat was a human one.

✯

The sudden wail must have made the Seveners think the Navajo had captured a member of the family and scalped him. It was a long, hoarse scream, full of pain and horror, a gash in the soundscape saying that it was already too late. To be heard, the wail had to have been louder than the kettle's whistle or the clatter of the sewing machine in the kitchen where the mother worked with her children nearby. It had to make its way between the hammer blows the father was striking below the guardrail. It had to travel over the hills and above the bellowing steers to reach the boys rounding up the herd that grazed three miles away. No doubt an echo reverberated against the valley walls, amplifying it just enough for a shudder to run through each family member in the same instant.

The horses began to neigh, the dogs to bark, and the baby to bawl. The father went upstairs while the daughters, armed with guns they had never fired, closed the shutters and hid beneath the kitchen table. The mother picked up a cast-iron skillet, sobbing because the newborn in her arms wouldn't stop crying. The women heard the floorboards creak overhead as the father moved from room to room, poking the muzzle of his hunting rifle through each window, scanning the horizon with no idea where the enemy might appear.

⚹

The Seveners had never been attacked by the Navajo or any other tribe. Those peoples had all been pacified and parked on reservations, except for a few bands of Apache. But with Indians it was like with ghosts: you didn't need to see them for them to keep you awake at night.

In Paria, people used to say that at one time surprise Apache raids could turn a perfectly thriving hamlet into a ghost village overnight. Its inhabitants were left ossified in death as if moulded in blood, and for weeks no one disturbed their slumber.

In times of peace, fear faded away. When it returned, people wondered how they could have forgotten it, so that such a lack of concern seemed to be based on self-deception. Then the fear would dissipate again, but this time people knew it would return. And when it did, they knew it would go away again. Fear was a season that the calendar left out.

⚹

The sun was beginning to set by the time the sons arrived home. Along the way, they had found a man lying unconscious at the side of the trail, face down in the dust.

His hands were gone. They had been severed, and the stumps cauterized. He wore a black tailcoat and riding boots; his clothes and hair, like something left lying too long beside the trail, were covered with a film of reddish dirt. When the boys turned him over, his face was so coated with orange sand you'd have thought this white man was trying to pass for a Redskin. The boys lifted the stranger and laid him across one of their horses, then trotted the animal home. The eldest carried the wounded man to one of the upstairs bedrooms. While the women tended to him, the men searched his personal belongings. They didn't find a single weapon, not even a knife. His bag contained only a Bible and a collection of sermons, from which they concluded that the stranger was a preacher.

That evening they thanked the Lord for finally sending them a man of God. It mattered little to which church he belonged, as long as he wasn't a Mormon.

"Good morning, Reverend." "With pleasure, Reverend." "What a long face you have this morning, Reverend." All the members of the Sevener family became accustomed to addressing him in that way.

✳

The Sevener homestead was a few miles from Paria. The first settlers had named their town "Pahreah," but one day a careless map-maker had written "Paria" on his maps.

Of the fifty or so families who bought their provisions in town, only a dozen or so called themselves Americans. The others considered themselves Mormons; they weren't ashamed of their town's name. Every Sunday the Americans planted the trunks of four poplar trees in the ground and stretched a tarpaulin overhead. They gathered under this canvas church-roof to show the Mormons that they too could pray, even if they lacked a clergyman. Oftentimes, a former miner, now the village drunk, would look on at the spectacle, his back against the adobe wall of the saloon and his backside in the dust. He entertained himself by balancing the neck of a bottle between his toes as he muttered inanities at the worshippers. "It's the women's fault if the gold's all gone," the old-timer said. "It's always the same. When the women start to arrive, it's goodbye to the gold. Blood and whiskey, that's what the earth feeds on, and the women drive them away."

Gold had never been found around Paria.

⚹

The Seveners made their eldest daughter, Astrid, serve as companion to the handless preacher, to do for him what he was unable to do for himself – everything, in other words. Of course she was not responsible for undressing or washing him. She can't have been older than twelve or thirteen. She was young enough to obey, yet old enough not to bore the cripple. As thin as a rake, she wore only dresses that were too big for her, most likely hand-me-downs from her mother's wardrobe. She gave off a subtle fragrance of lavender in a house that had no scent.

Ma Sevener never sat down and never spoke to anyone but her newborn. "Shush, shush ... Never worry, my precious. Soon we'll have a church of our own," she would murmur as she cradled him. When she went upstairs to visit the injured man, she would place the child in his arms. The Reverend had lost his hands, and looked like he had never held an infant before, but she left him no choice. "He'll baptize you for real," she whispered. "Soon, you'll see. The Reverend will be better soon." At meal-times she would come and go around the table. "The Mormons think this whole territory belongs to them, and that all the women should join their harem, but the day the army invades their houses and sets their women free they'll learn what's what. By the time you're grown up, we'll be the ones with a church, and the Mormons won't have one anymore."

The rest of the brood ate in silence. All the children, younger and older, wore the same calico print with green and yellow stripes. The Reverend noticed that someone had gone to the trouble of painting the wooden boards of the dining-room walls periwinkle-blue. Perhaps it had been assumed that one day there would be mouldings and artwork. The rest of the house was still raw wood, a starkness that the family took for granted.

Astrid fed the Reverend with a spoon, like a child. The father had finished his meal and was picking his teeth. The Reverend stopped chewing. Never again would he be able to do that.

✳

Most of the time the Reverend remained upstairs in the bedroom he shared with the boys, sitting at the foot of his bed with the Bible open on his knees. When Astrid was slow in turning the page he would become impatient, and she would beg his pardon. "No, I'm the one who should ask for your pardon, little one. It's not your fault if I've no hands anymore. Once ... I was known for my hearty handshake."

Through her guileless insistence, Astrid learned that the Reverend's name was Aaron. She asked if this was his first name or family name. "It doesn't matter," he answered. "When I was in Sacramento in '72, I met a town marshal named Eustis Marshall, which made him Marshal Marshall. So, when people asked for him, you never knew what they meant." No one asked him that again.

There were other, more vexing mysteries.

✳

The Seveners led a life regulated by the transit of the sun. The time of day mattered little, yet the father would take his watch from his vest pocket at least twice during each meal. The mother held the newborn in one arm while she stirred the contents of a pot with her other hand. The Reverend waited patiently at the table, back rigid and stumps resting on his thighs, while Astrid cut him a juicy piece of pork.

"So, Reverend, surely you're going to tell us one of these days who did that to you," asked Sevener.

"Don't listen, my pet, this is no talk for children's ears," said the mother, kissing the baby's brow.

The father glanced up at her, and then went back to looking the Reverend straight in the eye.

"It was the Matador."

7

"The who?" exclaimed the father.

"The Matador."

The father sat up on his chair. "Not a real bullfighter, I suppose?"

The Reverend chewed slowly. "What difference does it make?"

Astrid offered the Reverend a piece of potato on the end of a fork. She stopped halfway through the motion, one hand cupped underneath to catch any drips, as she waited for him to open his mouth.

"Likely none," said the father, returning to his plate.

The Reverend stared back at him, then took the mouthful that Astrid held out to him. He chewed it thoroughly before continuing, "If you go to Tucson, they'll tell you he's called the Matador because he's a great sleepwalker. Apparently someone overheard him talking in his sleep, saying something like 'Even if the blood flows, they've come from near and far to see me.' "

✳

The Sevener home contained several treasures: a light fixture with three oil lamps hanging above the dining table; a chair with a padded seat, covered with a fine lace antimacassar; a little chest of drawers with curved legs; a silver serving tray; two books with heavy bindings; and a china vase in a cupboard otherwise filled with items for cooking or sewing.

Unlike some pioneers who became attached to fragile possessions because they had survived the journey, the Seveners seemed to have forgotten about theirs. For a long time now the usual visits had not really been social events. It took the Reverend's arrival for young Astrid to be seen dusting off these vestiges of a social life.

✳

Nothing prevented the Reverend Aaron from going out, but he preferred to look at the outside world from the window, as if it were easier to take in when divided among four panes of glass.

To find grazing, the menfolk had to drive the herd all the way to the recesses of the canyon, where an ephemeral stream watered the rusty soil. They spent their days on horseback a good distance from the homestead. The Reverend would be at the window when they set out – and when they returned.

Never again would he be able to ride a horse.

In the evenings, the father and sons played dice at the kitchen table with the contented air of men at the end of their daily grind. "So much for just this," the Reverend said to himself the first time. The second time, he felt like joining them, but then he remembered he had no hands, not even for gambling.

✴

The Seveners had a piano, but it was permanently out of tune because of the climate. No one played it except Astrid, who had taught herself. A collection of pieces had been left on the music stand, but she never opened any of them.

For the third time in succession she was picking out "Sweet Betsy from Pike," the only tune she seemed to know. The Reverend imagined himself closing the lid on her fingers. He drew back close to the window to hide his shame.

✴

The eldest boy was named Leroy, but everyone called him Lee. He found the Reverend outside in the shed, an open lean-to. A cloudless sky stretched to the horizon. A California condor croaked. A wheelbarrow and a cartwheel caked with dried earth rested against the house. The Reverend stood staring at the objects heaped up on a workbench before him: bowls, cleavers, a butcher's bellows, a metal shovel, pincers, a pastry cutter, and a whip.

"Need somethin'?" asked the young man.

"There's nothing there I'd know how to use. And even if I did, I can't handle things anymore."

"So it's true you was a preacher?"

"I was. I was one of the rare men never to carry a gun, even in places where gunfights were most likely. I'd pay prostitutes to get them to talk, but I never touched them. I chewed tobacco all day long, yet I swear no one ever saw me spit." He nodded into empty space as if to convince himself, and then sniffed. "Still, I was no example to anyone."

He refrained from explaining that he was obsessed by everything that people thought, except when it concerned him. He loved to bargain, but had no interest in money. He didn't gamble, but had the impression he was living in a game. He believed in God, but lacked faith. He would invite his congregation to pray for their neighbours, while he prayed only for himself. He also avoided mentioning that he had seen a little girl beaten by her father for not praying enough, and a woman beaten by her husband for praying too much, suspecting the preacher had cast a spell on her. How often had he sworn that no one wanted to go to heaven anymore, and that the most devout only wanted to ensure they had a place on the first page of the next Testament.

"You baptized a lot of folks?" asked Lee.

"No. I used to recite sermons. The other preachers went from camp to camp to show the faithful how easy it was to walk in the way of the Lord. I preferred to show them how difficult it would be."

"So you're not goin' lookin' for revenge? Forgivin' an' all that?"

He darted a sidelong look at the young man. "And what hands could I use to take my revenge?"

Lee shrugged. "I dunno. Mebbe someone else's."

※

One day, Astrid found the Reverend sitting on the foot of his bed, his head buried in the pillow. She had never seen a man in tears. She went closer; a floorboard creaked. The Reverend raised his head and the pillow fell from his lap. He picked it up between his stumps, stood up, and flung it on the bed before going to the window. He stood with his back to the girl with his arms folded as if he still had hands to cross. His shirt had come out of his trousers, his suspenders were loose.

"Why did they do that to you, Reverend?"

"You'd have to ask the Matador," he answered, sniffling.

"You weren't too lucky, anyhow."

"Luck had nothing to do with it. Luck would have taken one hand, not both of them. Folk pray for protection from bad luck, but they'd do better to pray against wickedness instead, for it doesn't only punish the daring. It afflicts the weak – cautious folk, in other words. Bad luck isn't something to be feared, for it's passive. It's when the elements deliberately align against you that fear takes hold. It's the intentions we attribute to things and people that make us afraid. It's like thinking you're free when you still believe in God. It's the reassurance you tell yourself that He doesn't interfere, but that if He ever did, His intentions would be good." He wiped his cheek with his forearm.

Astrid stared at the floor, and then broke the silence again. "You've really no idea why he took your hands?"

The Reverend straightened his spine and sighed, without turning around. "I'm aware of the circumstances that led him to me and drove him to assault me, but basically there's no reason. 'Why?' is a question you don't ask an artist. Truly, no one's to blame. By searching for people who'd deserve to have others act their parts, you end up going in circles. If New Babylon had existed, I'd still have my hands."

Astrid was telling herself for the first time that maybe the man was crazy, for she gave up trying to catch his eye and asked him nothing more except "Are you warm?" "Cold?" "Are you sleepy, Reverend?"

✳

"There was somethin' wrong about us comin' here," Lee confided in him one day. "I dunno how to put it. We're no poorer than before. It's not a question of money. My parents ... I think they just stopped actin' like we was respectable folks. I'm not sayin' they're not okay," he said, scraping the ground with his toe. "I'm just sayin' that in Missouri, we was well respected. Me, I'm not goin' to do what they did. I'm goin' to go somewhere else. I'm not goin' to give up so easy."

"If you could choose how to die, what would it be like?"

You could talk to a man for hours, about what had brought him to where he was, or about what he was looking for. About the way he dreamed of living. But the Reverend had discovered long ago that the best way to draw out exceptional people was to ask them how they dreamed of dying.

Lee shrugged. "I'm too young to think about dyin'."

"Me," said the Reverend, "I've always dreamed of dying in the desert. Is there a more honourable way to end your life than to die of thirst in the middle of nowhere? Collapsing where there's no enemy, no epidemic, where it's as if you were cut down by God's own hand? The desert wishes us no harm, yet for us it's always an adversary we can't lay a finger on."

✳

If the Reverend Aaron was finding that time was passing slowly, so did the people of Paria, who were eager to hear about God from someone acquainted with hope.

"You have to understand him; losing your hands is a terrible test, even for a preacher. A lot of men would rather die."

"Sure, but after all, his is the only profession in the world he doesn't need hands for," argued others.

Lee would often ask him when he was going to start preaching again, but he remained silent, never budging. Answering this question, even postponing it until the next day, seemed to require too much effort. Then one day he framed an answer – or rather a sentence: "Never. I'll never preach again."

Lee repeated these words to Astrid, who repeated them to her father. Then the Seveners began to heed the gossip that was going around: "What if the crippled clergyman wasn't a man of God at all, but a fraud? A thief? Why did they cut his hands off if he's not a thief?"

"But then why bother to keep him alive? Why didn't they just string him up like any other thief?"

"Surely because he's a preacher, and it would have brought bad luck."

Then one day the rumour became news. A few Mormons from Paria had heard from family members in Arizona that the stranger had lodged with families close to the border. He had never claimed to be a preacher while living among them, just a Mormon from Missouri searching for his elderly sister.

✴

The Reverend Aaron was brought to the table, as he was every morning. Someone else would say grace, because from the outset he had asked to skip his turn.

They all ate without speaking, and then the father cleared his throat. "We're not going to be able to keep you, Reverend. With the new baby, you understand ... The girls will pack up your things and then I'll drive you somewhere else. Wherever you like."

The Reverend had always known that this day would come, but not so soon, not so brutally. Not before he had worked out a plan for the future, or at least a plan for revenge.

"I can't do anything for myself," he pronounced, looking at the bowl in front of him.

"You must have family somewhere."

He didn't answer.

Sevener insisted. "You have a family, friends, Reverend?"

The Reverend nodded to Astrid, who took a spoonful of porridge and stuffed it into his mouth.

Sevener sat quite still, staring at him. He placed one elbow on the table, then the other. "There's no one here wondering what you did or didn't do, but I'm going to ask you a question now and I'm pretty sure you're going to answer, else it'll be for me to decide. So where do you want me to drive you?"

Looking back at the father, the Reverend swallowed his porridge, leaving a grey residue on the edge of his lower lip. "To a place where there's a big brothel with plenty of prostitutes."

The father bowed his head and closed his eyes. One of the daughters muttered a prayer. The mother, who was pacing around the table to put the baby to sleep, rocked the child even harder. "Just what I was afraid of," muttered the father.

Astrid, shedding a tear, wiped the corner of the Reverend's mouth, and not another word was said.

⁕

When the sound of the wagon was heard, announcing her father's return, Astrid went to greet him and asked where he had driven the Reverend in the end.

"South," was her father's only answer as he climbed down. "South of here there's places folks don't even know exist."

⁕

To this day the Sevener family and the community of Paria still have no idea what happened on the sixteenth of May 1881, immediately before the Reverend Aaron was found lying on the dusty trail leading to their homestead, with his hands severed at the wrists, but one thing they know for sure: the natives had nothing to do with it.

Most people will read this book to find out everything they can about Charles Teasdale. Mexican readers will want to learn the fate of Vicente Aguilar. Others will be looking to better understand Russian Bill, or Pearl Guthrie.

But this book is dedicated to the people of Paria, for only they will turn its pages to know more about the Reverend Aaron.

NOTEBOOK I

The Ten Hangings of
Charles Teasdale

BULLIONVILLE, 1880 ✣ PANAMINT, 1873

POTOSI, 1861 ✣ SAN FRANCISCO, 1849

EUREKA, 1866 ✣ AURORA, 1866–1871

CHERRY CREEK, 1874 ✣ VIRGINIA CITY, 1860–1875

CARSON CITY, 1875–1876 ✣ ELDORADO CANYON, 1876

HOSSEFROSS, 1876 ✣ HAMILTON, 1871–1876

PRESCOTT, 1870–1876 ✣ GREATERVILLE, 1876

✣ PIOCHE, 1880 ✣

I've nothing to say.
The dead aren't entitled to speak.
I know that to you I'm not dead yet, but for me it's all over.

BULLIONVILLE

JUNE 1880

Charles Teasdale had escaped hanging on nine occasions in his lifetime. But then one day he had had enough, so he hanged himself. Early one morning he was found in a stable next to the forge in Bullionville, though he had never set foot in the place before. Bullionville was a small town with neither a past nor a future. No one went there anymore – to live or to die.

He might have chosen to end his days in Pioche, ten miles to the north, where the silver mines were still yielding a few tubs of ore each week; or in Panaca, two miles to the south, a peaceful farming village lulled by Mormon hymns; or maybe less than a mile to the north, in the majestic natural beauty of the eroded clay formations in the gorges there. But it was in Bullionville, in a desert of red rocks and sagebrush, that Charles Teasdale's despair launched its final offensive at the very moment when even the most obdurate of the town's inhabitants were thinking of moving out. There, in a town with no post office, where the ore crushers and their smokestacks were falling into ruin, and where even the bushes, from a distance, resembled stones. It was impossible to say if the town's sandy soil was grey or yellow, but you could say without hesitation that it had the pallor of those ailing and on the brink of death.

So Bullionville itself had nothing to do with the life or the suicide of the somewhat notorious Charles Teasdale.

⁜

Old Duncan, the town's unofficial mayor and a confirmed bachelor, didn't know what to make of this good fortune. His only pleasures were praying and contemplating the finest views. Even people who had known him since he'd first arrived in town could never have suspected that he would transform Teasdale's suicide into a widespread conspiracy.

A proud descendent of the earliest Dutch settlers, Duncan had spent his entire life loving work and accumulating his nest egg. One by one he had sold off the mining concerns that were the source of his prosperity and had moved into an enormous mansion. From it he could admire the wall of monuments that Mother Nature had carved out of the white clay and which evoked the elegance and grandeur of old-world cathedrals. All he lacked in his isolated retreat on the outskirts of Bullionville were companions with similar interests and the same level of education with whom he could discuss politics and philosophy – though he couldn't bear those ladies from great families who wore feathered hats, insisted their water be poured from a crystal carafe, and obeyed the dictates of fashion with greater fervour than he did those of religion. Every evening, he prayed that a journalist from the East would come along to vaunt the beauty of the site in a Boston or Philadelphia newspaper, attracting future pioneers. But he was aware that the Indians and their strange customs were the only things of interest to the excessively wealthy who indulged in the joys of tourism.

⚹

The Bullionville blacksmith followed Duncan's manservant into the dining room, with its bay window and white walls devoid of decoration. The old man was carving slices of roast beef which he ate with little appetite. Wearing a close-fitting grey jacket and a blue shirt attached at the collar by a single button, he looked as sedate as the manservant. They could even have been confused, if the latter had not been a black man. "You're quite sure it's him?" he asked, signalling to the manservant to saddle up his horse.

"As sure as I'm standin' here, Mr. Duncan. Ah've bet on him too often in Virginia City to forgit that face and them cauliflower ears."

Duncan sent the blacksmith to Panaca to fetch the photographer, while he himself rode to the county courthouse in Pioche. It was rumoured that he entered the office of the Justice of the Peace and laid before him three bundles of banknotes. This is how he supposedly obtained authority to transfer and escort two prisoners who were serving a two-month sentence for selling liquor to the Indians. When the jailer unlocked the cell door and Duncan informed the condemned men that they were accused of the murder of Charles Teasdale, one of them replied, "Sure, we killed Charles Teasdale. And Abraham Lincoln. And Napoleon and the King of England too. We murdered the lot of them."

The town council, confronted with a *fait accompli*, decided that for the good of the community old Duncan's version would be the true one. It meant that pilgrims in their hundreds would come to visit Teasdale's grave. People would pay dearly to visit the hotel room where the outlaw had last slept and to see the stable where he had knotted his rope. That same year a museum would be founded, and an exhibition entitled *Life and Death of Charles Teasdale, Arsonist of the West* would be created. Bullionville would become famous beyond the state borders, and the town's name would always evoke the unfading image of the eccentric bandit.

Duncan shut himself in with Teasdale's corpse and fired a bullet into the still-warm heart, adapting appearances to his story. There was very little blood. Some dead bodies coagulate faster than live ones.

※

In Nevada, large numbers of people believe that if Southern folk mourn more spectacularly than Northerners, it's because of the heat – which doesn't leave them time to watch over the departed. The heat accelerates everything, amplifies everything, including decomposition of the remains of their nearest and dearest.

Teasdale's body was laid out on a wooden plank covered with ice cut from the heights of the Sierra Nevada, but this was not enough to prevent putrefaction. The photographer immortalized Charles Teasdale wearing clothes that were soaking wet and a white shirt darkened by a sepulchral perspiration. Initially, those who had never met Teasdale in person were skeptical. The photo showed a man with burn marks on the left side of his neck and a thick brown beard – a mature man's beard on a still youthful face.

The first time he was arrested, Teasdale was still beardless. By the time of his second arrest he had begun to grow a moustache, and later a beard, but it had been singed in a fire he himself had set. As a result, all the wanted posters that circulated from then until the end of his life had shown him with no hair on his chin and a young face devoid of blemishes. After his first two escapes, amateur law-enforcers were no longer able to recognize the barely pubescent arsonist, though he was as wanted as ever.

A freshly painted notice on a wooden panel was nailed to a post and placed near the road:

Welcome to Bullionville
Last Resting-Place of the
Great Charles Teesdale
Firebug of the West

The town had reached new heights as legends go. Missives were dispatched to the four corners of the land. "Charles Teesdale has been murdered. Come and see where he breathed his last."

The deceased would have been disappointed to see his name misspelled, for throughout his life his signature had been his single source of pride.

✯

On the twelfth of June 1880, the Reverend Aaron officiated at Charles Teasdale's funeral. The most prominent personalities in the region were all present at the burial of this individual who was a total stranger to them. Their dark suits and impatient manner made them seem like vultures. The local folk gathered around the open grave, hats in hand despite the sun, sweat pouring down their backs. The women held their fans closed in front of them, as propriety required. Not one tear was shed.

The Reverend was the only speaker: "Charles Teasdale was a tortured man. He belonged to that first generation of settler children who never saw the East before reaching adulthood. The only family he knew was that formed by the patrons of saloons who, from town to town, are all alike, interchangeable.

"Like the savages," the Reverend went on, "Charles Teasdale was a nomad who spent his life far from our Lord's teachings. But no man is damned while he is alive. Against all expectations, Charles Teasdale heard God's voice through mine. I saw him change under my very eyes. I heard him wonder what he could leave behind as a reminder of his passage here on earth. He died as he lived, but first he was saved. And if an unscrupulous bandit like Charles Teasdale can be saved, anyone can."

At the time, the Reverend was still unaware that Teasdale had committed suicide. If he had known, this is what he would have said: "Teasdale, you sonofabitch. So I never saved you or defeated you. If you could see the state I'm in, you wouldn't have wasted all this time. You'd have hanged yourself sooner."

So many ways to die,
but not the slightest hint of fear.

PANAMINT

JULY 1873

You knew you'd arrived in the valley because of the constant wind. Its howl was as fluid as a river that flowed between the rocks and as shrill as a woman's cry. The Indians called it Chinook, believing that its voice haunted places where humans were forbidden to settle. Folks in the know were aware that the valley wind was the same as any other. The real difference was that there were no children's shouts and laughter to mask its sound. Some will tell you that people in the valley worshipped the same storms that drove them crazy. Cowboys would circle their horses and shoot their six-guns into the air, all for no good reason. Folks in the know said they did it to cover the sound of the wind. So they wouldn't go crazy without kids around.

In the heat of the day, you could douse your head with a bucket of water and ten minutes later your hair would be completely dry. Murders had been committed for a patch of shade. In the recesses of Surprise Canyon – an excellent spot for ambushes – the Indians used to practise a form of torture that consisted of tying a white man to a leafless acacia tree in the direct sun, in a place where no one ever passed. They would take off his hat and set it down where he could see it, but just beyond his reach. This was done to remind him that he was dying because he was white, for unlike him the Indians didn't need hats.

Panamint was situated in a place where the sand was so hot it could scorch a horse's hooves. It was hell out of doors. And when you entered the saloon, it was still hell. Because it was so unbearable, the miners' camp attracted the most daring and desperate. They believed that the simple fact of going there would earn them a heavenly reward, but in their disappointment they no longer hesitated to commit the slightest crime, for it was perfectly obvious that God had no interest in such a place.

✳

The Reverend Aaron entered the saloon in his shirtsleeves, his books hidden in the folds of his tailcoat. Displaying his Bible and his prayer collections in such a place was the quickest way to cast yourself as an outsider. There were two kinds of men: those who tried to forget their own perpetual fear by provoking fear in others, and those who preached the Gospel to convince others not to shoot them. The Reverend remained stock-still near the door, chewing his tobacco, long enough to let his eyes grow accustomed to the dark. Without turning around, two card players sized him up with a sidelong glance. Panamint was not part of the Reverend's usual itinerary. When he took stock of the clientele, he wondered why not.

More than one murder had been committed in this saloon. It was said to be the most poorly lit in the valley, so dark compared to outside that the miners might have felt they were back deep inside the mine. The only rays of light came from the ceiling, which was riddled with bullet holes. In the evening, the saloon-keeper would hang an oil lamp from a hook passed through one of the openings – insufficient to allow the customers to see what they were drinking. The Reverend headed for the rear and set his things down on the bar. The barman was busy arguing with a young woman in her working clothes – a nightdress and baggy knickers. The Reverend could barely make out his reflection opposite, in a mirror so large that it doubled the proportions of the room. It wasn't the noisiest of saloons. There was no piano, no music, and no horde of drunken girls filling the room with their forced laughter. Miners played cards, muttering and knocking back glasses of amber liquid. If he had wanted, it would have been easy for him to attract people's attention and let them know what God thought of their insignificant lives.

"You're nothing but a sonofabitch, Malvern," he heard someone say from the centre of the room. The man who had uttered these words was sitting with his back to the Reverend. He had long hair under a little soft-felt cowboy hat. Opposite him, the individual named Malvern wore fingerless gloves and a short top hat, the worse for wear. A vein throbbed in the middle of his forehead and his fingernails were yellowed and as thick as claws.

"Win or lose, we're all sonsofbitches to you," said Malvern without raising his voice.

"How would you know? You never lose."

"Like all the other sonsofbitches card sharps like you," answered the man in the soft-felt hat.

"You can write that up in your little paper then. Say that this evening you got beat again by another sonofabitch."

The Reverend stopped chewing his tobacco. The barman's eyes slid from the woman to his patrons. The card players at the next table stopped in mid-air, cards in hand, and looked over their shoulders. The woman turned around and walked backward to the end of the bar, ready to duck at the first swift movement. She would be sheltered from stray bullets there, but exposed to shards from the mirror. At that moment, a harsh, husky snore broke the silence. The Reverend surveyed the back of the room and made out a man sleeping on a chair in the darkest part of the saloon, quite unaware of the tension in the air. His head was leaned backward and his mouth was wide open. With paralytic slowness, the man in the soft-felt hat drew his hands from under the table and opened them, palms up. He was unarmed, but Malvern's hands were still hidden. His left eyelid twitched. "Go on, clear out," Malvern said, gesturing to the exit with his chin.

The other, with his hands raised, moved toward the door. The card players turned away and resumed their game.

The Reverend began chewing his tobacco again, squinting to get a better view of the sleeping man. "That's Charles Teasdale," the barman informed him. The sleeper's hat was sitting on the table. There was a spot of blood on one side of his head up to his widow's peak, but not as if he had bled – more as if someone had bled on him. He wasn't yet thirty, but seemed older.

"Even if they had fired, that guy would never have opened an eye," the barman added. "They say you can stand two paces in front of him and shoot at the ceiling and he'll not waken up any more'n he did just now."

"You've seen him do that – I mean go on sleeping when others are shooting at one another?"

"No. But that's what they say. When I look at him, it's not hard to believe. After all, horses sleep standin' up. He sleeps sittin' down."

It was in this very saloon that Charles Teasdale would be arrested two years later, dragged to Carson City, and incarcerated in the state prison to await execution for the ninth time. But right now he was sleeping.

※

Charles Teasdale was one of those who couldn't stand the silence of the valley. In fact, he couldn't stand silence in general, maybe because he was himself a man of few words. He never had anything to tell, but if as he rode along he encountered a rider heading in the same direction, he wouldn't disdain the stranger's company, even though it might be dangerous. He didn't mind wide open spaces. He loved campfires, but he refused to sleep under the stars. Yet he was incapable of spending a full night in bed. He needed a tavern and a steady noise unrelated to him, or else he would never have slept. They say that one evening he found himself in a community run by religious fanatics in which every establishment that served liquor had been shut down. When daylight came, he was seen near the steps of the hardware store, where there was the most coming and going. He slept on the ground, bare-headed, with his hat over his face. He spent the following night puking from sunstroke.

Teasdale trimmed his beard four times a year, but never shaved it off. In his pouch he carried sheets of paper, a writing case, a metal pen, and an ink well. His fingers were permanently ink-stained, the result of the hours he spent each day perfecting his signature by scribbling it on bits of paper. He never removed his boots except to take a bath – because of the snakes, he said. In the morning, when he awoke, he would sit down somewhere and feed stray chickens and dogs. He changed horses more often than shirts. Anyway, he never wore a white shirt, because white got dirty too easily for a man who had raised himself up among his fellows by attracting punches to the jaw.

He moved from mining camp to mining camp, but never prospected. He wouldn't return to the same town twice, except out of necessity or to set a fire. He never slept with the same girl twice. Each evening, he got as drunk as the night before. Apart from the fact that he was wanted in more than eight counties, no one could really understand why he liked to be on the move so much. Once you've reached a certain degree of inebriation, everywhere in the world must look the same.

I just took advantage of the fact that the others respected the rules. Ignoring them gave me a head start. In life, and toward death.

POTOSI

APRIL 1861

The first time Charles Teasdale escaped hanging was in Potosi. In the camp there, tents had sprouted at random as the miners arrived, attracted like flies to honey by the promise of work. It was a hamlet of mud and excrement. The mud swallowed shoes; it rose, it swelled, while the shoes sank into it, were lost, and lost their raison d'être. Mud, yes, if only you'd seen that mud. A fine, treacherous sand, everywhere. Excrement was the binder for these substances. Everything was in the excrement, and the excrement was in everything.

The saloon in Potosi resembled a marquee tent, with its unfinished wood frame and canvas roof. Daylight filtered in everywhere, reminding the drinkers of the military campaigns they had fled. You were never wholly outside it, nor entirely within. The mirrors in the tent were filthy and blurred. You could say goodbye to your fine little neatly trimmed moustache. You had to make do with coarse, approximate cuts. The razor – a sheath knife – also served as a kitchen knife. Eat, kill, shave: the same tool for all. This was a camp inhabited by men whose sweat stank of onions and whose nails were always black, even when chewed to the quick. Men who were likeable enough, though no one could say why.

✵

Young Teasdale was dragged by the ear and shut up in the only finished building in the entire camp: the tiny cabin of rough planks behind the saloon that served as a privy. "I don't need to go, mister," he protested through the door.

"It's the only jail we've got," grumbled the man who had volunteered to stand in as the jailer while waiting for other more influential men to return from the mine. "To think that in '49 you could find gold nuggets the size of billiard balls and leave them unguarded in your tent. I'd bet you wasn't even born in '49, you little asshole."

"Yes, I *was* born then, mister."

Charles Teasdale was barely twelve, and his voice hadn't broken yet. He had claimed to be sixteen to try to get hired for work in the mine, but no one had believed him. When evening came, he had offered to fight anyone in exchange for the kitty. The men had laughed and invited him to share their meal. He disappeared during the evening, and the foreman had caught him pouring away the contents of a barrel of whiskey behind the saloon. The foreman led him back inside by the collar, and the boy remained in his chair the entire evening, staring silently at the fire. Then he disappeared with two horses during the night, most likely intending to sell them. They caught him early next morning on the way to Fort Baker.

In those parts, stealing horses was punished more severely than murder. This was because without his horse a man was sure to die, and because, far from his brothers and cousins, a man had no one to avenge him or appeal to the court on his behalf. But then, unlike a horse, a man could defend himself.

"When the others get back, you'd best say you wasn't born yet, in '49. The younger you is, the less chance they'll hang you."

"I'm sixteen, I swear."

The guard shook his head sorrowfully. "You don't git what I'm tellin' you? If you're sixteen, you're goin' to die."

"Then I'd really like to smoke one last cigarette before I go."

With a sigh, the guard produced his tobacco tin. He sat at the base of the hut to make it easier to roll the tobacco, and struck a match. He opened the door to reach an arm inside, and handed the boy the lit cigarette. In the dark, the paper around the tobacco burned, the shreds turning red at the end – just as any celebration at the top consumes what it sits on.

"You'll suffocate, smokin' in there," said the guard.

A minute later the outhouse caught fire. Then the flames consumed a rope lying among the rocks separating the latrines from the saloon, and set fire to the sagebrush. In the confusion, Teasdale was able to make his escape. Ten minutes later, the saloon was on fire; soon it was the nearby tents, and then the whole camp.

It's a godawful time, but some folks will
still miss it when it's done.

SAN FRANCISCO

JUNE 1849

Charles Teasdale was born on the eighth of June 1849, onboard a ship sailing from the East Coast to California by way of Cape Horn. He spent the first hours of his life in the hold, where the passengers had to sleep side by side on the floor, stacked like logs waiting for the fire. Then his early years were spent in the taverns of San Francisco, a town where houses were piled one above the other, ready to fall like dominoes in a succession of fires. There were no cradles for the children, so babies slept in vessels normally used for panning river sand to separate out the gold.

He was barely able to stand on his two feet when he took up the habit of running along the muddy San Francisco streets behind the fire engines. The volunteer firemen were all notorious pugilists, and in his idolatry, the young Teasdale followed his heroes everywhere, including to the vacant lots where they could hold illicit boxing matches, hoping to evade the authorities. He was soon acting as lookout during the fights, running back to warn the organizers as soon as the police appeared.

Then his mother decided they had to leave San Francisco. Charles Teasdale would remember this day as the saddest of his life. Yet, despite seeming to be the freest man in all the territories west of the Mississippi, he had never returned.

If only gloves were worn and there was less blood, it would be a real sport, they tell me. I'm the one that does the bleeding, but you're the one that gets upset.

EUREKA

JANUARY 1866

For Charles Teasdale, North and South were compass points and blue and grey were merely colours, concepts too remote to stir the slightest emotion in him. For him to choose one side over the other would have been as nonsensical as to prefer Mars to Mercury.

He was sixteen. The gold rush was over, as was the Civil War, and young Teasdale had given up lying about his age. He had also given up looking for work in the mines. Not once was he seen with his feet in a river, turning over the sand. Instead, he lived in the mushrooming towns of Nevada, a camp follower of the mining world. When the promise of wealth became a frustration, prospectors would look elsewhere, and parasites like him lost no time in following them.

He changed names whenever he changed towns. He would pick the first name that occurred to him as long as it preserved his real initials, for he didn't want to change his signature.

He earned money building houses while the men were off digging, or watching over a concession run by some incorporeal mining company. He rarely took part in games of chance, but every night he allowed himself to be lulled by the sound of gamblers' voices. Often, he would fight bare-fisted. He was still too young and skinny to fight for money. He would listen to the conversations in taverns, trying to pick up a European accent the way others turned an ear to the sky when hunting for birds. When he found an adversary his own size, he would call him a dirty Irishman. Of all nationalities, he preferred the Irish. Charles Teasdale always managed to provoke the other, but no one could provoke Charles Teasdale. He didn't fight out of compulsion, but fascination. Sometimes he lost. Then, on opening his eyes, he would see a crowd of onlookers leaning over him, a well of light under a crown of top hats.

✳

He rode into Eureka one winter evening with the intention of satisfying all his desires. He called himself Caspar Tootsey, a name he didn't expect to have to keep for five years. In one saloon he spotted an Irishman called Shanahan. He planted himself behind the young fellow and tapped him on the shoulder with two fingers. Shanahan turned around, and Teasdale spat in his face. The man wiped his face with the back of his hand, grabbed Teasdale by the shirt, and threw him backward onto a table some distance away. A drinker pulled away his glass just before Teasdale landed on it. Teasdale got up and took a Bowie knife from his boot.

"What do you want?" asked the man, drawing a .36 Colt Navy.

The other drinkers leapt up from their chairs to get out of harm's way. Teasdale dropped his knife to the floor. He stood erect, panting. He had clenched his fists, the knuckles wrapped with worn socks. He had the hollow cheeks of a malnourished child and enormous eyes, as dark as a sea bed. Teasdale said very little, but his eyes spoke volumes.

The man lowered his revolver and unbuckled his belt. The other patrons rushed for the walls. Most spectators were as eager to flee from impromptu fights as they were to step on one another's toes to get closer to properly organized bouts.

Thirty-two minutes, three broken chairs, and a chipped mirror later, Teasdale cracked the other man's skull against the corner of the table. He didn't know it, but the young man he had just humiliated was a bemedalled veteran of the Union Army. As booty, he inherited his adversary's Colt Navy revolver. Teasdale never wore a belt, so he passed a cord through the weapon's trigger guard and tied it around his neck, an arrangement that allowed him neither to conceal the weapon nor to draw it quickly enough to have the advantage in a gunfight.

He left with his shirt and suspenders soaked in sweat and spotted with blood, and carrying his coat over one arm, impervious to the winter chill, although the people he met walked with their heads sunk deep in their collars. He entered the other saloon, passed the gun over his head, and laid it flat on the bar, intending to trade it for a solid night's drinking.

A hand appeared on his arm. "Forget it," said a voice behind his shoulder. "Keep your gun, sonny."

That evening, Charles Teasdale exchanged his instinctive neutrality toward the great American schism for a bottle of whiskey.

Years later, even after he had acquired a cartridge belt and a pair of holsters, he still wore his Colt around his neck with the pride of a Catholic priest displaying his cross.

※

The phantom cavalry was a vaguely defined band of mercenaries with no paymaster. Its founding members were a group of Confederate veterans who had refused to lay down arms and return to the monotony of life on the farm or plantation, brother veterans whose thirst for vengeance was satisfied entirely by pillage, rape, and drunkenness. In its ranks were lads of twelve who were mere infants when the war began. They had never set foot on the battlefield, yet they shouted their hatred of the Yankee from every rooftop. When the weather was cloudy, they would set off to pick a fight with other kids, because, they declared, they had filthy Yankee faces, and they would burn down their stables because, they said, their horses gave off a Yankee stench. And when they contemplated the inferno and their bloodied fists, they roared their bliss between gulps of hot liquor.

From the moment he was recruited by the phantom cavalry, Charles Teasdale, alias Caspar Tootsey, became one of those kids – except that he never claimed to have hated anyone.

Binges that leave a post-war taste.
Wars that feel like benders.

AURORA

JUNE 1866

The second time Charles Teasdale escaped hanging it was early morning. The air was still cool, with not a cloud in the sky. A beautiful day for dying. A day that began well for almost everyone.

Aurora was a mining town that had reached maturity. There were still just a few children whose ears had to be stopped against folly, but people had begun to hang drapes on their windows. They had acquired the habit of wiping their feet before entering homes.

During the Civil War, Aurora had been the most Yankee of all the towns in the state of Nevada. While soldiers were killing one another in the East, the inhabitants of Aurora had forced supporters of the South to swear allegiance to the flag they abhorred. A year after the war ended, the rebels of the phantom cavalry stormed Aurora. They dragged the most prosperous storekeepers into the street and shot them without further ado. They robbed the orphaned stores, carrying off the banknotes from the tills along with all the merchandise and bottles of alcohol that they desired. Then they set fire to a few strategic buildings to make sure that nothing that couldn't be stolen would survive.

A posse was sent to track down the pillagers. It managed to catch a few laggards, namely Charles Teasdale and three other hapless greenhorns, before it was shaken off by the rest of the gang.

✳

The evening before, the sound of sawing and hammering had resounded through the northerly part of town, where every building had been burned to the ground. New structures of brick and wood resembling the old ones began to rise, crowded together in the nakedness of dawn as if to shelter from the cold. Everywhere the ground was still dry and cracked like a biscuit fresh from the oven. The inhabitants were still spitting ash.

At the end of the main street a gallows had been erected on a wooden platform that was used both for vaudeville performances by touring companies and for public executions. The townspeople gathered to witness the final moments of the ruffians who had stolen all their possessions. Even the tardiest risers were up at cock crow.

On the scaffold, a clergyman railed against the condemned men, showering them with his spittle. "You are savages. Worse than Indians. It's no excuse to have been born where you were born. You were baptized, you were suckled by a white breast, and you speak the same language as us. You understand the meaning of the words 'sin' and 'damnation.' You have no people of your own, for you're neither Indian nor Christian. You don't deserve to have anyone pray for your souls."

The hangman put the rope around Teasdale's neck, and then around the neck of his neighbour to the left. As he approached the two men on the right, a rumble rose from the ground, making the gallows shake. Two clouds of dust could be seen approaching, one at each end of the street. A pair of bullets hit the executioner in the arm. A wave of panic ran through the crowd, the good folk pushed one another aside to escape, but the crowd was surrounded by thirty or so horsemen aiming their ordnance at them. One wore the grey tunic of the Confederate Army: its gilt buttons still shone, but the garment had been patched with brightly coloured bits of cloth. A teenage boy on a white mare had donned a jacket that was in better condition, but too big for him. Another had the grey kepi of the volunteers on his head, but otherwise wore tanned leather. An old man missing an ear had a patch over one eye and wore a sling cut from the Confederate flag. Among them, four riderless steeds were led on ropes. Four horses: one for each prisoner.

Seeing his companions ride to his rescue, Teasdale realized that he truly belonged in the phantom cavalry. As soon as they were released, the four condemned men rejoined the ranks of their comrades and galloped without a qualm until they were out of sight of the citizens of Aurora.

A few individuals in the crowd were killed, some struck by stray bullets not meant for them, while others were trampled by their peers. A woman with dishevelled hair was wailing "Why, Lord? Oh why?" Later that evening, she cried to her husband, "Why? Why didn't you go after them? How can we go on living now?" Another woman knelt by a lifeless body, and wept as she smeared her face and clothes with blood while the vast circle of her skirts rustled in the wind-blown sand that followed the carnage.

✶

The phantom cavalry had two modes of operation: like an army the moment it went on the attack, and like a band of dissolute brothers at other times. Between raids, the riders led an independent existence, entering towns in groups of three, never more. They pretended not to recognize one another when they met one another at corrals or in red-light districts, even though a few miles farther on they would ride side by side as they headed in the same direction. By operating in this way, they were able to plunder villages and isolated ranches for five years without ever wearing masks. They never rejected any male who wanted to join them, even if he was barely past puberty, which is why, despite deaths and executions, they reached the record number of twenty-two members in '66 and '67, before splitting into several smaller gangs.

Their leader was Darius Cole, a former cutler forced into retirement by the advent of firearms. Compared to the other veterans, he had a relatively wholesome air about him. Yet at first glance you could see he had known real war by the way he kept a straight back, mounted knives on his guns to serve as bayonets, rolled up his sleeping blankets in an instant, raised an arm before giving the signal to attack, and, when returning a man's stare, spat into the fire without ever missing his target.

❋

After freeing the prisoners in Aurora, the band rode south all day until they reached California, and then the deserts of the Sierra Nevada, north of Lake Mono. Along its shores they found grass to graze the horses. At the time, the railroad had not reached that far. It had not been forgotten that grass was the traveller's most crucial resource, for without it cattle, horses, and mules had nothing to eat and therefore no source for the energy required to keep moving and to haul their loads of humans and freight. The band set up camp at the lake, though the water was too brackish to drink. In the evening, they hunted wild animals roasted on the rods used to tamp powder in the bottom of their aged guns. At several spots across the lake, they could see the scattered lights of a camp, maybe even a town.

Teasdale began to saddle his horse outside the circle of light. He felt cold metal brush his cheek, and then heard Darius Cole's voice behind him. "Where are you off to like that, sonny?"

Teasdale glanced over his shoulder. The gun barrel pressed harder into his cheek. "Into town," he answered.

"What you think you're goin' to do in town?"

"Drink, and sleep awhile. I'll be back before you've opened an eye, boss."

"And what if a posse found us while you're away in town, who'll be here to keep watch? Did you think of that? If it wasn't for me you'd have died this mornin'. Mebbe you've never learned about this because you've never fought a war, but when a guy saves your life you owe him a debt. So no, Tootsey, I don't think you'll be goin' into town." Cole lowered his gun.

Teasdale remained motionless, with his back turned. "When will I have paid my debt to you, boss?"

"When you've saved the lives of all them that saved yours," Cole shot back before returning to the fire.

Charles Teasdale had a specialty: lighting and stoking fires, both campfires and destructive blazes. He knew where to place a fiery brand so that the flames would spread quickly, which structures would collapse first, and in which direction he should retreat to avoid suffocation.

Even in a town like Aurora, where the buildings were mostly of brick, he was able to recognize the flammable materials in shanties and hardware stores. He would roam the streets after dark when there were lights in the houses, and identify the ones with a decor of glue-soaked wallpaper, muslin curtains, and rosewood furniture. He developed strategies which he then conveyed to his comrades by sketching maps in the sand with the tip of an acacia branch, or, when the ground was too dry, with the muzzle of his gun.

Fire was his strength and his downfall. Before the pillaging began, he would be at his most calm and concentrated, for his pleasure depended on the precise application of his expertise. Afterward, it was he who had to be watched as the glow of the conflagration shone in his eyes, and when the others would take him by the arm to drag him away, he would shake off their grip and continue watching the blaze. It was in such mesmerizing moments that he would fall into the clutches of the authorities; he would stand entranced, mouth agape, his features wild and glowing red from the heat and splendour of the flames. Ironically, on several occasions his comrades had to set fire to the roof of the makeshift prison where he was being held in order to free him. The more often he was captured and then liberated by his comrades, the more morally indebted to the gang he became.

The deeper his debt, the less he resisted arrest and the less effort he made to escape. The others were beginning to tire of this and pleaded with Cole to let them stop rescuing him. No doubt Teasdale would have consented. But Cole couldn't plumb the unfathomable eyes of this Caspar Tootsey. Besides, the arsonist knew the gang's hideouts, haunts, and tactics. Darius Cole had been through the war, and had been advised often enough never to lose sight of his enemies.

✳

SEPTEMBER 1871

They returned to camp at Lake Mono, on the very spot they had chosen four years before. Now only nine mercenaries were riding with Darius Cole. Remorse and scruples, rapaciousness and crises of confidence had infected the gang. Despite the discord, Teasdale continued to be the perpetual outsider. No one had tried to make an ally of him before leaving. The phantom cavalry was now reduced to attacking small villages and isolated ranches where defenders were few and poorly armed. To survive, it had to space out its misdeeds more and more between raids, to leave people time to forget.

The men were again preparing to attack Aurora, which was now a town in decline. One by one the surrounding mines were closing; houses and businesses were being abandoned by those who had built them with their own hands. There remained just enough people in Aurora for the phantom cavalry to claim it was driving the final nail into the coffin of the most Yankee town in Nevada.

A line of orange sunlight was still visible to the west of the lake. Immersed in semi-darkness, some of the men were cleaning their weapons; others were playing their mouth organs. Teasdale was busy scraping gunpowder against a rock to light a fire. Cole laid his saddle on a log, sat on it, and rubbed his hands.

"So, Tootsey, what does that make, seven months since the last caper? I hope you remember what to do."

Teasdale continued scraping his rock without speaking. A spark formed, and he jumped back as the fire caught at his feet, exactly where he wanted it. His only answer was to glance over the flames at the gang leader.

"I suppose you haven't forgotten how to get caught neither," added Cole. A harmonica player broke off in the middle of a refrain. A deathly silence fell as the crackling of the fire punctuated the tense atmosphere.

Teasdale sat cross-legged on the ground and stretched his neck, playing with the cord of his Colt Navy. "Come on, boss, don't be unfair," he finally said.

Cole laughed. "Unfair? No, but tell me what's stoppin' me from shootin' this guy down where he stands!"

"Mebbe you feel you owe me something. For all the times I've risked my life for you. There's no one here has taken as many risks as me ..."

Cole looked him straight in the eye. "Filthy scum," he muttered, shaking his head, and then spat into the fire as the last rays of the sun were disappearing behind the Sierra Nevada.

⁂

The next day they entered Aurora, scrutinizing the faces of the inhabitants who were looking on, trying to recognize familiar faces. The scaffold was in place, but the gallows had disappeared. Perhaps it too had finally been used for firewood.

Everything went according to plan, except that Teasdale wasn't captured. There was no one in authority in Aurora to take care of that.

It was Teasdale's final raid.

Now the surviving criminal members of the phantom cavalry were beginning to carry out their exploits independently and sporadically. The same offences were committed, the same wounds reappeared, and the same crimes were perpetrated by former members, or others. The cavalry lived on, but it had become a phantom indeed.

Once, we saw a dead baby between two empty barrels.
She said to me, "You see, that's the difference
between me and a whore."

CHERRY CREEK

FEBRUARY 1874

In Cherry Creek, Mrs. Pumkin's house was the only building without a view of the still snow-capped mountains of the Cherry Creek Range. It was a two-storey place, with windows on every side. All the ones in the rear were boarded up. No one in town knew precisely why, but everyone had their own theory.

Originally, Mrs. Pumkin had named the establishment after herself. In time, the customers had renamed it the Crazy Girl Whorehouse because it had become the setting for fits of rage by one of the girls. No one really knew what triggered her outbursts. The crazy girl would begin to moan and groan as if pursued by a demon, with arms swinging and a tear-soaked face. Then the others would shut her up in a bedroom until she came to her senses. Her howls were arresting and had the power to chill the ardour of most customers – even those who usually needed to hear their girl cry out. At the height of her fits she would pummel the walls with her fists and feet, disturbing conversation on the ground floor. People would be chatting about so-and-so's new brooch, someone's bald spot, or laughing at the latest ludicrous accidents that had befallen the usual drunks. Gunshots, barking dogs, braying mules, or street-vendor cries couldn't disturb them, only the crazy girl's awe-inspiring outbursts.

Mrs. Pumkin had personally removed the young woman from her native village somewhere on the Mexican border and brought her to this no-less-godforsaken country. She said it was too late to cast her back into the desert, like a captain refusing to throw a disagreeable passenger overboard. Quite a few suspected that beneath her exterior as an impeccable madam, Mrs. Pumkin envied the crazy girl for having found a way to strike fear into men.

✻

That day, the town was alive and the streets were crowded with shoppers. Outside places of business, lineups zigzagged around the horse droppings. Men awaited their turns in front of the Crazy Girl Whorehouse. The Reverend Aaron, holding a holy book, was in the last quarter of the line when a quarrel broke out between two miners. It seemed written in the stars, as predictable as the ending of a dime novel. One miner pushed another, provoking a cascade of "Hey there!" Guns were drawn.

"Just like kids," remarked the man behind him. "I tell you, there'll never be a clergyman too many in this town."

"I imagine that's your way of welcoming me."

"For sure you're welcome, Reverend."

"Even if, obviously, I'm in the line to enter a whorehouse. Am I really the kind of preacher you want in your town?"

The Reverend didn't wait for an answer but turned away and stuck his nose back in his book. When it was his turn to go in, he asked to see the girl Charles Teasdale had chosen the evening before. "I'll wait if I have to," he added.

"Well, yesterday, truth to tell, he didn't really choose her," said the man behind the bar.

This was the third time the Reverend had turned up at the Crazy Girl Whorehouse with the same request.

A girl standing at the bar who had not enjoyed the good fortune of being chosen made a sarcastic comment. "So, if I understand right, the girls Mr. Teasdale picks are paid for twice: once to sleep with him, and the second time, with you."

Charles Teasdale was extremely popular with women, despite his unkempt beard and cauliflower ears. He forgot to cut his nails, except before fights. He was neither seductive nor charming. He had no interest in his good looks, of which he remained

49

unaware. It was a tragic beauty, as any superfluous beauty is tragic. You might think that in the sphere of his existence that sort of thing didn't matter, since women were won with fists or ready money, and since, whether dragged by the hair or willing to fornicate in order to survive, they didn't enjoy the luxury of choosing their lovers according to such superficial criteria. But the women did have their preferences. An experienced prostitute could size up a customer with a single glance. She could tell which one would push her against a wall and compel her to perform the most obscene acts, after which she would be left to shout insults – "Shit! Sonofabitch!" – from the top of the steps as he departed through the front door. Or she could recognize one she might fall for – a gentle, strong man, one who would whisper compliments and amorous words, whose departure she would observe with tear-filled eyes, quite unaware that as he went on his way he would smile to himself and say, "Poor fool." And then there was the one who would promise her marriage and children but not show his face again for months. When she saw him she would curse him too: "Shit! Sonofabitch!" No matter what kind of man it was, the same insults would be heaped on him in the end.

But for people reading these lines, and who live in a different world, such details are of capital importance. Yes, Charles Teasdale was good-looking, but he would have been happier to be ugly.

✳

The Reverend found himself in a little room at the back with boarded-up windows. In the middle of the dusty room, a rope-strung bed seemed on the point of collapse. A chest of drawers made of grey unvarnished wood, a likely source of splinters, completed the crude furnishings. Above the bed, a picture depicting the French Alps swung to and fro whenever the door banged.

The pale young woman, wearing a chemise, corset, and white knickers, drew a thin linen shawl across her bosom. He had already questioned many girls like her, the kind that knew what men were trying to hide. Nothing was kept from them, for they were not considered witnesses. Instead, it was their job to absorb men's ugly secrets without throwing them back in their faces. The Reverend would lend an ear like a golden spittoon, and as a bonus the girls could earn forgiveness for their sins.

She told him how Teasdale had staggered up the front steps and collapsed on a table near the bar. The young woman had rushed over to him, abandoning the customer she had been trying to lure. She placed herself beneath him and wrapped him in her arms, murmuring a few words to him in French. His cheeks were swollen and his eyebrows bleeding. Cradling him, she pleaded with the madam to allow her to take him upstairs without paying, so that she could care for him and pamper him.

"You knew he'd just won four hundred dollars? That he'd just won a boxing match?" asked the Reverend.

She shook her head, gazed at her hands on her thighs, and scratched the arch of her thumb. "I thought he was a drunk that had just been in a fight. He didn't pay nothing. No tip, no gift, nothing."

The Reverend walked across the room, hands behind his back, as if the walls and furniture formed an equation to which he was seeking the solution. He turned around and contemplated the picture of the Alps above the bed. "It looks like them, doesn't it?"

"Like what?" said the girl, astonished.

"The mountains, outside there," he said, indicating the rectangle of nailed planks with a nod.

"What mountains?"

I imagine I'll be in my proper place in hell,
but not for the reasons you think.

VIRGINIA CITY

SEPTEMBER 1860

In nature, all things that combat one another are equal in their
own way. When you look at the desert, you see that every spot
is a potential centre. The desert is an infinite number of focal
points. Add a human settlement and immediately it becomes the
heart of the landscape. That was the effect produced by Virginia
City. It gave the impression of being at the centre of the universe.

Charles Teasdale went to Virginia City for the first time the
year after the Comstock Lode was discovered. Back then there
were still no lamps in the saloon, only candles that melted, ran,
and ended as pyramids of wax in the centre of the tables. Actually
they weren't yet tables, just planks laid across barrels. The body
of a wooden wagon, which had been pulled to the top of the ravine
by mules before it finally gave up the ghost, served as the bar.
The saloonkeeper doled out the liquor with a ladle. As an eleven
year old, Teasdale had witnessed a boxing match between two
strangers in the open street. One of the adversaries had choked
on his own blood, spat out a few clots, and then insisted on fighting to the death.

✳

AUGUST 1875

Fifteen years later, everything had changed. The sheds had been
replaced by brick buildings, and those with adobe walls had made
way for wooden structures three or four storeys high. The miners melted into the throng of businessmen and other speculators
in tailcoats and derby hats – the kind of men who smoked cigars

in saloons and had exchanged their brass knuckle-dusters for gold rings. Seen from the surrounding hilltops, the town had become an endless grid of streets, a checkerboard on a mythical scale, dotted with chimneys, clotheslines, and telegraph poles.

Very close to Virginia City, the camps of Gold Hill and Silver had also grown up around the ore deposits. From the outset, rivalry among the three towns often took the form of boxing matches. By the end of the Civil War, Virginia City had become the boxing hub of the entire American West. In the ring, the dice weren't loaded, and every man had an equal chance – in reality more than in principle. "Let the best man win," went the saying, and the winner was always the best man since he was the only one left standing.

Sometimes fights would turn into free-for-alls, but no one participated unwillingly. Each blow delivered was a cause rather than a consequence, an act of communion rather than of self-defence. In this harmony, public order was never really compromised, except when suspicions arose of fights being thrown. Then the spectators did indeed become soldiers marching for their revolution. The free-for-all would become a tidal wave with purpose, driven by the same anger as a lynch mob carrying flaming torches and ready to break down the door of the police station to ensure justice was done.

✳

The discovery of a major talent is always staggering, especially when it takes the form of the destruction of another man by bare fists. Those who have boxed know that instinct isn't enough. Fighting is an art that has to be learned.

Charles Teasdale must have been initiated by someone somewhere, but to watch him perform you might have thought the contrary. The essence of his technique consisted in bobbing and weaving rather than in power, but he seemed to have been born to it, with fists clenched from the cradle. He left the definite impression that his skill owed little to any apprenticeship, or even to an inherited ability. Even those who disdained violent sports couldn't help seeing at a single glance the affinities between this lethal dance and a conversation with God – that is, if there was any such thing as God in Teasdale's head.

The American miners took to him because beneath his black mop of hair Teasdale had milky white skin. As men who spent their days beneath the earth far from the sun's rays, they recognized themselves in that pallor, as well as in the fact that he rarely spoke. And when he did say something, they understood his rough language, devoid of any accent and the much-despised flourishes employed by the educated. They recognized themselves in what Teasdale didn't have, or didn't do.

He wore a grey and yellow scarf around his waist. In it, the miners saw the colours as gold and silver. For Confederates these colours recalled the Southern rebels, while for Yankees they evoked the arid landscapes of Nevada. When the miners asked Teasdale why he had chosen those colours, he shrugged. "Because I'm colour-blind."

⚹

For almost a year the Reverend had attended all of Teasdale's fights, in Virginia City and in many a one-horse town in the middle of nowhere. The Reverend would stand among the crowd, as close to the ropes as possible, arms crossed on his chest. Motionless, he chewed his tobacco, pursing his lips whenever the muffled thud of a devastating blow was heard, yet he never uttered an exclamation and applauded with restraint. Despite this discreet behaviour, his religious books attracted attention. By always staying on the same side, among Teasdale's supporters, he eventually got himself noticed.

"So, Reverend, what does God think about all this violence?" a spectator installed beside him would occasionally ask, as they waited for the opponents to appear.

"And you, what do *you* think he thinks about all this violence?" was his only answer.

Teasdale fought his most memorable bout on the sixth of August 1875. Though he seemed thoroughly beaten, he got back on his feet to shouts from the crowd, which had roared itself hoarse. Bare-chested, his suspenders stained with sweat, grease, and blood, and his beard dripping, he unleashed two uppercuts to the chin of his adversary, who fell unconscious into the arms of his seconds. After this victory, Teasdale went up to the bar in the saloon and ordered a bottle from the bartender. A Mexican waiter began to mop up the spot where the fight had taken place, wiping away the stains of fluids the wooden floor had not absorbed. The Reverend was already sitting at a table in the middle of the room. Teasdale held a cold-water compress to his cheek and another to his nose. He turned and leaned his back against the bar, noticed the Reverend, and nodded to him. The Reverend responded likewise. A reporter from the *Gold Hill Daily News* approached Teasdale and asked him about his fighting style. "I let the other guy tire himself out," he summarized.

The reporter, after wiping up the splatters of blood that had fallen on his notebook, asked Teasdale to what kind of fighter he compared himself. He shrugged. "Some folks say I fight like a woman."

This was the quote that ran on the front page the next day.

※

OCTOBER 1875

Late in the afternoon of the twenty-fifth of October 1875, Charles Teasdale's fans were waiting to see him in his hour of glory. He had never fought against any of the Eastern champions, nor even against one of the self-proclaimed champions of the West, but he was preparing to confront an Englishman called Lyman Brettle. The simple fact that his opponent was a proud subject of Queen Victoria had been enough to unite the gamblers behind him, whether they were American or Irish. Only the Mexicans, who were only interested in cockfighting, failed to understand what was at stake.

Posts strung with ropes were set up on an empty lot behind a block of buildings. Spectators began to assemble around the ring.

The Reverend Aaron, who didn't like having to fight for elbow room, took his place among the few supporters of the Englishman who had gathered on one side of the arena. Some of the regular fans stared over the ropes at the Reverend and whispered among themselves. The two contenders arrived simultaneously, and the crowd parted to make way for them. The two pugilists threw their hats into the ring before passing under the ropes. Teasdale lost the toss and found himself facing the setting sun, with his adversary bobbing and weaving in a halo of light. Blinded, Teasdale took a blow between the eyes when the fight had barely begun.

For almost two hours Teasdale's supporters winced, as much to see their favourite being battered as to realize that senseless courage was not enough against a professional who had the advantage of a private trainer's advice. The blood on Teasdale's face turned brown, covered with the dust he stirred up every time he hit the ground.

For a third time, Teasdale had difficulty getting to his feet. His defeat seemed inevitable when a shot rang out among the crowd. "This fight is fixed," someone shouted. The crowd rumbled. The referee protested. More shots rang out. The town marshal entered the ring to announce that the fight was cancelled, and his deputies began to disperse the crowd. The men went off angrily, spitting over their shoulders. The Reverend remained motionless, his arms crossed. The marshal gestured to him to make his escape, and the referee caught him by the shoulder. "This fight wasn't fixed. Look at the shape he's in," he pleaded, pointing at the half-dead Teasdale. He had one knee in the sand and the other hand on the ropes, while blood trickled from his chin to the ground.

The referee and the marshal placed Teasdale's arms around their necks and dragged him to St. Mary's Hospital. Two deputies accompanied them, guns at the ready.

✴

The Reverend went into a café and sat near a window overlooking the empty ring. He was eating a rhubarb tart when three men appeared around his table. "Well," they said, "if it isn't the guy who was in on the deal."

He laid down his fork and wiped his mouth. "I imagine you're referring to Charles Teasdale's defeat by Lyman Brettle. Frankly, I don't see what makes you think that fight was fixed."

"That's it, say what you like. We thought preachers didn't cheat."

The Reverend looked at each of the men in turn. "Not only do preachers worthy of the name not cheat, they don't gamble either. I didn't have a bet on anyone."

"So you say, but you've been seen at every fight in the Washoe Valley. This is the first time you've been seen on his opponent's side, and just by chance it's the Englishman wins."

The Reverend lifted his tin mug, took a swig, and set it down again. "So I'm responsible for something just because it happens in front of me?"

"Still, it's strange, don't you think?"

The Reverend sighed. "Of all the things you've witnessed around here, is it what's strange that upsets you most?"

⚝

It was after one in the morning when Teasdale entered one of the saloons. His face was devoured by stitches and some of his beard had been shaved close to the jaw. He ordered a bottle of whiskey, settled down in the back of the room, and closed his eyes. When he opened them, the saloonkeeper was standing in front of him, fists on hips and his apron pushed behind him, like a cape. "We don't serve crooked fighters here. Go find yourself somewhere else to sleep."

Without a word, Teasdale grabbed his hat and bottle and made for the exit. In the doorway he turned around, took a swig from the bottle, and spat it out before him. "I wish you a good evening, ladies and gentlemen," he said, before raising his hat and setting off down the street.

He spent the night wandering from saloon to saloon. In one he managed to get an hour's sleep before two customers with cartridge belts slung over their shoulders threw him out, under the passive gaze of the employees. Teasdale tried his luck in all the dives, taverns, and gambling dens in the town before suffering his final rejection. "You understand, my customers are real pissed off. I don't want no problems," the saloonkeeper explained.

"All that's left for me now is to make a campfire," Teasdale concluded. "Can I at least take a bottle with me?"

As he wandered in the streets, Teasdale had to hold on to his hat against the wind blowing in off nearby Mount Davidson – baptized the "Washoe Zephyr," as if it were a predatory animal on the prowl, or maybe a god that ruled the valley. Teasdale pulled the cork from the bottle with his teeth, and after a quick gulp placed his thumb over its neck. He advanced against the sand-laden gusts, and stopped in the middle of the street just as the first rays of light were breaking through. He moistened a finger as if to check the direction of the wind, and laughed to himself before taking another swig.

At five in the morning, though he had never slept in a bed before, he entered Kate Shea's boarding house and asked to rent a room on the top floor, overlooking the street. Of all the business people in Virginia City, maybe Miss Shea was the one who should have turned him away, for seven minutes later the roof of her boarding house was on fire. By the time the flames reached the opera house, Teasdale was walking slowly in the opposite direction to the volunteer firemen who were rushing to the scene with bells ringing. Teasdale climbed the lowest hill and sat on the ground, clutching his knees. He took one last drink from the bottle as he watched Virginia City burn. Daytime fires had always been his favourites. Orange flames licking the azure morning sky. The pillar of black smoke rising, linking earth and sky. Daytime fires were the most obscene.

Charles Abner Teasdale Jr. That's my signature.
I add the "Junior" for my own pleasure.
I've never been anyone's junior.

CARSON CITY

NOVEMBER 1875

When he was told that Charles Teasdale had been captured at Panamint, Jewett W. Adams, lieutenant governor of the State of Nevada, let out a deep sigh – for he was also the *ex officio* governor of Carson City jail. "Here we go. Now the problems begin," he declared privately.

The founders of Carson City had made every effort to make their piece of country the state capital of Nevada. They had planted poplars along the streets to make the town verdant and shady.

The owner of the Warm Springs Hotel offered to house the town's first prisoners. The hotel became the state prison, and its proprietor the prison governor. With the passing years, increasingly higher and thicker walls had been built around the prison using huge yellow stone cut from a quarry within the prison limits. The prisoners themselves quarried the sandstone that served to confine them more securely.

Despite these efforts, Carson City had failed to make itself the certain choice as seat of the capital, and ambitious men had been dreaming more and more of transferring the honour to the livelier and more populous Virginia City. So, when Adams learned that the latter city had been burned to the ground, he was unable to suppress a slight smile before loudly expressing his sympathy for all those Virginians left to live on the street, or whose businesses had gone up in smoke. Having been elected lieutenant governor of the State of Nevada, Adams was obliged to rejoice publicly at the capture of Charles Teasdale, the Virginia City arsonist, while knowing that it would only mean trouble for him. The voters of

Virginia City would demand a hanging, though the sentence was more likely to be life imprisonment. Only those found guilty of first-degree murder could be condemned to death. But anyone demanding vengeance merely needed to form a vigilance committee, catch the criminal, and lynch him before the authorities had time to lock him up. But lynching gave the impression that the justice system was weak and the politicians incompetent. If he wanted to be elected state governor one day, Jewett W. Adams would have to find a way to have Teasdale executed legally.

The Reverend Aaron knew all this because he was the sole confidant of Adams's mistress, a young German singer who resided in a respectable hotel. Adams did not want to be seen in her company, so the entire time that the lovebirds had together was spent within the confines of her room. He would not allow her to stoop to working, and forbade her all visitors. In any case, she knew no one. One day she reproached him, saying, "The hotels in this town are becoming prisons, and its citizens are your prisoners."

✳

Jewett W. Adams followed the jailer along the corridor leading to the common cell into which new prisoners were crammed while awaiting transfer to the main building. He had to repress the urge to vomit, so overpowering was the smell of sweat and urine. The few rays of light that filtered above the heads of the eight crowded prisoners did not allow him to distinguish their faces. Some muttered prayers, others shouted for them to be quiet. In the gloom, the lieutenant governor's outline stood out without his features being visible, yet one of the men recognized the part in his hair and the full, white moustache that fell on both sides of his chin. He nudged his neighbour.

"It's the lieutenant governor," he said.

The jailer opened the cell door.

"Charles Teasdale," he called.

Teasdale rose and came forward heavily, with the walk of a man whose legs have been shackled so that he can more readily be ordered to move faster. The jailer closed the cell door behind him. Teasdale was led into the empty courtyard. Above the prison wall, the peaks of the Sierra Nevada were sprinkled with white. He was stripped and placed on a chair. His hair and beard were shaved off – a treatment to which all the prisoners were subjected in order to control the epidemic of lice that infested the pillows. A bucketful of water was poured over his head. He shivered for a few minutes before being thrown a towel, followed by his prison garb. He first pulled on the trousers, decorated with wide vertical white and grey stripes, then a shirt with horizontal stripes, and finally a buttoned sleeveless jacket, also striped: the dress of a perfect gentleman, but designed to make fugitives immediately stand out among honest folk.

Teasdale was dragged through the oldest building along a corridor lit by lamps screwed to the walls at regular intervals. "Not a candle in the whole damn place," he remarked before getting a shove in his back.

He entered an almost-empty room containing a mahogany desk and a few chairs. The decor seemed unchanged since the days when the room had served as a tea room for hotel guests. The walls were covered with sage wallpaper and the floor with a Persian-style carpet. It was easy to imagine the sofas and low tables of yesteryear, with the ornaments and porcelain tea services that graced them. The curtains were heavy and ornamented with tassels. Adams drew them back to let the light in, and Teasdale could see that even these windows had bars. He was seated on a chair facing the desk, his cuffed hands crossed on his belly. Adams picked up a pile of posters with photos of men wanted for murder. He brought each sheet up to Teasdale's face, trying to find a killer for whom he could pass. But even without his beard, Teasdale had unusual features, with a well-defined nose and unusually large eyes. The precision of the photographs made any confusion impossible. Adams took another pile from a drawer, this time older posters of wanted men, mostly pictured in sketches rather than photographs. He repeated the exercise, taking time to scrutinize each drawing. He stopped for a few moments on a poster for Caspar Tootsey, and then shook his head.

He went through the rest of the pile faster and faster, becoming increasingly exasperated. "Dammit," he exclaimed, "surely there must be someone in the world who looks like this man!"

Teasdale shrugged. "Not that I knows of, there ain't," he said.

✳

The door closed behind the lawyer. He wore a chestnut brown suit, a derby hat, and a black tie. Teasdale, in his striped three-piece suit, had his back to the wall, squatting on his heels, arms stretched out above his knees to maintain his balance. An oil lamp, its glass chimney blackened by soot, sat on the ground beside him. The feeble light it cast softened the corners of the room and magnified the shadows. The words "Charles" and "Teasdale" had been scratched all over the whitewashed walls. "May I?" asked the lawyer, pointing to the bed.

He sat down, took out his pocket watch, opened it, and then put it away. "I've been brought in from Salt Lake City to defend you," he said. "Cases like yours are my specialty."

"What does that mean, cases like mine?"

"It means ... The cases of accused men that everyone hates."

"Really?" said Teasdale. "So you can get me out of this place?"

"That depends on what you've told them since you got here."

"I've told them nothing."

"You've neither denied nor confessed?"

"I've said nothing."

"That's good. It's very good. Now then, I won't beat around the bush. Are you innocent, Mr. Teasdale?"

Teasdale shook his head.

"Thank you for your honesty," said the lawyer. "Though not everyone who admits to a killing does so out of honesty."

"I ain't got nothin' to hide. I'd rather be dead than spend the rest of my days in this place."

"Have you ever killed anyone?" Teasdale closed his eyelids and then slowly reopened them, as if overcome by a sudden weariness.

He stretched out his legs and scratched his Adam's apple. His razor burn was still visible, as was the red imprint left on the sides of his neck by the cord of his Colt Navy. He crossed his arms.

"I was in the phantom cavalry till '71."

The lawyer examined his client with narrowed eyes, saying nothing.

"Apart from that, it was self-defence. It was them or me."

The lawyer took off his coat and stood up, stroking his moustache.

"Does anyone know that you killed these … people you're speaking of?"

"There's some in Hamilton."

"They know it was self-defence?"

"Even better. They think it was for their protection."

"Very good. Now, have you got any enemies? Are there folks with a grudge against you outside of Virginia City?"

"I dunno. I ain't inside their heads."

"But there are people who have reasons to wish you ill?"

Teasdale nodded, gazing into space.

"Where?"

He shrugged. "All over."

The lawyer went back to his seat on the bed and crossed his arms. "That's not going to be any help."

Screwing his eyes tight, Teasdale sized up the lawyer and decided that he was the bottom of the barrel. "I thought that was your specialty." He looked away. "Anyhow, what's it to you? I ain't even payin' you."

"Someone is paying me, but I'm not allowed to tell you who. That's part of the deal."

Then Teasdale stared wide-eyed at the lawyer. "I've no family or friends, Mr. Lawyer. If there's someone payin' you to save me from the rope, it's got to be he wants to kill me himself later on."

The lawyer sighed. "So I imagine churchgoing isn't one of your habits, Mr. Teasdale?"

JANUARY 1876

Charles Teasdale's jury trial lasted two whole days. The Reverend Aaron was called to the witness box on the second day. He abstained from chewing tobacco for the occasion, although most of the jurors had cigars in their mouths and clouds of smoke drifted across the room.

"You say you were in the company of the accused during the night of the twenty-sixth of October? Tell us about it," asked the prosecuting attorney.

"After he was thrown out of all the taverns, according to what he told me himself, Charles Teasdale went to the Presbyterian church, where I was. He had no thought of getting his revenge for the injustice inflicted on him that day. He pleaded with me to help him give up drinking and find real work. You see, he never had a father, no one was ever able to teach him what he needed to pursue a trade or business. He learned to live on the street and in the saloons, but it's not too late to save him. He pleaded with me to show him the way. I invited him to pray. The man you are accusing was communing with the Lord at the time when the fire was started. Those who thought they saw him in Kate Shea's boarding house were mistaken. In any case, everyone who knows this man is aware that he never sleeps in boarding houses or hotels, so ..."

"Yet Kate Shea states not only that she let her room to Charles Teasdale, but that she saw his signature in her register. It's her word against yours."

"Then show me this register. But let me guess: I imagine it went up in smoke like the rest of the town. I'm a minister of God and she's a woman of ill repute who is said never to have refused a lodger. Which of us are you going to believe? Who do you think would dare perjure themselves on the Holy Scriptures?"

Charles Teasdale was acquitted. In the light of the evidence provided, the jury concluded that doubt about his guilt was more than reasonable. A week later, to avoid any unconvinced citizens getting their hands on him, he was escorted outside the town under cover of darkness.

For months, each evening before going to sleep, Jewett W. Adams continued to leaf through the wanted posters. Every time he came to the one of Caspar Tootsey he lingered a little longer. Then he would sigh and put out his lamp. Yet one day he was elected governor of the State of Nevada.

It's my father's fault if I die, for I never had no father.
The only one I had was Sam Ambrose,
and Sam Ambrose never existed.

ELDORADO CANYON

FEBRUARY 1876

Eldorado Canyon could have been a mining town like any other, afflicted since birth by picks and mattocks and abandoned at the first indication that the ore was exhausted. But there was something else about it, strewn as it was with signs left behind by unreasonable folk – folk for whom fate was an adversary to be provoked.

It was early morning, just after the revellers had gone to bed and before the early risers were up. The Reverend Aaron arrived at the camp and made for the river, leading his horse by the bridle along the pebble-strewn dirt road. He passed an abandoned barn, an enormous wooden structure, all of four storeys high, with a sloping roof. Only its walls and roof remained. All the doors were gone. Through the openings, little red and grey piles of rock could be seen, and farther back, the miners' shacks. At the very the top, from the empty little window on the facade, a baby puma had been hanged by the neck. It was only a wild cat, but it gave the Reverend goosebumps, precisely because it was just a cat. Who could possibly bear such a grudge against this feline that they were prepared to climb a ruined building and create such a gallows? Perhaps the Reverend had heard an animal caterwauling the night before but hadn't paid any attention. And anyway, who can claim to tell the cry of a cat that's fighting from one being hanged?

✴

Neither Charles Teasdale nor the Reverend Aaron had a specific destination. Each believed himself to be free, but both were

69

looking for the same mining towns. The men would lose sight of each other for weeks, but then chance would put them side by side at the bar in some saloon, or lining up outside a public bathhouse.

The Reverend entered the makeshift saloon during the midday rush hour. The hubbub of miners, part-time bandits, and other fugitives could be heard from well outside the long cabin, whose thatched roof rested on uneven tree trunks. It served no food. In Eldorado, corn liquor and cheap brandy replaced the main meal. In the corner across from the entrance, Charles Teasdale dozed, his head leaned back against the wall and his mouth open, his saddle sitting on the other chair as his only companion. His hat was jammed between the wall and the back of his head. His hair was growing back and beginning to cover his scalp. Around him, men in soft-felt hats, some bare-chested beneath their suspenders, were drinking and playing cards; a man wearing goatskin chaps had removed his boots and was filing his toenails; another was polishing his gun, a long rifle with notches showing how many he had killed – all of them ordinary living beings who had grown up far from any concern for hygiene or from a mother's love.

At one time soldiers had been stationed in this hamlet to ensure the miners' safety, but later they were recalled to serve in the war. Indeed, numerous deserters remained among the civilians. Those who stayed behind had to learn to defend themselves against repeated attacks by the Paiute – avoiding one war only to be caught up in another. In a place like this, surrounded by men equally familiar with the precise colour of blood-soaked sand, Teasdale didn't allow anyone to bother him. These were men without ties except to the spirits of those they had killed, men who could all compete for the title of freest man between Santa Cruz and Santa Fe.

✷

Early in the afternoon Teasdale rose, picked up his saddle, and left the saloon. The Reverend found him again a few hours later in a gambling den. All evening, he watched Teasdale knock back drink after drink as he moved from one game of faro to another, losing his stake and then winning it back. Later, Teasdale disappeared for an hour, probably to pay a visit to the brothel. Then he returned to play one last game before ordering a bottle of whiskey and pulling up an isolated chair, which he placed with its back to the Reverend. Teasdale took a swig. The Reverend pretended to read his Bible. Teasdale took another swig; the Reverend turned a page. This ploy continued until Teasdale rose and came toward the Reverend. Placing his two fists on the table in front of him, he leaned forward. "Had enough of watching me sleep?" he asked in a low voice, so that the other gamblers couldn't hear.

"What makes you think I'm watching you?"

"I can't sleep if you stay here."

"Well then, go somewhere else."

"I was here first."

"So? Do like everyone else and rent a room."

Teasdale gripped the back of the chair in front of him and leaned his weight on it. "Let's make a deal, me and you. In future, whenever we cross paths, the first to arrive has the right to stay where he is, and the other has to leave."

"But I couldn't care less if you're in the same place as me. It's your problem, not mine."

"You keep followin' me wherever I go. I could make it a problem for you too."

"I'm a man of God, and you're an outlaw. No one will defend you."

"You ain't even a real preacher. I ain't never seen you preach."

"And I've never seen you prospecting."

"You've got a nerve for a guy that don't carry a gun."

"Unlike you, I have no need of a weapon."

"The day I've had enough of feelin' you're always on my heels, mebbe then you'll need one."

The Reverend laid down his Bible and crossed his arms. "I saved your life, and that's all the thanks I get?"

"I never asked you for nothin'."

"But you're alive, and a free man. And I've never asked you for anything either. You can do what you like, but I'm not budging."

Teasdale turned on his heel and threw his saddle over his shoulder. He turned around, stared at the Reverend, then picked up his hat and bottle. He backed out of the room, never taking his eyes off the preacher.

Three weeks passed before they met again.

There are fruits without stones,
so there must be men without souls.

HOSSEFROSS

FEBRUARY 1876

Once there was nothing in the place: just men, on foot and half naked. Later, men on horseback came, and the half-naked ones rode horses too. And then the men on horseback armed themselves with guns they could carry with them, so the half-naked men on horseback also equipped themselves with guns they could carry with them. And lo and behold, at every turn, on every young kid's hips, you found revolvers and derringers mass-produced somewhere in Connecticut, and the half-naked men had no choice but to wear clothes so that they could carry guns on their hips too.

The Moapa Valley was one of the rare places where there were no Indians anymore, but for all that the whites were no more numerous. The Reverend Aaron was crossing the valley when he was offered hospitality at a tiny ranch where the animals were starving – a property consisting of a house and a barn, hidden in the hollows, sitting there like a thing someone had dropped along the way.

The rancher, who was called Hossefross, hadn't left home in two years. He had travelled there with his wife in the hope of founding a family, at a time when the call of the West was less a dream than an imperative. The West had an expiry date. You had to take the big leap before it was too late. His wife had died of smallpox three weeks after they arrived. Since then he had lived as a recluse, selling his cattle to those who approached him.

Honour-bound to obey the rules of hospitality, Hossefross put a lamp and crocheted placemats on the table, and served a stew for the evening meal. The two men ate in silence. The

Reverend told himself that, even if he had wanted to, he wouldn't have known what to preach. It was easier to preach to women or couples, for there would be at least one woman to ask him to teach her something, to which the Reverend would reply that he had nothing to teach people who welcomed their fellow men with such generosity.

The two men were swallowing their last few mouthfuls when they heard a rider approaching. Hossefross went out, banging the door behind him, causing the lace curtain chosen by his late wife to flutter. Outside was Charles Teasdale, who had also come to take advantage of the ranch's hospitality. Hossefross swallowed his mouthful noisily as he watched the newcomer dismount. He observed the long-barrelled gun attached to the saddle, the cartridge belt, and the Colt Navy swinging on his chest. Teasdale raised his hat with one hand and then, with ill-concealed annoyance as the Reverend emerged from behind his host, returned it to his head. He greeted the Reverend with a nod.

"You know this young man?" asked Hossefross, turning to the Reverend.

"The Reverend Aaron saved my life once," Teasdale put in, which had the immediate effect of rekindling confidence in Hossefross's eyes.

The two travellers sat at the table, across from each other. Hossefross placed a third bowl in front of Teasdale. Soon he was the only one chewing, with eyes lowered on the stew.

"So how did it happen, when you saved his life?" asked Hossefross.

The Reverend tore a piece from the loaf in the centre of the table and mopped up the inside of his bowl. "To tell the truth, I didn't do much. I just convinced some folks not to kill him. I did my duty as God's servant. A pastor's role isn't restricted to saving souls. You sometimes have to start by saving lives."

"Sometimes there's no soul to be saved, even when folks are alive. You wasn't the first to save me from hanging."

At the word "hanging," Hossefross looked away.

"There's my old companions of the phantom cavalry saved me from the rope too," Teasdale went on. "I owe them my life not once, but eight times over. Basically, I should have stayed with them forever, or at least till I could settle my debt by saving their lives in return."

"And you did?" asked the Reverend.

Teasdale laid down his spoon. He looked at the Reverend, swinging on his chair, balanced on its rear legs. "No. I ran out of patience. I killed the lot of them."

The Reverend returned his gaze without a word. Outside, a mule began to bray. Hossefross took a breath, stood up, and began to gather up the bowls. His hands were shaking; the dishes knocked together and clinked against one another. He turned away from the two men and set everything down in a bucket beside the sink. "Don't take it wrong," he managed to utter, "but I have to tell you there's nothing to steal here."

"Never you worry, Mr. Hossefross. We'll sleep outside, in the open. That's nothing new for you, isn't that right, Mr. Teasdale?"

Teasdale brought the front legs of his chair back to the floor. "You know me too well, Reverend."

✳

The two men camped outside around a fire, away from the corral, but no one closed an eye that night. Through the windows of the only room in the house, they could see the pale light of the oil lamp that Hossefross carried with him wherever he went.

A shot rang out during the night. They found Hossefross behind the house, among his cattle, bleeding from his lower leg. He had shot himself in the foot with his rifle. "I had a pain in my little toe. I've had enough of my little toe hurting," he repeated, sobbing.

Teasdale helped the Reverend to harness up a cart. There was no doctor in Overton, the nearest stopping place, so they took Hossefross to the Utah border, where it was said you could find a brothel that was home to an abortionist with a healing touch. It was only a rumour. There was indeed a brothel, but no abortionist.

The sun was coming up as they arrived. The Reverend's lanky frame filled the front of the cart. Teasdale rode alongside on his own horse. Their hats were silhouetted against the rosy horizon. Only the knocking of the wheels against the stones and Hossefross's groans were heard. They brought a woman from the brothel back to the ranch to look after the wounded man. She was not very conscientious: she couldn't wait to be done and get back to her brothel, maybe because between two lousy jobs the one you know best is the one you prefer.

We've all grown up in dumps left behind by the mining companies. They used their money to pay for countless parties and whoring, and what do you know, a little later we were born. They made off with what's owed us, and we made it our duty to get it back. Every time we rob a bank, or hold up a stagecoach, we're just reclaiming part of our inheritance.

HAMILTON

OCTOBER 1871

On the fourteenth of October 1871, the seven remaining members of the phantom cavalry set up camp in a clearing in the valley east of Hamilton. "Clearing" was just a way of saying that in that spot there was less sagebrush and fewer thorn bushes than anywhere else. They hunted hares all afternoon, and at nightfall lit a fire to roast their catch. All evening, they worked on a plan to attack a wagon train heading for Hamilton, north of the rocky spur.

Charles Teasdale kept watch while the others slept. There was no moon, and the sky was so black that nothing could be seen beyond the circle of light cast by the campfire. In the darkest of the night, Teasdale got up and positioned himself between the fire and the men, who lay strung out in a row on one side, sheltered from the north-easterly wind. Darius Cole slept in the middle of the row, one hand on his belly, close to his revolver. Teasdale could have remained there, back to the fire, and fired a bullet into the head of each man. He would have had the advantage of discerning every movement they made, lit by the flames, while to them he remained in shadow as they stared into the light. No doubt some would have leapt up at the sound of the first shots, confused momentarily by the sight of their murderer's dark bulk silhouetted against the red embers of the fire and thinking they were having a nightmare. But he decided instead to go behind them and cut their throats with his Bowie knife. He began on the left. Ezra Whitaker, who was last on the extreme right, woke up just as Teasdale was finishing off the man next to him. He leapt from his sleeping bag on all fours and drew his revolver. Teasdale threw himself on him, and the gun fell farther back, behind Whitaker. The two men crouched, Teasdale brandishing his knife in one hand as Whitaker inched backward to pick up his weapon. When he bent over, Teasdale rushed him. They struggled on the ground. Whitaker tried to strangle him with the cord holding the Colt around his neck. A shot was fired in the darkness. Whitaker collapsed.

Teasdale remained on his knees, recovering his breath. The fire continued to crackle, its warm light dancing over the inert bodies. Teasdale picked up his knife and wiped it off on his pants before casting a last glance at Whitaker's corpse, lying apart from the others – the only man to be startled awake between sleep and death.

Though Teasdale had rid himself of those who wouldn't let him sleep, he couldn't close an eye for the rest of the night. At dawn, he piled two corpses on each horse and roped the animals together, one behind the other. He headed for Hamilton, the county seat, where he had a good chance of finding the sheriff. He entered along the main street; curious onlookers observed the funeral procession. A woman brought a hand to her mouth. A man removed his hat and wiped his brow. Teasdale tied his horse to a rail, while the others pawed the ground behind. The bodies laid across the last horse seemed to be slipping. He rebalanced them across the saddle and walked to the sheriff's office. A moment later he emerged accompanied by the sheriff, who examined each body in turn. Teasdale was awarded a total of seven hundred dollars, including five hundred as his reward for capturing Darius Cole.

With this money he was able to wander for four months, doing nothing but drink, sleep, and drink some more. When he ran out of cash, he began to beg. When he had exhausted the charity of the citizens of Hamilton he changed towns, started to borrow, and then changed towns again. He kept going like that until the day when one of his creditors decided to give him a thrashing, resulting in one of the most splendid free-for-alls ever observed thereabouts. Then, as he was puking his guts into a metal boiler behind a saloon, he was offered a fight against the reigning champion of Lander County, who just happened to be looking for an easy opponent.

Charles Teasdale gave up stealing and begging. These were not occupations to be pursued for an entire lifetime. Nor was boxing. But no one knew what Teasdale was to make of the rest of his life.

⚜

MARCH 1876

The Reverend passed through Hamilton without dismounting and continued up the butte toward Treasure City, grafted on to the mountainside. In front of him, a convoy of merchandise transported on mule back was heading for the same destination. The mules were panting, stubbornly pausing to graze on the little green shoots that managed to pierce the soil between the rocks.

The buildings of Treasure City appeared one after another, with their facades of blackened wood on the western slope. Some seemed abandoned, appeared to have lost their roofs, or were invaded by sagebrush. The brown and grey peaks of Mount Hamilton loomed to the west like the successive surges of an age-old tidal wave of rock. To the south was the furrow traced by the winding road, shrinking until it disappeared.

Perched on a particularly steep hilly outcrop a man was squatting, his buttocks resting on his heels. The Reverend approached him, and though the man's back was toward him, he recognized Charles Teasdale by his spurs, his plain flannel shirt, and his too-short jacket.

"Go ahead, do what you came to do," said Teasdale without turning around.

"I came to admire the view."

"Sure!" said Teasdale with a laugh.

The Reverend lifted the tails of his coat and sat cross-legged on the ground. "What did you think I came for?"

Teasdale didn't answer. He spat in front of him, and his saliva disappeared into empty space. "There ain't nothin' here. You've no cause to be here."

"Nor do you. Maybe I'm here for the same reason as you. Maybe I'm a thief too. Since you're convinced I'm not a preacher."

"To start with, I thought you was a promoter from the East come scoutin' for fresh talent. You're no promoter. I dunno who pays you. I dunno what you want. But you can kill me, what do I care."

"You're lying. If you weren't afraid of dying you'd have no difficulty sleeping, even in my presence."

Teasdale looked over his shoulder out of the corner of his eye and then turned away.

"Have you given any thought to your dying words?" the Reverend went on.

Teasdale shrugged.

"Really, if I hadn't gotten you out of Carson City Jail, wouldn't you have prepared a few words? A thought for a loved one?"

"Never been my style."

"You see, Charles, even the most miserable of pickpockets can't help taking advantage of his moment of glory, just before they pull the bag over his head. Most times people in the crowd never stop shouting insults at the condemned man, who ultimately doesn't speak to anyone, except maybe God. But for you, the crowd would have gone quiet. People would have wanted to hear your last words. And you'd have said nothing. We have one thing in common, you and me. I'm a preacher, so people expect me to preach at them. And when they grab my tailcoat and plead with me to talk about the emptiness of their lives, I don't say anything."

Teasdale turned around and stared at the Reverend. "For God's sake, who are you?"

"I'm not here to haunt you, Charles, but to save you."

Teasdale turned away and began to sob. He buried his head between his knees. "Why?" he finally pronounced.

"Because I think that usually you're afraid of nothing. I think you're capable of sleeping through a gunfight. That's an extraordinary talent. I'm no fortune teller, but I can guarantee you one thing: the next time you're on the gallows, the crowd will be silent. And maybe in that moment you'll remember me."

The Reverend got up, mounted his horse, and rode down toward the road, while Teasdale followed him with red-rimmed eyes.

If I keep coming back to this rotten state where they want me dead, it's because I think I'm invincible. And it just gets worse with time. For me to keep from going back for the thousandth time, I'd have had to die there the first time.

PRESCOTT

AUGUST 1870

In the very heart of Arizona, the town of Prescott seemed like an oasis with its tall grasses and forests of ponderosa pine.

"I'm amazed you've never been there," mocked Larry Udall, in the days when Teasdale belonged to the phantom cavalry. "There's nary a Mexican in the place. Just nice white folks that attend church and all, aside from a few black guys to shine your boots," he went on. "There's wood everywhere. You won't see a single brick house around there, not even the governor's. And like it was on purpose, they've put wooden pickets for fences around two-storey houses, like in the Midwest. And they store barrels of gunpowder in their basements, like bullets wasn't invented yet. You'd set fire to the town just lookin' at it."

✴

AUGUST 1876

Charles Teasdale and the Reverend Aaron were accustomed to riding side by side when heading for the same place, but they never ate dinner together, as if to remind themselves that ultimately they were headed in opposite directions.

Teasdale was moving on southward from town to town without changing anything in his late-evening rituals, except that he spent more and more time practising his signature. On the way to Hiko, he admitted to the Reverend that the idea of choosing his last words, which he had found childish at first, had grown on him.

"What I have to say before I die is nobody's business. On the other hand, it's true it might be a good idea to choose my last thoughts. Since I won't be goin' to heaven for sure, my last thoughts is likely to be my last. I'd better not screw up. Imagine if the last sight that came to me before I died was ... I dunno ... a pig gettin' slaughtered. Or the ugliest girl I slept with."

In Barclay, he went into a clothing store and emerged wearing a white shirt for the first time in his life. His jacket still lacked a watch chain and the old Colt Navy still swung on his chest, but now he was served faster in diners, and in brothels he was offered younger girls.

One day he went so far south that he crossed the Nevada frontier. He entered the Arizona Territory with a new identity, as Charley Monday Jr., abandoning his precious initials, and in doing so breaking the only rule he had always imposed on himself. With his new alias, he claimed to come from a pioneer family in Oregon. People guessed he was a professional gambler – an impression he didn't always dare to correct, as if claiming to be a professional boxer would have meant challenging fate. He had been so many other things that he wasn't yet certain about what he wanted to be.

✳

The Reverend Aaron entered Fort Date Creek, a former army post converted to an inn. It was a favourite stopping place for both travellers of substance and the down and out, since anyone who didn't want to pay for a bedroom could camp inside the perimeter of the fort for less money.

The smell of candlewax floated through the dining room, mingled with the aroma of baked ham. The whitewashed walls seemed yellow under the only light, which came from a candelabra suspended from the ceiling beams. The room was occupied by two long tables of varnished wood with no tablecloths. Teasdale was sitting at the back of the room. The Reverend greeted him with a nod. He found a place at the other table, near the door, taking note of two men seated in the middle who were watching him suspiciously from under their big soft-felt hats. The Reverend was bent over the menu when he recognized the characteristic clink of Teasdale's spurs approaching. Teasdale set down his plate and, swinging his legs across the bench, sat down in front of him and went on eating, as if he had finally decided that there was no harm in being seen in the preacher's company.

The waiter came to take the Reverend's order. In the meantime, Teasdale pushed away his plate and took his sheets of paper and his pen from his satchel. The waiter went away. The two men in big hats ate on in silence. The Reverend looked at them, and one of them stared back at the Reverend. He withstood his gaze, thinking to himself that Teasdale would enjoy jumping on the man.

But Teasdale seemed indifferent to the roughneck's challenge. "They told me that if I won in Prescott I could fight in Cerbat, in a tavern where there's no ring, but a stage. Can you imagine that? A fight seen from only one side? If that's the future ..." he said, tossing his head. He began scribbling on his sheet of paper.

The Reverend noticed that he had kept the scraps of paper on which he had practised back when he still signed "Charles Teasdale." "It's not very wise, all that stuff," the Reverend concluded, gesturing to the metal box with his chin.

"What use is it runnin' everywhere if there's no one to run after me?"

The waiter put a steaming plate in front of the Reverend, who began to eat while watching Teasdale continue to fill the sheet with more or less identical signatures. The Reverend stared at the top of his bent head. He hadn't seen him without a hat since his hair had grown back to a respectable length.

"Tell me ..." Teasdale needed a few seconds before going on. He sniffed. "If I manage never to steal anythin' again and never to set a fire nowhere again ... D'you think there's a chance I won't be hanged?"

"Is there a way you'd rather die?"

"Given the choice, I'd rather die in the ring. I'd rather die in the ring tomorrow than be hanged a hundred years from now."

The Reverend nodded, took a swig of water, and set down the mug. "Then it's simple, you have to maintain your new reputation, so that no one will want to kill you outside the ring."

Teasdale gave a faint smile. "Larry Udall would be disappointed to hear that."

"Larry who?"

"Larry Udall. One of the guys in the phantom cavalry. The third one whose throat I cut."

＊

When the Reverend entered Prescott, a ball game was in progress, with the local team playing the soldiers from Fort Whipple. The Prescott players, dressed in white with socks up to below the knees, were waiting at attention, hands over their hearts, as the brass and drum band announced the start of the game. Prominent in the background was the garnet tip of Thumb Butte, like the neck of a giant bottle above the avenue that contained all the saloons in this well-planned town.

Employees of the sawmill and budding politicians had gathered around the baseball diamond. Some breathed through kerchiefs when a player sliding close to them kicked up the dust. Ladies in their Sunday best fanned themselves, taking up twice the room of the men because of their bustles and their trains that swept the sand as they went. A solitary laugh, racked by coughing, rang out from the heart of the crowd, though for the most part the spectators were serious and attentive. Nothing was less ridiculous than a baseball match. The Reverend stood on tiptoe and saw that Teasdale was the source of this outburst. He had never heard Teasdale laugh before.

The home team scored a run. "Ways to go! Good job!" Teasdale shouted, clapping louder than anybody, before again starting to laugh all by himself. When he moved away from the crowd, grumbling "It's all foolishness," the Reverend could see that he was wearing a white shirt under his jacket.

＊

That evening, Charley "Silverfists" Monday fought Crazy Euphenor Bagby in a dive on Montezuma Street.

The Reverend sat astride a chair close to the ring, his jacket unbuttoned, his hands on his knees. All the lighting was concentrated on the ring. Behind it, the shapes of faces could barely be made out in the semi-darkness. A cloud of cigar smoke floated around the boxers. The Reverend slowly chewed his tobacco, no matter what jabs hit their target, what masterly feints Teasdale pulled off, or what sledgehammer blows he received, as if the spectacle taking place before him was a still-life painting. There was indeed a future for this Charley Monday, this respectable fellow who really held no interest for the Reverend, but who would serve to launch the immortality of Charles Teasdale. This man who could enter Prescott without setting it on fire.

✭

The next morning, the Reverend questioned the wench Teasdale had treated himself to after his victory. She had very white skin and very black hair, and spoke with a foreign accent impossible to identify. She probably came from one of those minuscule kingdoms that kept getting invaded without anyone paying much attention. "He left me this," she said, holding out the scrap of paper containing Charley Monday's autograph. "In my country," she went on, "I never went to school. I asked him to teach me to write my name. He answered, 'It's no use being able to write your name if there's no one to remember it'."

They died in the thousands during the war and were laid to rest in national cemeteries. Folks say they was heroes, but no one even knows their names. I'd rather have a grave with my name over it, even if it means crowds will come to spit on it.

———————◆◇◆———————

GREATERVILLE

OCTOBER 1876

In Greaterville, you could with impunity blow tobacco smoke in the face of the señoritas, enter saloons without dismounting, and hammer on the door of the hotel in the middle of the night. Life in the town was punctuated by conflict between the American and Mexican miners: pickaxe blows struck between the eyes of a neighbour unlucky enough to have sung in the wrong language, avenging bullets fired into the back of someone who had dared to badmouth the other.

In these parts, men died young, while the cacti lived a hundred years. The tall, triple-branched saguaros, standing like signposts, were the dominant species in a region where nature was able to keep men in their place. More than one Christian had died from a wound inflicted by the spines of this plant. Through the valleys, stocky Mexicans transported canvas bags full of water on donkey-back to slake the miners' thirst. The Apaches never bothered the Mexicans, for the Indians were perfectly able to manage without water. In certain tribes, the traditional training required young braves to run for miles with their mouths full of liquid without swallowing a drop. No, despite its scarcity, water had little value for the Apaches in the area. What interested them was alcohol. One night two muleteers transporting whiskey and mescal from Tucson reached the town with bleeding feet, crying out in Spanish that they had been attacked by the Apaches. A party of volunteers was organized and set out at daybreak to capture the Indians. Even the saloonkeeper, for whom the stolen cargo had been intended, removed his apron and took a rifle from under the bar. Drunks readying their firepower to deal with a few natives as drunk as themselves.

✳

The Reverend happened to be in an eatery patronized only by Mexicans, a cellar of beaten earth with a woollen blanket for a door and a square hole cut in the top of the wall as its only window. In summer, it was a popular haunt because it was cool. In winter, you needed an iron will to linger there, even wearing an overcoat.

For the first time, the talk there turned to something other than the treachery of the Americans. "You can never trust the Apaches," someone said in Spanish. "If you see an Apache on his own with no weapon, you can be sure it's a trap. If their tracks lead to open ground, it's a trap."

"When you're fightin' savages, you have to behave like a savage. You have to develop their instincts. Get used to burying your shit and stop laughin' about nothin'."

"The Injuns only laugh when they're drunk," added another.

"Problem is, no one's willin' to pay any more. When I was young there was governors in the South would give a good fat purse to anyone brought in savages' scalps still warm, no questions asked. Nowadays they pay us to shoot stray dogs, and that's it."

"And there's another problem. It's only dogs can hear the Apaches comin' to attack afore they gets here."

"These days, killin' Injuns is a waste of time. There's no reward no more. It's a bit like goin' to the privy."

"And you, Preacher, what's your opinion of the savages?"

The Reverend pretended not to have heard, but with all eyes fixed on him, he sat back on his chair and looked at the ceiling as he searched for an answer, and then for the way to translate his thoughts into Spanish. "I think those who fought in the war will never get over it, and the others will never get over not having been part of it."

Staring into space, the men nodded under their Stetsons or sombreros, and returned to their own discussion.

✳

The riders returned empty-handed to Greaterville after three days, and after the eighth day fights began to proliferate. The mining company therefore decided to organize a bare-knuckle contest between an American and a Mexican as an outlet for aggression and to calm the homicidal urges.

The fight took place in the open, on a circular patch of ground that formed a natural gathering place in the centre of town. A marquee had been erected, more as shade from the afternoon sun than as a shelter from unlikely rain showers. The Reverend attended the fight, immersed in the crowd of miners and storekeepers who had closed up shop. The fight lasted four hours, until the Mexican could no longer get to his feet, and the American was proclaimed the victor. Around the posts and ropes of the ring, the crowd dispersed like a receding tide. Only Charles Teasdale remained on the opposite side; he seemed to have spotted the Reverend first. The two men doffed their hats to each other.

The next day, the Reverend learned that Charley Monday had received an offer of two hundred dollars from the mining company to face the American in a future fight, as soon as the latter was fit again.

✳

The Reverend was sleeping lightly when the first two shots rang out. As he climbed down from the upper bunk, the brass structure creaked. Yet in the bottom bed, the miner, sleeping fully clothed, with no sheet or blanket, seemed dead to the world. A stench of alcohol and vomit wafted through the dormitory. His hat and clothes under one arm, the Reverend stepped over two men in pink combinations who were snoring near the door, looking like plucked chickens, crumpled on the ground as if a hay mower had lifted them up and dropped them there. He was getting dressed in the corridor when a third shot rang out, and other sleepers streamed toward the first floor. Men carrying torches were advancing toward a saloon farther down the street. Orange flames stood out against the shades of blue that heralded dawn. A crowd had gathered around the saloon. The saloonkeeper was in the middle, and kept repeating, "They're gonna pay for the damage; they won't get away with it like that."

The Reverend approached a circle of men wearing buckskin and asked them what had happened.

"Paddy and me, we was in that saloon there. We was chattin' peaceful-like when this guy came in and planted himself in front of big Wilbur, who was drinkin' all by himself. The guy brought his hand to his belt and you heard a click comin' from Wilbur's direction. We don't know how it happened, for everyone made for the door. I guess we'll never know. Both of them are dyin'. They've lost too much blood. It smells of death in there ..."

The Reverend noticed Teasdale leaning against the hitching rail outside the general store, apart from the crowd.

"And that man over there, what was he doing?" he asked, pointing at him.

"Him? He had nothin' to do with it. He was asleep. My God, you can't pretend to be a-sleepin' like that, and you droolin' that way. But all the same, he got out like everyone else. He can't be any crazier than the rest."

"Did someone wake him or did he waken on his own?" inquired the Reverend.

The man stared at him before answering. "For sure he woke up on his own. There was guys shootin' at one another in there. What do you think, he should have waited till someone pulled him by the beard?"

The Reverend thanked him and moved away from the group. He stood motionless for a few seconds, observing Teasdale from a distance. He was taking gulps from his bottle, one hip resting against the rail, as if he had all the time in the world. As the Reverend walked away, the men in buckskin continued the conversation they had most likely begun inside, which was about why no one had ever died from dehydration when they drank only whiskey and mescal.

⚜

DECEMBER 1876

The fight between Charley Monday and the victorious American miner took place four days before Christmas – a Christmas smelling of chili con carne, with no gifts distributed to anyone. The Papago Indians who went from village to village selling items of pottery and woven baskets lingered in front of the saloon, hoping to find buyers, holding their merchandise over their heads, and offering to dance in exchange for a few cents. The Reverend and Teasdale had not crossed paths since the shooting incident three months before. Since then, Teasdale had fought and won two other fights in other towns in Arizona and New Mexico.

During the Christmas fight, the Reverend remained inside the cantina, wrapped in a blanket, listening to the other drinkers babbling in Spanish. From there he could hear disappointed shouts from the miners when they saw their fighter lose strength as the fight went on.

Teasdale came into the cantina with the Stars and Stripes around his shoulders; he quickly took it off and rolled it into a ball. He met the gaze of the Reverend, who greeted him as usual, but Teasdale looked away. He ordered himself a bottle and sat down with his back to the Reverend and crossed his arms.

"Seeing your peachy complexion, I'd say you had an easy time of it," said the Reverend.

Teasdale took a swig. "Where you been all this time? Found other folk to save, I bet," he shot back over his shoulder.

"You'd like to know you're not the only one who can be saved?"

"I don't give a damn about you. You've never saved no one, includin' me," he said, before turning farther away.

"Yet I saved you from the gallows."

"Yeah. Mebbe that time."

The Reverend closed his book. "Anyone would think you hold a grudge against me, Mr. Monday."

Teasdale shrugged. "Why would I?"

The Reverend smiled. "For the same reason as you fight people you don't know. Because you hate everybody, and nobody."

Teasdale spotted a bronze spittoon sitting beneath the nearby table, pulled it to him with his feet, and spat into it. "Until today I was glad I never shot at you."

The Reverend let the blanket fall from his shoulders, rose, and went across to Teasdale's table. He was preparing to draw up a chair when Teasdale put his feet on it to stop him. He put his hands on the table and leaned toward him. "Tell me, Mr. Monday, is it really true that you slept all the way through a gunfight?" he asked in a low voice, so that no one else could hear.

"I dunno. When I'm asleep, I'm asleep."

The Reverend nodded and drew back. "Truly, I just can't tell if it upsets you that you have a reputation, or if you do it on purpose."

"I don't see no connection," said Teasdale, wiping his nose on a corner of the flag. "You're the craziest preacher I've ever come across, for sure."

The Reverend smiled and held out his hand. "And you're the craziest of all the professional boxers, for sure."

Teasdale stared at the hand, hesitated, and then shook it, looking away. In a gesture of blessing, the Reverend rested his other hand on his. "What are you looking for, Charley Monday?" he asked, gravely.

"I want to fight. What about you?"

The Reverend released him, picked up his hat and books, and left the cantina. That was the last time he saw Teasdale alive. He no longer saw the use. There were already lots of talented boxers in the East.

"I'll never marry an outlaw, whatever law's involved,"
my mother used to say. "Well, I hope you're proud,
because your son's a bandit today, and he's to
be hanged a few hours from now."

PIOCHE

JUNE 1880

The rest of Charles Teasdale's history is a mystery with only a few sparse clues. We know that in '77 a certain Charley Monday lost a fight badly in Harrisburg, and almost won another in Natchez in '78.

No doubt Teasdale continued his journey eastward, attracted by legends of towns with a thousand saloons, the promise of fights well covered by the press, and of gymnasiums to train in. Maybe he became one of those second-rank fighters whose name nobody knew and who were served up on a platter to heavier boxers with superior teams to help them rise through the ranks of the bare-knuckle gladiators, leaving him to languish at the bottom of the prize list. Or maybe he changed his name again and again, making himself impossible to trace.

What is certain is that he didn't like the East, for he returned to die among the familiar strangers of his great nowhere land. On his grave the people of Bullionville inscribed his original name – or at least the earliest name they knew.

✳

DECEMBER 1880

The courthouse in Pioche was a red brick building of rather modest appearance, though the million dollars it cost to build it left no doubt about the magnitude of the bribes exchanged. It was the perfect building to accommodate the trial of Charles Teasdale's murderers.

The coroner had received death threats. The jury was made up almost entirely of local storekeepers. The witnesses came directly from a San Francisco theatre troupe. Even the defence lawyer had been bribed to make the least possible effort. The most corrupt trial in the history of Nevada was about to begin. Church pews had been added to the courtroom to accommodate the host of spectators. Most had to remain standing. Some had come from as far as Virginia City to kiss the hand of the accused, others to spit at them. The place was so crowded that despite the cool weather the windows and the door were kept open. After the first day it was forbidden to smoke cigars in the courtroom. The trial was all the more entertaining in that one of the two accused had admitted his guilt, while the other proclaimed his innocence.

"My brother lost everything in the Virginia City fire. The law has already had a chance to do its job, but it didn't. So I gave that bastard Teasdale what he deserved," said the first.

"Your brother died in the war, you fool!" retorted the second, before the judge silenced him by striking his gavel on its block.

The Reverend Aaron attended the entire charade. The more layers of perfidy that were piled up to establish the guilt of the two accused, the less the Reverend believed in it. He was witnessing a betrayal – the spectacle of a community creating its own legend. After the verdict was announced, a journalist from Virginia City asked him what God thought of this trial.

The Reverend's silence was never more eloquent.

⚹

On the morning of the execution, the Reverend offered his spiritual assistance to the accused. He went up to the second floor of the courthouse and the sheriff opened the door of the single cell for him. The first rays of sunlight passing through the window cast the shadow of the bars on the white wall. The floor of softwood boards creaked beneath his feet. The condemned men were weeping, uttering anything that crossed their minds, from pleas to prayers and to curses. After they had both calmed down, the Reverend asked the one who had proclaimed his guilt why he had chosen a lie and death instead of the truth, and life.

"They was goin' to hang us anyway. Might as well die famous," he said, wiping his nose on his sleeve.

That man would have wished for his name to be mentioned here.

NOTEBOOK II

The Thirty Marriages
Pearl Guthrie Never Had

PEACHTREE, 1881 ✣ ST. LOUIS, 1874

SHAWNEETOWN, 1874–1876 ✣ GUTHRIE, 1877

KANSAS CITY, 1877 ✣ TOPEKA, 1877–1882

FREDERICK, 1877 ✣ DODGE CITY, 1877

MONUMENT, 1877–1878 ✣ AUBREY, 1878

Sometimes there's no difference between always moving on and going in circles. Like everyone, I'm here because I wanted to live a thousand lives in one, but I ended up living the same one a thousand times over.

PEACHTREE

FEBRUARY 1881

In the escarpments of the Paria River canyons, among the desert of red cliffs, there were no roads, but every trail led to a single destination: a large two-storey stone building, its front coated with white stucco, the only human construction for miles around. This place had no name and was not marked on any map. Everyone called it the Peachtree.

At the entrance, an old mestiza woman kept guard, her face crumpled by a hundred years of sunlight. She answered to the name Guadalupe, and everything that came out of her mouth was repeated in several languages: Spanish, English, and an Indian language that the Reverend had never managed to identify. Even when you told her which of them you understood, she persisted in translating into the other two, as if she was addressing not only you, but all of her clientele – in other words, the entire world.

Going through the door and taking off your hat, you grasped where you were, or rather it was the place that grabbed you. Everywhere, on each table, on each step of the staircase, sat a girl. On each chair sat a man with at least one damsel on each knee. There were not enough bedrooms for everyone, but most of the patrons were happy to be immersed in the bounty of the main hall. It was a place where men had to pay court as well as cash, for it was up to the girls to choose the rare customers who would enjoy the special intimacy of a bedroom. Occasionally, within a few minutes of being chosen, one of the select few would fall under the bullets of a drunken rival. More than one girl had died even before she could reach the staircase, shot in a fit of jealous, resentful rage by a man who desired her. But for a woman wishing to stay alive, there was no problem. She merely had to refrain entirely from choosing a man, and allow herself to be loved equally by all, never yielding to the promises of wealth and everlasting bliss that customers whispered in the hope of buying themselves a night upstairs, and therefore remaining on the ground floor, where she had little to hope for in terms of wealth or happiness but where it was possible to earn a living without coming to any great harm.

Pearl Guthrie was one of the women who never glanced toward the upstairs. She had eyes only for the pages of her books. She never made a move toward the patrons. They had to approach her, and then, before closing her book, she would make them feel that they were a considerable nuisance to her. She barely eked out a living, but she survived.

✯

One evening, the Matador entered the Peachtree, took off his hat with one hand, and held it before his face as he smoothed his moustache with his fingertips. He put his hat on again and looked around the room with the calm of someone who didn't mind being seen to do nothing but observe.

He approached the bar, ordered a coffee, and asked to speak to Russian Bill's widow. The barman pointed with his chin to the back of the room. "Name's Pearl," he said. She was sitting alone at a table, her face lit by a candle close to burning out. She drew a shawl around her shoulders. Three or four times a year the temperature outside would approach freezing point. Then the girls, most of whom wore a sleeveless blouse that fitted tightly over their corset in order to hug its shape, would show goose-bumps amid the lace of their plunging necklines.

The Matador fumbled in his jacket pocket and laid a few more coins on the bar. "A coffee for her too."

He walked over to her table, following closely on the heels of the waiter and detouring around girls who almost hit him with their gesticulations.

"I have to talk to you," he said.

The noise was so deafening that he had to make two attempts before he could make himself heard.

"Go on," she said without looking up from her book. He pulled up a chair and sat down in front of her.

"A man will come to see you, a preacher. He'll want to know everything about your late husband," he said, speaking excellent English, though with a strong Spanish accent.

She shut her book. "How did he die?"

The Matador leaned toward her to make out what she was saying, and then drew back. "You didn't know your husband was dead?"

"He wasn't really my husband."

"He was hanged in Shakespeare, New Mexico, by a vigilance committee."

"Of course," she said. She wrapped her hands around the cup, more to warm them than to drink its contents.

The Matador respected her silence for a few seconds before continuing. "So a man will come to see you. You'll be tempted to talk to him, and he'll offer to pay you, but you should refuse to speak with him."

"This preacher, what is he, a Pinkerton agent?"

"Something like that, but he doesn't work for anyone."

"What does he want to know about Bill, now he's dead?"

"Everything. He's a liar. You can't trust him."

"So if he's a liar, as you say, this preacher won't need me because he doesn't need to know the truth."

"On the contrary, he needs to know to be a better liar. So he can better distort the truth about your husband."

She shrugged. "Bill was a liar himself. Maybe it's what he deserves."

The Matador shook his head. "The preacher won't tell you this, but he wants to celebrate Bill's memory."

Pearl tapped on her cup. She wanted to ask her interlocutor who he was and why it was so important to him to warn her like this, but in the Peachtree it was forbidden to ask customers such questions.

"It wouldn't upset me if Bill's memory were celebrated. In any case, it doesn't seem to upset me as much as it does you."

"You wouldn't be here if you had had a happy marriage, isn't that so? Also, I know what happened in Santa Fe."

Pearl frowned, and then looked at the stranger. "Nothing happened in Santa Fe."

"Fine. Just don't tell *him* that."

"Why should I believe you but not him?"

"Because I'm not asking you for anything. I'm doing you a favour."

"If this man wants to pay to make me talk, then you should pay me more to keep quiet."

The Matador stared at her. "Are you saying that because you're a real *puta*, or because you're a real wife? Maybe you really liked your husband after all, and it would suit you fine for lies to win out over the truth."

"Oh mister, if only you knew. The truth doesn't matter in the least when the only entertainment you have is other people's stories."

⁕

JUNE 1881

The Reverend Aaron entered the Peachtree, not for the first time, because, like everywhere else, he always chose a girl for what she could tell him. But this was the first time he was entering a brothel to choose a girl for what she was able to *do*.

It wasn't yet ten in the morning. Half the tables were still stacked at the back of the room. The rest of the floor was covered with mattresses on which girls were asleep, some of them half naked. One early riser was playing solitaire. Pearl was sitting near the window, with her back to the Reverend. He had already met her in Topeka four years before, but he didn't recognize her immediately. She had one shoulder bare, wearing her blouse Mexican-style. A plait obscured the nape of her neck. Her back was straight, in the posture of a well-trained child.

There was no flower behind the ear – nothing superfluous, apart from the dizzying pile of books in front of her. You didn't need to be a preacher to see that she would rather be somewhere else – outside in the sunshine that fell on one side of her face, revealing her swollen eyes. But in spite of this she was not out of place in the environment, like a prisoner who enlivens a jail by attempting to escape. She had fled a village of mourners, tired of being surrounded entirely by women. And after all that to end up in a brothel, populated entirely by women who, when they weren't drunk, spent their days weeping. But what do you expect a woman to do who was married thirty times before she was twenty-one?

The Reverend knew that in addition to finding the person he was looking for he had found the hands he lacked. He needed a young woman who could write. So his choice fell on one who could read.

One of the first things she said to him on noticing the stumps at his wrists was, "I remember you, but not your hands. Yet I'm sure you had them."

"That's because there was nothing special about them." He refrained from adding that they used to look like the hands of a doctor who in the daytime cares for women in labour and welcomes the newborn, and spends his evening dissecting newly disinterred corpses to perfect his knowledge of anatomy.

Sometimes I'd ask my mother, "Why are we leaving again?" She'd reply, "It's dangerous here." I'd answer that it was dangerous in other places too. She never listened to me. I was always right. One day she said, "It's to give you the best life possible." The worst part is that she believed it.

ST. LOUIS

MAY 1874

It was a time when girls were baptized Jewel, Rose, or Mercy and then decked out in lace and flowers, when ladies tried to look like birds and play down their membership in the long, uncouth line of descent from the apes. Gifts brought from afar would be heaped on them, such as exotic fruit that had survived the journey from California and needed to be peeled before they were eaten – minor wonders with a fine, delicate skin, to be daintily consumed. If you punctured them, the juice would spurt in your eye. Then the ladies would laugh, happy to be enjoying a fruit in their own image.

Her name was Pearl Guthrie, and she was not yet fourteen. She had never set foot outside Gallatin County or the district around Shawneetown, where she was born. She was preparing to spend the summer near St. Louis, at her cousin's, whose husband was waiting outside in his buggy. Pearl embraced her mother, who wept as if her daughter were setting off to war. Then her mother drove this absurd notion out of her mind so that she could force a smile. "You come home again soon, now."

She might have added, "Don't be like men, who don't come home till you no longer need them."

Girls did not go off to war. Even when they began to fall in love with men who loved war. That was why they were christened Jewel, Rose, Mercy, or Pearl.

In St. Louis, Pearl toured the city in a carriage. The tour lasted an hour, and did not pass the same place twice. She ate nougat and candied fruit. She heard music played by instruments she never knew existed – huge violins that had to be held upright and long pianos that could have served as banquet tables.

In St. Louis, she had a dress made the likes of which she had never possessed before. A bodice and skirt of cream-coloured silk with an ascending floral pattern embroidered in green. A dress in a colour too light for any kind of work, meant to be worn on picnics, despite the risk of grass stains.

In St. Louis, she saw rats creeping along the windowsills and, in the market, the old and withered scalp of a Sioux Indian in a glass whiskey jar. She visited a fun fair with magicians and mind readers. She took part in a mass hypnosis session. The hypnotist lined the curious participants up one behind another, and they all collapsed on their knees like human dominoes when the magician waved his hand in front of their faces. All of them, that is, except Pearl, who would be troubled by the experience forever after. For when everyone around you collapses, men included, and you are the only one left standing, you must have missed something. There is such a thing as magic, but you've been excluded from it. You aren't one of those mortals lying on top of one another like corpses thrown into a pit. You are the odd one out.

In St. Louis, women of all ages regularly suffered fainting fits. They all carried with them a little sachet of powder that they could sniff to recover from a weak spell. Pearl brought a box of it home. Three years later she had not yet had any occasion to use the stuff. She was still waiting to encounter something that could cause an emotion strong enough to render her unconscious.

I don't know if in the East they hang us with kids looking on. Here, I never see any kids. Just from the gallows, when they're getting ready to hang me. I've often wondered if those kids were really there.

SHAWNEETOWN

MAY 1874

In other towns, red brick chimneys were rising, silhouetted against the grey skies of large cities. Country folk were becoming factory workers, attracted by the bright lights of industry shining through an increasingly dense pall of coal smoke. In other places, grazing lands were being developed, dividing the boundless landscape into fenced properties. The ruts gouged by the pioneers' passage had become roads. The more points of convergence, the more people there were to converge, as if each mountain hid a mecca that exerted its power to attract pilgrims. First come, first served. History would not repeat itself.

And all this time no one was heading for southern Illinois, near the Ohio River, a region too young to have made an impression on people's minds but already too old for anyone to want to put down roots there. Shawneetown had once been a metropolis, the largest city in the nascent state of Illinois. When there was a flood, when the river rose until the town was entirely flooded, it was not rare to see steamboats sailing up the middle of the main street, transforming Shawneetown into a modern Venice. Back then, several times a day the Guthries could see teams of mules passing their house on their way to the port, drawing carts laden with a cargo extracted from the local salt mines. They would leave a trail of salt behind them, an abundance of grains marking the way between a seemingly inexhaustible supply and an eager market.

But that day was gone.

First came the gold fever. By 1851, already there were very few men still around to make children with the local women. Bitten one by one by the bug, they had deserted the salt mines in order to stumble over one another in the nugget-bearing rivers of California. Thus, Pearl could count herself fortunate to have been conceived. Old Man Guthrie was one of the skeptics who resisted the call of the gold. Maybe it was from him that Pearl had inherited her propensity to disdain what many others desired, but in fact she had no idea. She had never known him. In '61, a few months before she came into this world, the Civil War began, and this time, Pa Guthrie couldn't resist the deadly fever. Nor could Pearl's brothers, who one by one joined the ranks of the 18th and the 6th Cavalry. A father and three older brothers. A demolishing of father figures and a plethora of desertions. By the end of the war, Pearl was old enough to understand the difference between men and women – it was just that the cripples who began to flow back in '65 were no longer men.

She might have been happy in Shawneetown if she had not been the prettiest girl, for she was the youngest. If only she hadn't been surrounded in school by pupils older than she, had not made rapid strides through the grades, nor begun to indulge her thirst for romantic novels before an appropriate age. If only she hadn't been made to think that she deserved better than a one-armed man with flat feet, or a stammering deserter thirty years her senior.

✳

SEPTEMBER 1876

On the last Friday of each month, Pearl Guthrie asked to be photographed in front of the columns at the Shawneetown bank. In a town with no future, nothing was more handsome than the buildings of yesteryear.

The Shawneetown photographer, an aged, talentless army veteran, was one of the better-off townsfolk. In the absence of young representatives of the male sex, the photographic plate was the final haven where young ladies could find a last justification for their beauty. In the first months after she returned from St. Louis, Pearl's eagerness to be attractive got her up and about before dawn. She would put on her cream dress and go to watch the sunrise. In the morning, she would go into town to make a few trivial purchases, but especially to show herself off. Then, toward midday, she would seek out the photographer before an emptiness developed in the pit of her stomach, causing her to ruin the portrait with a mournful expression. She would pose on the steps of the bank, an open parasol resting on her shoulder. The photographer would set up his tripod, lean over the camera, and draw the black cloth over his head, extending his right hand beyond it, trembling but ready to release the shutter at any moment. Pearl became expert at the art of keeping her eyes open, even when dazzled by the sun or the flash.

She would return home in the late afternoon to find her mother reading the *Shawneetown Mercury* in the hopes of finding proof that one of her sons, or maybe even her husband, was still alive. Every day, Ma Guthrie managed to reinterpret a piece of bad news as manna from heaven. "Thank you, Lord!" A bandit originally from Illinois was freed from San Quentin after eight years in jail: "Please, Lord, let it be my Ruben under a different name." Of all the pathetic habits kept up by her mother, none exasperated Pearl more than this.

One day, as Pearl was tidying the kitchen, her mother told her that the Shawneetown photographer had died. She dropped her cloth, walked over to the table, and tore the page out of the newspaper. The following day, a Friday, she donned her black dress instead of the cream one and went into town to attend the funeral. She couldn't examine her reflection to touch up her hairdo even once, for all the mirrors had been covered with opaque cloth in case anyone should glimpse the dead man's spirit in them. From the back of the crowd she could only make out the edge of the wooden coffin. The room in which the body was laid out could barely contain the throng of dark veils. The dead man had been elderly, but young women were weeping too. One man less in the town also meant that there was one woman more. The photographer was dead, and there was no one to immortalize the drama.

When I was small and we still lived with Sam Ambrose, my mother and him used to organize parties and invite people from all around to come dance and sing until the small hours. They'd leave their shawls and coats on a bench. It made a mountain of down for me. I'd climb onto it and fall asleep, with the laughter and a scraping violin as my lullaby. Later, when my mother and me started to move about, we would always sleep where there was a lot of noise. Often she'd forbid me to go to the bedroom upstairs, so I got used to sleeping under tables, in the room where the cowboys and good-for-nothings stayed awake all night. Anyway, by the time I was ten I was ashamed to be following my mother everywhere she went and still not be a man.
So I had no use for the bedroom any more.
They'd have had to pay me to go upstairs.
Bedrooms are for women.
I've never needed one.

GUTHRIE

MARCH 1877

Beyond the edge of Shawneetown stood a large house several storeys tall, surrounded by oak trees. It had once been an attractive home, painted yellow and white, but the porch roof and main roof now were covered by some green growth. A sign bearing the word "In" swung and creaked with every gust of wind, the second *n* having disappeared, along with the prosperous years when guests were numerous. The Guthrie house had been a crowded inn in the days when there was still a ferry on this part of the river – and there were still men around to spank the children. But by 1877, it was just a saloon where the same seven regulars came to get drunk too far from the town for their wives to go there on foot and drag them home by an ear.

If you overlooked its dilapidated state, the Guthrie saloon offered a decor not unlike those of the taverns found in the town, with textured wallpaper on only the upper part – because that was the fashion and because the lower parts were subject to water damage. Lamps on the tables cast a subdued light, separate pools of brightness that made the remaining gilt on the wallpaper sparkle. Around the circular tables, only a few chairs were left. When a chair leg broke, in summer the solution was to throw the chair into the river, and in winter, into the fire. No one felt it necessary to replace seats that would never be occupied. The mother and daughter lived upstairs, reduced to the unappealing role of saloonkeepers.

"What would your father say if he saw us now?" the mother would often complain. Then the daughter would clench her teeth to refrain from answering that a man shouldn't expect a woman to remain in her place when he abandons his.

It would have been wrong to think Pearl Guthrie was indifferent to gossip. The proof came years later in what she admitted to the Reverend Aaron. "You travel miles and miles, you find yourself on the other side of the world, but basically everything you do is on account of the tittle-tattle that will reach back home. Just like going to bed with one man to hurt another. I imagine that for you men it's like shooting some bastard that reminds you of another bastard who got away."

Except that in a region in decline, back when she was still just a virgin wearing dresses with bustles, she would never have dared to use such words.

✳

The Guthrie inn was built on a sloping site that dropped off into the river. The saloon was in the basement, and to enter it customers had to go around to the back of the house, which faced the water. The way to it led past a row of windows belonging to the unoccupied bedrooms. Knowing that even Ma Guthrie never set foot in them, some townspeople claimed that these rooms were haunted. The fact that Pearl's mother kept the downstairs curtains drawn but the upstairs ones open may have had something to do with this.

But no gossip was needed to make you feel uneasy around the Guthrie house. Most evenings, Mrs. Guthrie herself would serve the liquor in the saloon, but she wasn't the kind of barmaid to listen to drinkers' complaints. The slightest whiff of nostalgia brought tears to her eyes the way peeling onions does to others, and at that point she would entrust the saloon to her daughter's hands and take refuge in her bedroom, immediately above. Her sobs could be heard through the ceiling.

The second of March was one such evening. A man shut the tavern door behind him, and a cold draft reached the back of the room. The patrons turned to watch him shake off his hat. He was Charles Teasdale.

He removed his overcoat and threw it on a chair in front of him. A metal object hung on his chest. It was such an unusual adornment, it took Pearl a few seconds to realize that this was a gun. The revolver the man was wearing like a pendant shone in the glow of a lamp. It had been a long time since anyone carried a gun around Shawneetown. Standing at one end of the bar, she continued peeling a potato, her eyes moving to and fro between the tuber and Teasdale. He approached the bar and ordered a whiskey. From the bedroom above their heads, Ma Guthrie uttered a brief, painful moan. The man looked up at the ceiling.

"No, it ain't all fun and games around here," said the drunk in an oversized top hat who sat at a table behind him. "But at least in this place you've no cause to fret about appearances."

The newcomer turned around, raised his glass in the old man's direction, and downed its contents in a single gulp. Then he turned toward Pearl and lowered his gaze. "I'll take a bottle of that," he said. The tone was steady, the voice soft and deep, almost timid – a voice that negated the menacing impression the Colt had made. He turned to go to his table.

The top-hatted old man followed him with his eyes as he went by, then turned around and watched him pour himself a second drink. "Tell me, where do you come from, exactly?"

Teasdale stared at his glass before answering. "I've come from Harrisburg."

"Is that so? I could've swore you was from out West."

"It's not clear where I'm from. But what's clear is that where I come from, folks never ask you where you're from."

"That's true enough. Back there, it's not like here. In minin' country, you can turn up and say you're George Washington's grandnephew or Christ's descendant and no one'll ask no questions. It's not like that here, no way, believe you me," he cried, raising a finger to assert his expertise in the matter. The old man took a gulp and wiped his moustache on his sleeve. "Back there, the past don't matter," he went on. "You can always start over with a clean slate. If folks ask no questions, mebbe too it's cuz they don't want to be asked no questions back. Anyhow, mebbe that's what they think to themselves, that the past don't matter. I doubt they think it for other folks, though." He turned away and leaned his elbows on the table.

Teasdale looked at the back of the old man's top hat the way others might have rolled their eyes. "Anyway, who'd bother to reckon the importance of his ancestors in a camp full of brothel kids?" he exclaimed.

The old guy glanced over his shoulder, thinking he had acquired a plain-speaking interlocutor. "And better not forget the savages," he added with a nod of conviction. "Any bastard from around here is a prince out there compared to an Injun. Me, I'd never bring a woman to a place there's savages," he went on. "Know what they do to white women there? It takes a pretty tough guy to defend his wife against them devils, and above all it takes a guy tough enough to kill his wife before they carry her off. Myself, I'm fond enough of my wife, but not that much."

Teasdale searched in his pouch and took out a sheet of paper, a penholder, and a little box from which he extracted a metal nib that he set down in front of him. Pearl sensed that it would be risky to pay him too much attention. She avoided meeting his gaze, observing his hands instead: swollen joints that you could hear crack just looking at them, and ink-stained fingers with freshly cut nails. She had always believed that she would recognize the man meant for her by his hands. She would laugh at this later, when she was with the Reverend Aaron, both of whose hands had been amputated.

✻

A little before one in the morning, Pearl rang a handbell. "Ten minutes, gentlemen!"

One of the regulars muttered a few unintelligible words. The old guy swigged down the rest of his bottle.

Teasdale stood up again. "Is there some place open all night anywhere in town?" he asked, gathering up his coat with one hand and his bottle with the other.

"We're the establishment that closes the latest in the whole county," replied Pearl, not without a hint of entrepreneurial pride. Teasdale looked around the room with his large eyes, mouth slightly open. Upstairs, her mother's sobs had given way to snores.

"If you're interested, we have a room upstairs. It's less expensive than in town," suggested Pearl.

The regulars exchanged a glance. No one had stayed at the Guthries' since '73.

The man rubbed the ridge of his nose, sighed, and answered without raising his voice, "I've never paid to sleep in my whole life, and I'm not goin' to start now."

Of course! Pearl said to herself. If an Eastern dandy would be out of place in the lawless West, the reverse should be equally true. This denizen of the open prairie must have slept under the stars or taken advantage of the hospitality of the people he met along his way.

"Do you know about horses?"

He nodded, skeptically.

"We have a horse that has to be put down. The room will be free if you stay to help us tomorrow." Pearl gestured toward the customers heading for the door.

The man thought for a moment, chewing the inside of his cheek. "Then I'll take a last bottle for the night."

※

With Teasdale behind her, Pearl climbed the two flights with a lamp in one hand and a ewer full of water in the other. They went along the corridor and came to a wall covered with so many pictures that the wallpaper behind was barely visible. There were rectangular frames, and a few oval ones, in the centre of which were photographs of young soldiers in kepis with sabres at their hips, a few paintings of bucolic landscapes, and a photograph of Pearl in front of the Shawneetown bank – the last taken before the photographer's death.

In the room at the end of the corridor, she placed the ewer inside a basin on the chest of drawers close to the bed, and then set the lamp on the floor. Teasdale remained in the doorway with a second lamp in one hand and his whiskey bottle in the other. A chair with a woven straw seat filled the empty corner of the room; a pair of plaid trousers hung over its back, the only evidence of a departed presence. He ran a finger over the cloth and rubbed it against his thumb to dislodge the dust.

"With a river view," said Pearl, pulling back the drapes, two curtains of heavy, multi-layered lace.

"There's really folks that want that, a river view?"

Pearl shrugged. "It's my brother Ruben's room. When my mother's well, it's the best-kept room upstairs. So if you can manage not to disturb anything ... My mother's ... Anyway, you've heard her."

To signify his agreement, the man merely gestured with his chin. He threw his hat on the chair and lay down on the bed, his hands behind his head and his legs crossed. Pearl stared at the soles of his boots with their traces of dried mud and the left heel in direct contact with the bedspread. The good housekeeper in her wanted to express her outrage. The rebellious daughter wanted to cry victory. She wished him goodnight, picked up the lamp, and grasped the door handle.

"I've a question. What happens if your brother Ruben comes home durin' the night? He sees a stranger in his bed and fires at me. Unless of course I shoot first, as would be my right. Except I've no way of recognizin' him, so mebbe I'd kill someone else that wasn't even thinkin' of shootin' me, like you or your ma, for example."

Pearl blanched. She felt her hand beginning to sweat against the door handle, and her heartbeats pounded in her ears. The threat she had denied until then had just struck her with full force. She didn't dare turn around, though the worst thing to do would probably have been to turn her back on him. Then she heard a muffled laugh. He was making fun of her.

She sighed. "Don't worry, mister. My brother's never coming back."

She was still trembling as she went along the corridor. She went into the room where her mother was sleeping and kneeled in front of a chest by the door. She winced as she opened it, even though her mother's snores were several times louder than any sound she might have made. From the chest she unearthed an ancient pistol that had belonged to her father and a burlap bag weighed down by a roundish object. She shut the lid and tiptoed from the room. Once she was back in her own room, she shook the pistol to check that it was loaded, then hid it under her pillow.

She pushed back the edges of the burlap bag to reveal the Guthries' treasure: a twenty-pound gold nugget that her brother Ruben had brought home in the '50s before setting out again for God knows where – a rock the size of an eggplant, with lethally sharp corners. It had always remained hidden at the bottom of the chest, awaiting the day when the Guthrie women could no longer afford what they needed. Sometimes her mother would take it out of its wrapping and lay it on the table to contemplate it and remind herself that she had once had a son who hadn't abandoned her. At such moments, Pearl told herself that her mother would rather have starved to death than sell this treasured mineral. Pearl hid it under the covers at the foot of her bed, and lay stretched out for nearly an hour without shutting an eye. There was an armed man in her house. There was a man in her house. She could feel the solid shape of the pistol through her pillow.

Between a few snores and a couple of moans of the wind, she heard the ceiling creak. Teasdale was awake too. Then the staircase creaked in turn. She held her breath when the footsteps made the floor in front of her door tremble. She watched her door – the little chain that served as a bolt, and the handle – knowing in advance the exact sound it would make. Then the footsteps moved away and another door opened farther on.

She got out of bed, lit her lamp, and went out. In the corridor, she shivered for a moment. The man was gone. She went upstairs to see if he had taken anything. The lamp by his bed was still burning. The bedspread was crumpled, but the bedclothes had not been disturbed. There was no trace of the whiskey bottle, nor of the saddlebag; only the little box the man had taken out in the tavern had been left behind on the chest of drawers. Pearl tucked the box under her arm and went downstairs, intending to catch the stranger before he went too far. She regretted her generous impulse as soon as her first slipper came into contact with the chilly grass. She hopped to the rear of the house and saw that the man's horse was still tethered at the entrance to the tavern.

She froze, her white nightdress incandescent in the dark. Her breathing grew faster, and she looked down at the box she was holding. The man had probably gone to relieve himself, and now she would have to explain how the box had come into her possession. She would probably have chosen to tell the truth if he hadn't displayed his firearm like the antlers on a hunting trophy, or if she had known how to use her own. Then she got the idea that she could take the box into the tavern so that she could claim that he had left it there. She went in, set it on the table, and drew up a chair. She tried to doze, her face cradled in the crook of her arm, but she knew that nothing would calm her. She went up to the house and climbed the stairs with an assured step. The bedroom door was ajar, so she did not even need to dismiss the possibility that the man might fire at her. She found him sitting on the floor, his back against the bed, and the bottle between his thighs. He was smoking a cigarillo, using the chamber pot as an ashtray.

"I lied to you. There's no horse to be put down tomorrow."

He barely started.

"I told you it wouldn't cost you anything to spend the night, and I'll keep my word," Pearl went on. "There's another way to repay me."

He frowned.

She swallowed. "Take me out West."

Teasdale's beard parted in a smile. He took a puff at his cigarillo. "There ain't no West, darlin'. Ain't you well off here?"

She shook her head. "There are no men here. They've all left and gone to work in Missouri for half the year and in Mississippi for the other half."

"Then why not go to Missouri or Mississippi? Or New York? Paris?"

"Because out West there are only men, no women."

He pinched the cigarillo between his lips and pulled his saddle-bag from under the bed. He took out a few coins and held them out without getting up. "That should cover the cost for the night."

She sighed and crossed her arms over her chest. "I don't need money. I just need an escort."

The man rubbed his eyes and scratched the whiskers that grew down his throat. "If it's too dangerous to go there on your own, it's too dangerous to go with an escort. Didn't you hear what the old guy was sayin' earlier?"

"I don't care about the danger; I'm talking about what's proper."

"Then you need a more proper companion than me."

"There'll be no one after you."

Teasdale shrugged and turned away to continue smoking undisturbed. "Go back to bed, darlin'."

"I'll pay you if I have to."

"Out West, it's not the women that pays. It's the men pays them."

He planted a steely gaze in the young woman's eyes, and then shook his head, staring at his knees. A gust of wind stirred the branches outside, and they scraped against the windowpanes. "To go out West, you've got to act like the Westerners," he continued. "Take the money I owe you for the night, and then it'll be up to you to pay me for the journey. The way women pay out West."

She stood frozen for a few seconds as the outline of the deal he was offering took shape in her head. She picked up her lamp and turned on her heels. "Good night, mister. I shouldn't have disturbed you. I'm sorry."

Pearl locked herself inside her room and remained motionless, her arms tight against her chest. Then she gripped her bedspread in both hands and buried her face in it to muffle her sobs. Not a tear dampened the cloth.

The gold nugget and the pistol lay on the bare mattress. She chose the object she knew how to use. She went upstairs and knocked on the door a second time. With a trembling hand she held out the nugget to him. "Here's what I can offer you for the journey."

Teasdale considered the nugget for an instant, and then gazed at Pearl, at once strait-laced and brazen in her nightdress. He smiled. "I don't want your nugget. But my offer stands, all the same."

She drew the nugget to her, embracing it like a child hugging a doll. "If there's really nothing else I could offer you in exchange, then I accept. I'll do what you want, as long as you tell no one. My reputation must be intact."

"Don't worry about your reputation. I've forgot your name already, anyway."

"Might I ask yours, mister?"

He stood up, took off his cartridge belt, and threw it on the bed. Pearl clutched the nugget tighter, its rough edges scraping her stomach through the material of her sacrificial gown.

"Charley Monday."

He went over to her and stopped so close to her that only the nugget was between them.

"I'll need the first instalment this evening, and the rest when we arrive."

He caught Pearl by the collar and kissed her full on the mouth, as if taking something from her, but giving nothing in return. In this snatched kiss that tasted of alcohol and tobacco, the only thing given was the fact that he asked for nothing more. "Till tomorrow," he said, looking down at her, without stepping back.

Pearl closed the door behind her and took refuge in her room, her heart pounding. She packed her bag and dressed in her travelling clothes. She returned Ruben's nugget to its burlap bag, intending to bring it to her mother first thing in the morning, just before bidding her goodbye. She lay down again fully dressed, with no hope of finding sleep. Minutes, perhaps hours, went by. The ceiling creaked again, then the stairs. She rushed out of her room and found Teasdale in the kitchen, near the back door, his coat over one arm, his hat on his head, and his boots in one hand, as though he had taken them off with the failed intention of not alerting her. He went outside, pulled on his boots, and began to untether his horse.

Pearl stopped him. "Hey! Let me get my bag and saddle up!"

He stopped in his tracks. "I dunno where I'm goin', but sure as hell I ain't goin' back out West."

Between the moment when the man mounted his horse and when he set off, Pearl began to yell. Later she would not be able to recall in detail the insults she hurled at him, but she did remember running down the trail and continuing to shout after him as he rode away.

Turning around on his horse, the man answered her, "Keep it up, darlin'. That's just the way the girls holler out West."

※

Ma Guthrie got up around ten, as usual, seemingly oblivious to everything. Pearl checked and double-checked: the man with the pendant didn't seem to have stolen anything. She could have convinced herself that the outlaw Charley Monday had never set foot in the house. Nothing had changed.

Pearl, however, began to change. She rose later in the mornings. She ignored her mother for entire days. The two women ate dinner each evening in a silence punctuated by the ticking of the clock. Pearl would open the curtains in every room of the house, her mother would close them back up, and then Pearl would open them up again. Some of the tavern patrons expressed concern for the girl, who had abandoned her mask of forced smiles.

One afternoon, Pearl found her mother reading aloud from the *Shawnee Herald*.

"**An Omaha man has returned home after making his fortune in Denver**," her mother read out, satisfied, without any comment. Pearl slowly rose, grabbed the newspaper, and tore it up, without any show of emotion.

"Whatever has come over you, dear?"

The young woman threw the paper in the stove.

"I'm not like you," she retorted.

The same scene was repeated every day for a week.

"The killer was tall, and some witnesses noticed that under his hat he wore ginger sideburns," the mother read before continuing. "Just like my Ruben."

The mother, seeing her daughter approach, would crumple the newspaper and shield it against her bosom. Pearl came around the table and tried to snatch it from her. Shreds of paper tore off, but most of it stayed tight against the mother's increasingly ink-blackened bodice. Pearl continued to pull; a page tore off, and the young woman fell backward onto a chair, still holding a scrap of newspaper. On it was a small ad saying, "Schoolteacher needed in Alpine, Colorado."

The next day, Pearl didn't try to destroy her mother's newspaper; she even began reading it herself. In her impatience, she sent a reply to every job offer for young women that she came across, as long as the workplace was "out West."

Two months later Pearl left her mother and Shawneetown behind for good, taking the gold nugget with her. Initially, she considered it a loan. She told herself that once she was married she would send home three times the nugget's value. She carried it with her for miles and for years without feeling even the slightest prick of guilt. All the way to the doors of the Peachtree she fought to pursue her quest while avoiding the pitfalls of sin. She had sworn to her mother that the nugget would only be used as a last resort, like a return ticket. Gold had taken her menfolk from her. It had better bring her daughter back.

But Pearl was determined never to return. The theft had been committed even before the nugget was placed in the bottom of her bag, and her failure was carved in stone.

✳

Years later she would hear tell of an Indian whose tribe had been massacred by the Spaniards and its children raised by missionaries. One child was forced to take a Christian name because the missionaries wouldn't tolerate his being called "Biting Dog,". Then they were shocked when the child planted his teeth in their hands. "What a savage! What a little beast!" they lamented. Even today this story reminds Pearl Guthrie of the night when she offered a bed to an armed outlaw. When she has had enough and feels like moving on, she thinks back on that night, on the time when she slept with a pistol under her pillow, just a few feathers separating her temple from the muzzle.

It's not my tendency to always be on the move that makes me a nomad. It's that I never return to the same place.

———————◆—◆—◆———————

KANSAS CITY

JUNE 1877

Out West, the people were generous, the men were brave, and the nature of the dangers was known. So Pearl Guthrie told herself in the days when she still dreamed of a house deep in the woods where she could sit by the fire and mend the clothes of the man who would be her husband. Nowadays she wonders what women dream about as they sit by the fire mending their husbands' clothes.

No one was able to say exactly where the East ended and the West began. Fifty years earlier, the Mississippi River had served as the border separating civilization from untamed territory, but this frontier had been crossed long ago. For the Reverend Aaron, the West began on the bridge across the Sweetwater River, where one day he had noticed that all the streams and rivers flowed toward the Pacific. For most of the people Pearl consulted, the East ended at Kansas City.

The first job offer that appealed to her came from a banker who was looking for a governess for his children. She had leaped at the opportunity, forgetting all the other offers to which she had replied. In Kansas City, she lived in the family home, a brick house with several storeys, white-painted cornices, carpets smelling of cigar smoke, and large mirrors in each room showing that feminine vanity was looked upon with favour. The only concerns of those who inhabited the house were to preserve appearances, shield themselves from outside noises, and decide who would be first to use the carriage and driver to go shopping. Pearl has preserved few memories of this experience, with the possible exception of the evening parties attended by well-dressed young entrepreneurs, of which all that reached her was the music, for she was shut away on the top floor minding other people's children. She gave arithmetic lessons in a library as well-stocked as a pine forest, in which the books were lined up one against the other and could only be reached using a ladder. All around, a lack of space and things stacked high – nothing resembling the horizontal lines of the prairies.

"This isn't the West," she said to herself every day.

Pearl aspired to become the only ornament, the only flower to be picked in the midst of this total aridness. She was searching for a land as virginal as herself. A place so lawless that it would be a challenge just to remain alive. When she would at last be inhabited by her fear of the Comanche, of the Apache, of outlaws, of wounds becoming infected and guns jamming; only then would she be free of her inability to escape from herself.

After just three weeks as a governess, she handed in her resignation. In the train that was supposed to carry her farther, deeper, closer to her objective, she thought of her mother. She hadn't written to her since she left home, because for now there was nothing to write about. The old woman never received news of her daughter. On the other hand, she did receive hundreds of letters that had been delayed, all addressed to Pearl and all from potential employers who would also never receive any reply from her.

Always going to the same whores means
watching them grow old.

TOPEKA

APRIL 1882

As a general rule, young women lowered their eyes when they encountered a man, unless he was a clergyman. In the latter case, they would walk up to him, greet him, and beg him not to leave so soon, just as they would have done with a family member. They would converse with him, assail him with questions. As for the prostitutes, they acted in the contrary manner, approaching men as if they were family members – except for clergy, whom they avoided like the plague.

"I've never liked the clergy, and preachers even less," Pearl Guthrie would admit much later. "As for you, Reverend, I disliked you right away. But not for the same reasons as the others."

✳

JULY 1877

The workshop of Zottman the tailor was a room of austere simplicity. Apart from the black stove, the working tables, and the rolls of cloth, it was entirely white from floor to ceiling. When Pearl donned the white smock she wore as an apron over her dress and looked at herself in the mirror, she had the impression she had melted into the background.

Often, when changing behind the screen, ladies would complain, "Heavens! It's cold in here!"

"It's because you're not used to white, madam. White makes it colder," the tailor would answer.

"It's a little bare, don't you think?"

"That's the way I wanted it, to attract a male clientele, which, unlike you ladies, is leaning more and more toward the ready-made," he explained.

❉

Pearl was cutting a piece of cloth on the work table when the bell above the door tinkled. The Reverend Aaron entered, carrying a pair of trousers over one arm. He greeted Pearl and pointed to his legs. The trousers he was wearing fell in waves around his ankles. "They're too long. They need altering."

"I'm sorry, sir. You'll have to wait till the tailor is in."

"So you know how to cut cloth, but not how to shorten trouser legs?" said the Reverend, surprised.

"That's how it is in Mr. Zottman's workshop. He takes care of men's apparel, and I do women's."

"Even when he's absent?"

Pearl nodded.

The Reverend looked at her, chewing his quid of tobacco, a habit that conflicted with his appearance as an impeccably dressed man of the cloth. "I'll give you two dollars to do it right away. I won't say a word to your boss. I'm leaving Topeka this evening."

She blushed, and stammered, "The thing is, you see, I'm not very good with men's garments. I can do anything for ladies, from the first petticoat to the final bodice. But as for trousers, well ..."

The Reverend stared at her silently, which made her blush even more. "I'll give you two dollars, even if you make a mess of it."

"Very well then, since you insist."

The Reverend got up on the stool while Pearl went to fetch some pins. She knelt in front of the stool like a slave at her master's feet.

Some customers would stand with a rounded back, ill at ease on their pedestal. Others kept a straight back, with an air of having merited such a platform. The Reverend adjusted his tailcoat, examining himself in the oval mirror.

"I know what you're thinking," he said, watching her turn up one trouser leg after the other. "I wouldn't have needed any alteration if I'd avoided ready-made. But what choice do I have? There are places where no tailors have reached yet."

"What sort of places?"

"The sort where you wouldn't have any work, because there are two hundred men for every woman, and the few women there are spend their days without much on." She stood up and adjusted the mirror to allow the Reverend to judge the length. He got off the stool and went behind the screen to take off the pinned trousers.

"Do you often go to mining towns?" she asked, removing a pin from her mouth.

"I spend my whole life in mining towns."

"I imagine that's where you're most useful. I'd really like to go there too. I think that's where I'd be most needed. Not as a seamstress, I mean. As a virtuous woman."

The Reverend emerged from behind the screen and handed her the trousers. She went over to the table and began to sew the hems. The Reverend crossed his arms and wandered around the workshop as if it were a room in a museum.

"What keeps you here?" he asked.

"Well, here I have a job. There's no one there to welcome me. It wouldn't be very proper. Anyway, I'm talking as if I was thinking of a specific place ..."

The Reverend turned toward her.

"If you like," he began in a pause between spells of the sewing machine's chatter, "I know a respectable lady who could hire you for the rest of the summer."

"To do what kind of work?"

"Odd jobs, I suppose. Actually, I have to visit her very soon. I could mention you to her."

"Oh Reverend, would you? I'd be so grateful. What town does she live in?"

"Dodge City. It's not a mining town, but you'll see, it's even better."

Two afternoons later, as she was out for a walk in her best dress, Pearl saw the Reverend across the street, disappearing into a building of red and white brick with no awning or sign. "A tavern," she concluded. He had lied to her. He hadn't left town as he'd promised.

It was a wide, busy street. Pearl had to look each way and make a dash for it to avoid the carriages that were ploughing up the ground and leaving deep ruts behind. She had to pass some riders wearing suits, ladies holding up their skirts with one hand and clutching their flower-trimmed hats in another, and a black man pulling a wheelbarrow. She closed her parasol and stopped at the door. The voices of men speaking more loudly than necessary reached her, but she couldn't make out the Reverend's. She hesitated. It was no place for a lady, and it wasn't because she had kept a similar establishment in the Shawneetown woods that she was indifferent to appearances. She re-opened her parasol and wove her way along the street, gazing intently at the store windows. She loitered like this until, out of the corner of her eye, she saw the Reverend emerge, carrying his tailcoat over one arm. She called out to him, but he didn't hear.

She walked behind him for a good distance. The neighbourhood began to change. Brick houses gave way to rundown wooden ones, then to slums with tumbledown front porches and clotheslines improvised in doorways. In front of them, black women in calico dresses went about in their soiled aprons. Their children, in short pants, ran barefoot in the mud and threw pebbles at dogs and chickens. The Reverend turned off and walked to a boarding house that seemed as basic as the rest of the district. If he was obliged to lodge in such a place, Pearl said to herself, he couldn't be a very gifted preacher, but the kind who garner only insignificant offerings.

Pearl lived over the workshop with Zottman the tailor and his wife. The two women were awaiting a visit from Mrs. Quigley, a friend of the family. Pearl was reading aloud underneath a lamp, while the tailor's wife worked on a doily in her embroidery hoop. The knock on the door resounded so urgently that both of them rushed downstairs. They opened the door to a breathless, distraught Mrs. Quigley.

"Quick, shut the door!" she said.

"But for the love of God, what's going on?"

"A wag –" She caught her breath. "A wagon was attacked by bandits close to town, on the Oskaloosa road."

"Lord save us! Quick, Pearl, bolt the door. Poor Mrs. Quigley. Come in and sit down."

The news had spread from one end of town to the other like the aroma of roasting meat in windy weather, overtaking Mrs. Quigley as she went.

"Oh, and my husband was in the saloon! How can he ever manage to get home now?" worried Mrs. Zottman.

"Really, Mrs. Zottman, do you think we're in danger here?" asked Pearl in her surprise, more excited than afraid.

"How would I know? I don't know how many of them there were."

"You think Mr. Zottman set off with the posse to try and catch the robbers?" asked Pearl.

The two ladies fell silent and looked at her.

"It's up to the sheriff and his deputies to run after outlaws. That's what they're paid for," the tailor's wife decreed in a decisive tone.

Pearl put the kettle on and the two ladies sipped their afternoon infusion, chasing away flies with their fans and remembering the days when stagecoaches frequently were subject to holdups. Pearl wondered if in the future this afternoon would be added to their repertoire of past adventures.

When it became evident that there was no real danger, Pearl excused herself and went downstairs, then out into the street.

This is a town of cowards, she said to herself. To hell with propriety. She entered the crowded tavern and stood on tiptoe, trying to spot the Reverend. He was by himself at the bar, swirling a glass of brandy under his nose. She threaded her way across to him.

"You heard about the holdup?"

"Like everyone."

"So why are the men still here twiddling their thumbs?"

"Because it's none of their business."

"But it's *your* business, isn't it? You should be talking to them, reminding them of their duty."

"And you think they'd listen to me? I'm sorry to have to tell you this, but it's only women who do what preachers tell them. And I doubt very much that you'd want to send members of your sex to be massacred by bandits."

He knocked back a glass and turned toward the bar. Pearl sighed, and readjusted an errant lock of hair.

"I thought it was only like this where I came from. Actually, it's the same everywhere." She refrained from adding that men are small everywhere. To become a great lady, you've got to choose a great man. A great man or no one at all.

"So you're looking for a place where men are still men? I'll tell you again, go to Dodge City." The Reverend nodded. "Let me tell you why no one's concerned. The wagon that was held up belongs to a family from Tennessee Town, where former slaves live. Even the sheriff and his deputies won't lift a finger. They'll tell you themselves that they've already done enough for those folk during the war. Now you'd best go home, missy. Everyone's looking at you."

After Sam, my mother never wanted to remarry. My mother's men friends, I've seen plenty of them swinging at the end of a rope while she kept busy doing something else so she didn't have to watch. It all depended if she'd decided she didn't give a damn, or just wanted to keep holding a grudge against them.

FREDERICK

AUGUST 1877

A year earlier, in the centre of an unclaimed plot of land, the proprietor had erected a two-storey structure to serve as an eatery, tavern, and hotel – but a tornado swept it away. After this misfortune, the proprietor exploded a stick of dynamite to excavate a cellar where his business would be safe from storms. This establishment in Frederick stank of damp more than any other in Texas, and it was the only tavern you entered by climbing down a ladder instead of going up steps. The ceiling was so low that when they stood, Americans had to stoop. Since there were no Mexicans in this part of the country, nobody had held their heads high in the cellar until Pearl Guthrie arrived.

It rained a lot that summer. Pearl could spend entire days in the tavern listening to the water splashing on the logs overhead. When it wasn't raining, the weather always found a patch of sky to darken, and someone would come along predicting a tornado, even if the season was over: "Take my word for it, she's comin'!" To relieve their boredom, the farmers would tell stories about the daily slog they had come there to escape. Pearl would rather have heard them talk about what was happening elsewhere: about settlements left abandoned for so long that the sand and dust had infiltrated the shacks, making it impossible to enter without leaving tracks. She would like to have heard about towns that didn't yet exist, deserts where no one had yet set foot, terrains swarming with a life at war with itself, fought over by serpents, scorpions, carnivorous plants, freezing nights, and sandstorms, about towns whose names no one could pronounce. Often Pearl would lose the thread and hear the Reverend Aaron's voice ringing over and over inside her head. "Go to Dodge City."

"What about you, would you live in Dodge City?" she once asked.

The drinkers looked for an answer in the bottom of their glass.

"No one lives in Dodge City. They want you to think they do, but it's a lie. In winter, everyone clears out."

⁂

When the sun came out and Pearl emerged from the dark cellar, the light was so harsh the grey rocks looked white. Then she would go around back carrying a basket of sheets and napkins to hang out to dry. There was no hope of the cloth remaining clean with the sand whirling about and clinging to it. But she enjoyed this moment of solitude, when she could feel the wind stir the ringlets on her nape. She loved the shadow she cast on the ground, which exaggerated her slender figure and enormous straw hat. Whenever she sensed someone looking at her from behind, she would watch out of the corner of her eye for a second shadow to appear on the ground. But she never turned around, fearing there would be no one there.

She was beginning to consider her gold nugget in a different light. It was no longer a lifeless relic that served as an anchor for her mother's depression. It was a bud that had taken shape underground at a rate imperceptible to humans. Between the moments when there was nothing and when the precious metal reached maturity, religions had been born, continents had been discovered, and empires had fallen. Entire civilizations had disappeared and others had come into being. It was a treasure that had spent the eons of its existence deep in a cavity that not only contained its latent brilliance, but always prevented it from shining because daylight had never struck it. Or perhaps it had been sluiced from the river silt, like other minerals discovered in California around the same time. Pearl didn't know. But she preferred to imagine it as a truffle buried excessively deep within the earth and grown hard over time. The nugget had had to wait thousands of years for its master before coming into the hands of a Guthrie.

The nugget was her assurance of liberty, her only wealth. If this town failed to supply her with what she sought, she simply had to go and look for it elsewhere. Thanks to her lump of gold, Pearl would never be confined to a single place, to a single type of work. She would visit every town until she found the right one.

She said a prayer of thanks to Ruben, the brother she had never known, for having lived and found gold.

✤

When the saloonkeeper was absent, Pearl looked after the cash register in the store and served the few customers. The bachelor farmers and the sons of good families would come to sit and drink, enjoying the simple pleasure of watching her as she washed the dirty glasses from the previous night's drinking. There was a young widow who sold her charms part-time from a barn three miles away, but she was not attractive.

In the course of a month, Pearl had to administer four slaps and received two offers of marriage but did not meet any man she considered worthy to be her fiancé. Since there was no other place to drink thereabouts, her rejected suitors all returned to Frederick. Once rebuffed, they no longer remained at the bar to stare at her. They occupied chairs at the back of the cellar and followed her out of the corner of an eye, scoring the wooden table with their knives, their jaws clenched and their legs twitching nervously. Often, united by their shared bitterness, they would play cards together.

"We're not good enough for her, that's understandable. But if the four of us join forces, she won't be able to resist."

Pearl's back was turned when she heard this suggestion. She finished polishing the glasses and went upstairs to pack her bag. Then she went back down to the cellar and stuck her letter of resignation between the cash register and the scales.

Some say my mother was a whore. I'm just sayin', but I don't see no difference between a whore that sleeps with all the men, and a goody two-shoes that goes shopping around but never makes a pick.

DODGE CITY

Summer was over by the time Pearl Guthrie entered Dodge City. She made her way along the boardwalk, looking for the Gondola. The street was quiet. Most of the store windows were boarded up. She backed out into the middle of the street to read the names painted on the false fronts or pasted to the windows in giant lettering – but perhaps also to keep away from the many dens of vice, for fear of being drawn into them. She liked to think that people entered such establishments of their own free will. But in these parts the wind was strong. You could easily stumble and find yourself on hands and knees at the feet of your sworn enemy.

When she presented herself at the front entrance to the Gondola, she was struck by the snug look of the parlour, the wealth of wall-to-wall burgundy, green, and black carpet that covered the floors and stairs and hung on a few walls in place of wallpaper. These coverings seemed designed to swallow noise and liquids that were too much for the floorboards alone to absorb.

Pearl was welcomed by the owner, a thin, soberly dressed lady with greying hair – a businesswoman who looked like a schoolmistress, with a watch in one pocket and a ruler in the other.

"You've come too late, Miss Guthrie. The season is over. Half of the girls have gone back to Kansas City. I don't understand why the Reverend Aaron wouldn't have given you better information."

"To tell you the truth, the more I think about it the more I think the Reverend Aaron was laughing at me."

"Is that so?" said the woman, showing no compassion.

"The Reverend had mentioned a job as a general help." She looked down.

"And I fancy you're the kind of general help who generally isn't much help," the woman said, sarcastically.

They stared at each other in silence, both ensconced in a bodice buttoned to the neck, artfully exhibiting the prudish subtleties of New York fashion. The young woman examined the older one, wondering if she too had clung to her respectability, as she seemed to be doing that day. The older woman looked the younger one up and down, raising an eyebrow and thinking "Pity!"

Pearl bobbed with her bonnet, and turned away.

The owner stopped her: "You won't find any work in Dodge at this time of year, you know. Not as a general help, anyway."

"Then I'll go somewhere else."

"So you're going to become a drifter?"

Pearl held her breath, insulted. "Certainly not!"

"I can accommodate you till you find something else. I can't pay you anything in the off-season, you understand. But I could take you in, give you a roof over your head, and feed you, in exchange for a few domestic duties. Can you cook, Miss Guthrie?"

※

Given the responsibility of feeding the Gondola's girls, Pearl had to take account of their slightest dietary whims. One despised cooked carrots; another couldn't digest green onions. They all pushed away their plates as soon as they smelled garlic, saying they didn't want their customers to be repelled by their breath. One of them had made her surplus flesh a commercial advantage and demanded a double ration of bread and butter.

Each morning, Pearl would collect the empty bottles, hunt down corks in the four corners of the room, and recork the half-empty bottles. She would wipe up the sticky circles on the tables and sweep away the fragments of glass and the dirty tracks left by customers' boots. The first male voices would not be heard outside until after nine o'clock. The girls in the household would rise at three in the afternoon. Pearl did everything, while the girls did nothing. She went to bed at eleven, when the night's revelries were getting under way. But even then the girls would often come into her room and shake her by the shoulder. "Where's the champagne?" "I've a customer who wants pork jerky." "But yes, we *can* cook them a little something to eat if they're big spenders."

"Do you think she's pretending to be asleep? Just look at her. Even if she was wearing nothing but a feather fan, no customer would want her. What age is she, do you think? I'd say about twelve. Or maybe forty-eight."

Generally, she did what was asked of her, even after three in the morning. Often she kept her eyes closed, repressing a desire to grab one of the girls by the arm and pretend to read her palm: "You'll die by your own hand, like all the others of your sort, it's written in your palm."

When she ventured onto the streets of Dodge, she made every effort to hold her head high and mimic the walk of the European women she had once observed in St. Louis. But in order to stand apart from her colleagues, she also had to exhibit modesty, drawing her shawl around her shoulders and lowering her eyes when greeting people – behaviour she hadn't found it difficult to maintain in Shawneetown, but which in Dodge betrayed her desire to pass unnoticed. Yet she had nothing to be ashamed of. The fact that her virtue could remain intact in an establishment like the Gondola demonstrated her strength of character. But how could respectable men – the sort she might have married, the kind that didn't frequent the establishment – be sure that she wasn't tarnished goods, like the other employees?

※

In the summer months, the ground in Dodge City would quake. The streets were invaded by herds of cattle trampling the ground, a stream of hoofs all galloping in one direction as if heading for Noah's ark (when in fact they were making for the railroad car that would take them to the slaughterhouse).

Every night the hubbub of their bellowing was replaced by a confused cacophony of accordion and piano music, joyful shouts, and the sound of breaking glass. The taverns and gambling dens were bursting at the seams with cowboys wearing the tanned leather skins of animals other than the ones in whose close company they had spent long months, men who had nothing very human about them anymore, except for the tunes they whistled to fill the silence of the prairies and the worn photograph of a sweetheart or an actress that they kept crumpled deep in a pocket – men so happy to be back in civilization that they couldn't wait to demolish it, and who, like animals, could only be called to order by a few gunshots.

✷

It was Wednesday. The first customer arrived at seven o'clock. When he opened the door, the last rays of sunlight swept across part of the room. He wore a wide-brimmed hat and high boots. The girls came down the staircase and took up their places in front of him, one after the other. Pearl would remain to watch the ritual followed by each new customer when making his choice. This was her own little game – guessing which girl would be chosen. The man removed his hat. A several days' beard framed his face. Pearl had often heard the girls of the establishment complain to one another about such hairiness, for it left red blotches on their skin. The Gondola's girls were professionals: they had long given up venerating signs of their clients' virility. They preferred signs of wealth – and of weakness.

Pearl sat at the top of the staircase, hunched up in the semi-darkness to escape notice – untouchable, but excluded. The man undid the top button of his jacket; sweat poured down his neck. The girls, dressed in floating lace, were lined up as if on parade. However, unlike soldiers, they didn't stand at attention but rolled their shoulders and fluttered their eyelids.

The man approached and pronounced his judgment before each one. "Too thin. Too fat. Too tall. Much too skinny. Too drunk. Too dark." He said nothing to the girl he chose. He nodded toward the room – the only sign of approval that came from him, the nearest thing to a compliment.

Thus ended the ignominious parade. Upstairs, Pearl kept out of the way as the girls returned to their rooms, and then, as soon as the coast was clear, she returned below to her kitchen.

✳

The man with the prickly beard came back at the same time the next day. He was dressed in the same way as the evening before. The same choreography played out: sweat trickling in rivulets down the ladies' faces and their makeup cracking; plump arms moving to and fro, wearily fanning throats; triangles of lace held to noses, coils of hair falling over ears – but the heat had the last word as their cosmetics ran, as useless as all the seductive gestures that merely enlarged the damp circles under their armpits.

The customer was no more dignified than the girls, for it would have been easy for him to demand more – or rather less, by desisting when confronted with an inventory of such poor quality. But perhaps he enjoyed his hands being encrusted with cosmetics and dirt when he grasped the merchandise.

Without a word, he singled out the girl he had called too fat the evening before. In the dark, Pearl shook her head. This man had no consideration for anyone, she told herself, and no particular tastes. He consumed the girls the way you light a match and then throw it away. The day after that he came again, picking the girl he had described as much too skinny. The next day he took a girl he had previously found too tall. Each time he chose a different one. By the eighth evening, only two remained whose services he had not yet procured. He pointed to his companion for the evening, and Pearl felt a twinge of sympathy for the remaining one. She caught herself imagining what would have happened if she had placed herself at the end of the line. She saw herself in her dark dress buttoned to the neck and the plait falling down her back. She could only have been first, or last. She would have been the one he had always been waiting for. With a respectable girl, he would have been respectful. Or else he would have come to her, pronounced her overdressed, and showed no further interest, before taking her neighbour by the elbow. Then she would have returned each evening and remained at the tail end of the regiment of humiliation until she had worn him down. And each of his rejections would have been like a victory, for unlike the others she had no need to be the pick of the brothel in order to earn her living. She still had the gold nugget at the bottom of her bag.

✴

During the night, Pearl relived this scene in a dream, but the man's beard had grown and he introduced himself as Charley Monday. In her dream, the bandit stopped in front of her, looked her straight in the eye, and said, "I'll take this one." Until then it had been a pleasant dream. But once they were in the bedroom, which resembled the one in the house where she was born, in which Teasdale had slept, the man took her by the arm and pushed her against the wall. He grabbed her again and shook her like a rag doll. "Where's my box?" he repeated. "My box, I want my box, you whore." Teasdale let her go, but she lay huddled at the bottom of the wall, covering her head. "I'm not a whore," she said, weakly. He looked at the room, the unmade bed, the scattered dresses, the empty bottles and used glasses, and gave a wry smile – the sneer she would never forget, the last image she kept of him before he set off along the Shawneetown road.

"Maybe you're not a whore, but you're a slave to whores. You're the whores' whore." Pearl woke feeling sick to her stomach, her mouth filled with disgust. That afternoon she packed her bag and handed in her resignation before learning if the man with the prickly beard would return for the tenth girl.

I haven't learned a lot in my life, but I know that the brightest ideas come to you when you're walking, and the darkest ones when you're sleeping.

———————◆—◆—◆———————

MONUMENT

OCTOBER 1877

Monument was a town that could have been plunked down anywhere. It had no historical roots, nor did it sit on any natural resource. It existed only because the stagecoach company needed a station between Grinnell and Gopher. The company had decided to create one there, a place where travellers would have the leisure to break their journey halfway through and rest for a while. So Monument was a destination printed on tickets, but not a place anyone wanted to stay.

Pearl kept a list. Drawing on conversations between travellers that she overheard, she noted the names of places to visit, of masculine communities to astonish by her presence. She knew that Monument had nothing more to offer, but she had such a wide choice that she didn't know where to begin. Like everybody else, she had settled there only temporarily, employed as a servant by the hemophiliac saloon owner, a dreamer who preferred to experience adventure vicariously, through the uncouth epics related by migrants. Between the arrival and departure of each stagecoach, she lived in the hope that the considerable turnover of visitors would increase her chances of encountering her future husband. Her skirt was beginning to show wear, her complexion to grow darker. When she entered a place, people would frown and follow her with curious eyes. Her delicate hands and bearing no longer protected her from insults. A young woman on her own, neither widow nor prostitute, but lacking a family or a husband – the dove was on a questionable path. She had to talk to vindicate herself. So Pearl began to lie, initially out of her survival instinct, but ultimately out of habit. She lied to her employer, to the hotel guests, to her rejected suitors. She invented a fiancé, a father, a brother.

For five months she lived in Monument, trawling through the catalogue of potential husbands among the travellers while repeating to herself that the West was vast and the stock unlimited. She kept another list, which she kept secret in her head: a list of candidates. Each day she crossed one off because he had too much hair in his ears, because he smelled of talcum powder, or because his name was Earl (which sounded too much like her own). Every suitor she crossed off left a deficit, for she would cross out two for each one she added. Every rejection was a loan that had to be returned to the creditor, or there would be no list left.

She was overcome by doubt. Either God had arranged everything so that she would be free when she met "the right one," or else He was refusing her the thing she desired most ardently and which He had granted so many women less deserving than she. So she began to pray. During the day, she lied. In the evening, she prayed.

※

FEBRUARY 1878

One evening, an itinerant preacher named Fountain entered the saloon. His gaze rested inquisitively on each individual, and then, as soon as he had reached a decision, he pointed to Pearl and asked where her husband was.

"I haven't got one," she replied, in accordance with her latest lie.

"Then this is no place for you. How long has she been here?" asked the preacher, turning to the male customers.

"Five months," answered Pearl.

"Look at what you've done," said the Reverend Fountain, disappointed. "For five months you've allowed this woman to be corrupted. You have acted as profiteers instead of protectors."

"She came of her own free will," the owner replied.

"So? You've taken advantage of her liberty! But in fact she is not free, she's an orphan. If she had been your daughter or your sister, you'd have forbidden her to set foot in a tavern like this, full of men with evil intentions."

The preacher climbed onto a table. "Truly, this woman is all you deserve, for you're incapable of acting like men. You close your eyes; you block your ears. You refuse to see the unhappiness behind her forced smiles. Instead of going to bed with lost women, you should take them by the hair and drag them kicking and screaming back to their families, like lost sheep. But no, you never bring them back, neither women nor sheep, for you are a pack of thieves."

"That's enough! Nobody asked for your opinion," shouted a traveller.

"You're nothing but bandits," the preacher went on. "Good-for-nothings who think you're men because you ride on mules. You think you're Christians because you go to church once a year, but you spend the rest of the time in taverns. The only thing that should make you set foot in this place should be your desire to burn it to the ground. You are parasites."

Out of the corner of one eye, Pearl saw that her boss was unobtrusively moving toward the rear exit. She slowly drew back to join him. Just as she was closing the door behind her, she saw a man grab the preacher by the legs. Outside, Pearl and the hemophiliac tavern keeper sat with their backs against the rear wall, listening to the sounds of blows and breaking bottles. The owner could have reassured her or apologized for not having defended her, but he said nothing. Pearl might have begged forgiveness for the damage of which she was the indirect cause, but she said nothing either.

※

Once the tavern was empty, they discovered the preacher under a table. He was brought upstairs, to one of the bedrooms. Pearl bandaged his wounds. She could have spat in his cuts but refrained from doing so. "Have you any children, Reverend Fountain?" she asked.

"Yes, I have many children. They are all mine," he declared, keeping his eyes closed.

"I'd like to live a decent life, but I'm not able to find myself a decent husband. It's no use praying ... It changes nothing."

"As long as you remain in a town full of sinners, your prayers won't be answered."

The Reverend Fountain left the saloon a few hours later, in the middle of the night, as if nothing, not even total darkness, could make him lose his way. She never saw him again. Some say he died a martyr's death in El Paso.

One day someone said there was gold, and then folks started to look for it. Only a rare few found any. They must know perfectly well that they're the exception. But no, they'll be the first to preach and tell the whole world that if life has taught them a useful lesson, it's that you must never stop believing. Now if I had to preach something, it'd be that life teaches everyone a different lesson, and that preachers can stick their sermons you know where.

AUBREY

MARCH 1878

In the stagecoach sat Pearl, a young man carrying his things wrapped up in a bundle who had tired of walking, and a middle-aged lady with two children, a boy and a girl. The sun had just dropped behind the line of the horizon. The shadow of the rocks was gaining ground and the rosy sky was preparing to bid farewell. It was a time of day when even the eyes of remorseless criminals seemed to shine. The driver clicked his tongue to stir the mules, and the coach moved off. It advanced along the dirt road through fields of tall golden grasses that seemed to become greener as darkness fell. Pearl watched the town of Aubrey fade into the distance. It was a former army fort, now abandoned, of which there remained only a few sod huts and some stone buildings used by the stagecoach company's employees, left to their own devices in this uninhabited land.

"What's that?" asked the boy, pointing outside.

A white, unidentified marquee tent was taking shape away from the road. Behind it the line of the Arkansas River was visible, and farther on, the dunes of the South.

"Looks to me like a religious camp," his mother replied.

The young man leaned toward the window of the coach.

"It's pretty quiet."

Pearl leaned over in her turn, her gaze following the white triangle of the tent. She had never attended such a camp. She had never seen religious faith acting like a show. She rapped on the side of the coach and asked the driver to stop. She had to try a second time before he understood. He hauled her bag off the roof and set it down at her feet. "I don't think that's a good idea, miss. It's hostile territory around here," he said.

"Don't wait for me," she answered, turning around and setting off toward the tent.

"An' how are you goin' to get back to Aubrey afterward?"

She didn't answer and continued on her way without looking back, for that was how a person hearing God's call was supposed to behave. The driver, the young man, the woman, and perhaps even the children, had to spend a few minutes watching her silhouette grow smaller as she went, wondering if the poor girl was out of her mind – and asking why God didn't speak as clearly to them.

✳

By the time Pearl reached the camp, darkness had fallen. The tent was lit from inside, a solitary beacon deep in the night. She pushed back the canvas flaps and found ten or so people sitting on chairs, the men wearing brown suits with black, broad-brimmed hats on their heads, the women wrapped in cloaks or mantles under white bonnets with side flaps. Kerosene lamps sat here and there on the ground. The preacher at the front held an open book and seemed to be reading from it. He spoke softly, with few gestures.

She would have liked to see a preacher whose spittle flew to the back row, with the people weeping to the point of suffocation, to hear a chorus of Amens or to see some rascal release toads among the congregation and be invited up front by the preacher: repentant, he would fall on his knees, ask the Lord's pardon, and then accept Christ before everyone. She would have liked to hear a fiery speech that went straight to the heart, but the preacher was giving a very dull kind of homily, not unlike those she had heard every Sunday in the Shawneetown church.

She took a seat at the back. The walls of the tent flapped with every gust of wind. The faithful struck up a hymn that she herself had often sung. However, she remained silent, allowing the tears to course down her cheeks. Words and tones she had so often heard in her previous life now resonated in a strange land. She was still sitting in the back when the people rose to greet the pastor and congratulate him on his sermon before leaving, taking their lamps with them. Only one final lamp remained in front, near the preacher, who was putting away his books. Pearl uttered the word "Reverend!" in the gloom, and the preacher started. She went up to the light, threw herself at his feet, and asked for his help. The Lord refused to answer her prayers, though she had only one request: What should she do so that He would hear her? "You must pray, my child," answered the preacher.

The memory of her mother came back to her – her mother who prayed and wept every day, and wept and prayed. And the preacher who said exactly that: "Pray, my child." Then she pulled away from the preacher's hands and became angry.

"No! That's not enough. I have to do something. I have to pay, to bleed. Look ..."

Sniffling, she fumbled in her bag and took out the gold nugget. She held it up to the preacher, forcing him to take it.

"That's all I have. Now God will have no choice but to hear me." Seeing the preacher hesitate, she added, "Imagine all the churches you can build with this offering."

The preacher gripped Pearl by the elbow to help her to her feet. He examined the nugget, turning it over and over; his Adam's apple stood out when he swallowed. "The Lord will hear you," he said.

Pearl left the tent wiping away her tears and smiling beatifically.

It was a mistake. Even an imposter like the Reverend Aaron would have known that you can't bargain with God. Only pagan divinities were gratified by that kind of sacrifice, and they didn't exist. The One God had no interest in bleeding cattle or burnt grass. In her absence, or excess, of faith, Pearl Guthrie had just sealed her fate.

However, while not altogether answering her prayer, God did send her Russian Bill.

NOTEBOOK III

Russian Bill's Hundred Killings

CHARLESTON, 1880 ✤ PERRYVILLE, 1878

LA POSTA, 1878 ✤ O'DERMODY, 1878

VALVERDE, 1878 ✤ BIG BEND, 1878

LAKE CITY, 1878 ✤ TELLURIDE, 1878

ELIZABETHTOWN, 1879 ✤ SILVER CITY, 1879

NEW BABYLON, 1879–1881 ✤ SARAZIN, 1869–1881

✤ SANTA FE, 1880–1881 ✤

✤

It's not my fault if one man's victory means
another man's defeat.

CHARLESTON

APRIL 1880

Russian Bill entered a tavern in Charleston in the late afternoon one Tuesday in April 1880. Silhouetted against the light, holding his hat in his hands, his dark shape intervened between the daylight outside and the customers crowded inside. Only his ears allowed the sunlight through; they glowed like leather lanterns in the semi-darkness. Before they even saw his face, the customers knew that the newcomer was blessed with protruding ears.

"Have you any vodka?" he asked, without moving.

"We've got whiskey, mescal, and El Paso brandy," replied the barman.

Russian Bill approached the bar, his spurs clinking with each step, and ordered a whiskey. He was still less than thirty years old. Maybe twenty-five. He had bushy eyebrows, but a perfectly trimmed moustache. His hair was parted in the middle, though some recalcitrant whorls drove a few strands to rebel. A holstered revolver hung at each hip. The men watched him, trying to appear as if they were looking elsewhere.

"Too young to be someone important, too clean to be a cattle rustler," the Reverend told himself from his seat, a chair without a table farther inside the tavern. "The kind that shoots at the ceiling without the authority to do so, and the next day asks to go upstairs to see the holes in the floor."

"It's just impossible to find vodka around here," Russian Bill sighed, taking off his coat to reveal a double-breasted damask waistcoat and a white shirt. Around his neck was tied a large red bandana of raw cotton, a sign he belonged to the cowboy world. The Reverend categorized him as one of those Southern aristocrats who treat their inferiors the way they used to treat their slaves, but who keep their word whatever the consequences and are ready to die in a gunfight to defend their own honour or the honour of others. Among the cowboys were a lot of former plantation owners ruined by the war, but this man's clothes were too well-cut and his articulation too distinct, despite a strange accent. He expressed himself in an English that originated in old Europe, though his speech was peppered with Southern expressions. He rolled every fourth r. In this jumble of contradictions, it was difficult to distinguish the artificial from the authentic.

Russian Bill insisted that what he owed be recorded so that he didn't have to pay each time. The barman asked his name.

"William Tattenbaum. Or Russian Bill, if you prefer. That's what I go by around here. I imagine it's easier for you all to pronounce. And then you have to distinguish me from the other Bills, who seem to be legion in these parts."

The barman poured him a whiskey and then recorked the bottle, staring at him without uttering a word. The Russian knocked back the contents of his glass.

"My God, how I miss my own country," he said.

"So why don't you go back there?" asked a blasé individual from the other end of the bar.

Russian Bill took a deep breath before answering.

"Because, you see, they'd kill me. I left to escape the military police. I don't like talking about what I did, but I can't deny it. I slapped the face of a superior officer, a hussar who was a favourite of the czar's. I'm not proud of it, but there you are. I'd be a dead man if I hadn't left – despite being the son of Countess Telfrin. My title's useless here, but no one will ever make me give it up."

The line of drinkers standing around the bar looked him up and down as they went on chewing their tobacco and smoking their cigars. In Charleston, it wasn't usual for people to talk about their origins. Those who liked spinning yarns would say "In my hometown ..." without any further details. The most talkative would go as far as naming the state, but most said nothing at all.

"Life in the Russia of my birth is a lot more dramatic than here," he went on. "Peasants who disobey are buried alive. The nobility has unlimited power, and the oppression of the poor is boundless. Just the opposite of this America populated with semi-bourgeois self-made men, where even black men are free," he declared disdainfully.

"How do you say 'shut your mouth' in Russian?" called out one drinker.

The barman and the customers held their breath, waiting for the Russian to respond in the universal language by reaching for one of his revolvers. He contented himself with raising an eyebrow and lifting his glass very high as if he wanted to drink a toast with the whole world. He drew a breath and then uttered some unintelligible syllables of what must have been an improvised language. Disbelieving, the customers remained silent, then a laugh rang out, and another. A chorus of hearty laughter ran from one end of the room to the other.

In this place where you had to threaten to shoot if you didn't want to be shot, everyone had his own way of ensuring his personal safety. The Reverend Aaron did it by pretending to be a preacher, and Russian Bill, a buffoon.

※

The inhabitants of Charleston were mainly employed in the works where crushers pulverized the ore extracted from Tombstone's mines. They lived in hovels built of mud bricks or shacks of raw timber, and in daytime drove away the flies as they walked among the stalls selling red meat that hung from roofs made of branches.

Sometimes Southern troublemakers came to take advantage of the amenities. They were recognizable by their wide scarves and their mania for going into the saloons without dismounting, partly because they eventually forgot that they had a horse under them and partly because they liked to look down on the lackeys from the mines with a warrior's disdain. It had been like this since the Civil War, in Charleston as everywhere else in Arizona. Men would go into saloons and boast of having shot other men. It wasn't so much that they killed to see their adversaries' eyes glaze over, but rather to see a gleam in the eyes of onlookers. Men were ranked according to a shifting hierarchy, with those who had most killings to their credit at the top. Ones who had never killed were obliged to invent victims if they didn't want to languish at the bottom, and the ones who really had killed had to exaggerate by claiming they had done so dozens of times. Occasionally a man would be preceded by his reputation, in which case his entrance would be followed by silence, in a respectful atmosphere only the flies ignored. There would always be some curious individual to strike up a conversation with him and ask, "So tell me again how many guys you've shot?" Then he would throw a disdainful glance at the questioner and answer, "I don't think it's any of your business how many guys I've shot!"

It was these men that interested the Reverend Aaron – men who had understood that to recognize where shots came from, you first had to learn to keep your mouth shut.

⚹

Russian Bill boasted that he had killed about a hundred people. No one believed him. Nor did anyone pick a gunfight with him.

He often changed hats, saying that his headgear was the first and last thing that was noticed about a man, and that you could use it as well to conceal as to show yourself.

Though quick to criticize the quality of the liquor he was served, he actually drank very little and seemed to prefer flaunting the glass to emptying it. He would speak at the same time to everybody and to no one, and when he turned around to scrutinize those present it was with the sole objective of selecting the comment that would provoke someone into drawing his gun.

"There's a guy with a crooked nose. That's what happens when you fight someone tougher than yourself. And it must be that guy over there that stinks of the privies for miles around, or maybe it's the privies that stink of him?"

"It really kills my appetite to eat in front of guys like you," he once complained to a miner with pieces of bacon caught in his beard as he ate in the canteen.

"I just love arrogant little shits like you," was his bold way of accosting a cowboy younger than himself. "They think they're men already. I like to see to it that they never become men."

By first mocking himself with his picaresque tales of Russian nobility, he negated the effect of any subsequent insult. This was how Russian Bill became the only man in those parts who could say anything that came into his head. One day, he tackled the Reverend Aaron.

"Him again!" he said, feigning surprise. "He's going to have to tell us what he's doing here, this preacher man. I can tell you that in other places he talks even more than I do, but that here he's too scared. Isn't that right, Reverend? You're dead scared, aren't you? You know all too well that no one around here is afraid of hell."

The Reverend looked up.

"If you don't mind, I'll just go on reading and not talk to you."

"Oh, how nice of you to ask permission! Well, I'm not giving it. I don't like the way you look at me."

"Before you spoke to me, I wasn't looking at you."

"That's just the problem. Among folks who used to look at me, no one has ever been out to get me. So when people look away, there's nothing to say they don't want to shoot me."

"Leave it be, Bill," said a man behind him, between chuckles. "There's no way you can rile the Reverend here."

Bill went on staring at the Reverend, waiting for an answer.

"The day I start carrying a gun, I promise I'll start looking at you," assured the Reverend before returning to his notebook.

DECEMBER 1880

The Reverend Aaron was rarely mistaken about people, but he had misjudged Russian Bill. The Reverend had been blind to the anguish of a man broken by love, and whose craziness was genuine. He had failed to sense that, like himself, Bill was searching for treasures of no monetary value, and that his eccentricity was his only entertainment. Russian Bill was the kind of man who went to bed happy as long as at least one person had made a joke at his expense in the course of the day.

"That there Russian," the owner of a saloon in Charleston would sometimes say. "He's just like the whores from the back of the house. The more ashamed they are, the more they flaunt themselves."

The Reverend and Russian Bill had played all their games of chess in Tombstone, with one exception, in Charleston, when the saloon was empty. Bill asked the Reverend what he thought of him.

"Unlike you, I'm not used to telling people my opinion of them," he answered.

"Then what do you think other people think of me?"

"I think nobody believes you're a gentleman descended from Russian nobility."

Bill sighed, took off his Stetson, and put it on the bar.

"I care very little whether they believe it or not."

"Then why do you lie if you care so little what people think?"

"Because I'm telling the truth."

"All right, let's suppose you are telling the truth. Let's suppose you really have done away with a hundred people."

"Ninety-two."

"Then why do you need so badly for people to know it? You might have been satisfied to have done it, instead of boring others about it."

"Because I want to be famous, Reverend. After all I've been through, don't I deserve that?"

"But deep in your soul, what do you think you'll gain by becoming famous for being someone you're not?"

Amused, Bill smiled inwardly. He downed a glass of whiskey, choking on it.

"To be quite honest, Reverend, there are days when I'd rather not have killed a hundred or so people."

In all his phony career, the only mistake the Reverend Aaron made was to despise Russian Bill. But maybe it was a good thing. It reminded him he wasn't a god.

*I could have been a miner. Everywhere they were telling us that
with gold you couldn't miss as long as you had the right tools.
Everyone thought so. I've seen lots of mining camps, and the only
thing I ever heard was stories of good luck and bad luck.
There was nothing you could learn in the mines.*

———◆◆◆———

PERRYVILLE

APRIL 1878

The establishment served more as a tavern and gambling house than as a place to stay, but the word "Hotel" was painted in white letters on the front. Five letters, no more. No "Grand Hotel" – which would have proved to be untrue – as would any other qualification suggesting the slightest effort to compete.

The six beds on the second floor were occupied by permanent lodgers. The five round tables on the ground floor were occupied by regulars who in one evening would lose a sum and then return the following day to win it back from some other regular. Without any professionals to make the level of play more than mediocre, the hotel was no doubt one of the rare places where good or bad luck had the last word, the way a coin can fall only heads or tails.

It was late when Russian Bill entered the hotel one April Monday in 1878. The door closed behind him with a crash. The room was hazy with dust and cigar smoke; newspaper adorned the walls. A few kerosene lamps hung on the opposite wall, and candles stuck in bottles had been placed here and there on the tables. He set down his bags, which resembled the leather ones doctors carried, and then his Spencer rifle, which he might have used as a walking stick. He raised the turned-up brim of his homburg hat to take a better look at the premises. Near the entrance, a young woman of remarkable beauty was husking corn, with the leaves piling up at her feet. She greeted him with a timid nod. In one corner, an old man surrounded by empty glasses held a mirror up to his face as he used tweezers to pluck his nose hair.

Around a square table, six bare-headed men played cards, sitting so close together that there was little room for cheating. They all leaned forward with their black or brown jackets pulled up at the base of their spines, showing the ends of their suspenders. They were locals who seemed to have neither women to court nor men to intimidate. The girl with the corn had to be either inaccessible or easily bought. There was no one behind the bar. Russian Bill drew off his gloves one by one, tugging on the middle fingers, not sure to whom he should speak. He raised his voice for all to hear.

"Good evening, ladies and gentlemen. I'd like a room for the night."

"It's full," answered one of the gamblers, throwing a card on the table.

"At this time of year, permit me to doubt that," Bill insisted.

The card player threw an elbow over the back of his chair.

"Doubt all you like. I'm the owner, and if I say there's no room, there's no room."

"Very well, then you won't have any objection if I buy the lot across the road and set up some healthy competition. Since you seem unable to satisfy the demand," said Bill, taking out his wallet.

The innkeeper scratched his chin with the cards he was holding. His eyes went from the green banknotes the newcomer was waving to the revolvers hanging at his hips, and then to the Spencer rifle balanced against his leg.

"I'll see what I can do."

The five other card players had to draw back their chairs to allow him to leave the group. He made for the staircase, beckoning to the young woman to follow him. She got up, took off the serge apron she had pinned to the top of her bodice, and with her hand brushed away the corn silk still clinging to her rust-coloured skirt, which seemed almost brown against the greenish wood of the floor. She turned to go upstairs, revealing the ivory comb inserted in her hair, the only adornment in this sombre decor.

Bill drew up a chair in the middle of the room – an unusual choice for a man on his own who had not previously obtained gambling chips. In general, solitary characters were attracted by the tables at a distance from the others, where it was easier to conceal your boredom.

"Your room's the last on the right," said the innkeeper, coming downstairs a step at a time, clinging to the banisters with both hands. He returned to his place among the gamblers. Bill laid his hat down in front of him, placed his feet on the chair opposite, and began to hum what sounded like a Confederate lament.

"Hey friend, what about joining the game instead of hurting our ears?" inquired a regular with sideburns as thick as a fish's gills.

"No thanks."

The gamblers exchanged a glance over their cards. It was often said that a man who didn't have the guts to gamble didn't have much stomach for anything else.

"What I really like is to humiliate my opponents at chess," Bill ventured, "but there's not really any money to be made at that."

The remarkably beautiful young woman returned downstairs, avoiding the customers' glances. She collected the basket of corn and went out, returning a few minutes later with a basketful of carrots. The stranger began to whistle again, and the man with the sideburns turned to face him.

"Listen, I can't force you to join us, but it ain't the big city here, and there ain't nothin' else to do. I dunno how you keep entertained in other places but ..."

"I prefer to work," Bill interrupted.

"Oh yeah, as far as that goes, I like to work too," said the innkeeper, waving a couple of cards.

"Just like you-all, I'm working right now, despite appearances. I'm thinking, planning. You can laugh, but I'm sure that deep down you-all are sad at what's becoming of your town."

"There ain't nothin' becomin' of our town."

"Exactly! Now I find that's a pity. I bet it would suit you-all very well to have some new folks to compete with now and again."

"I dunno. We could do without guys like you," answered the innkeeper without turning around.

The card players froze in a tense silence. Only their eyes moved, shifting right to left, up and down. The only sound that could be heard was the knife strokes of the young woman cutting up carrots, simultaneously evoking the smell of a mother's soup and the furious rhythm of Northern industry. The stranger stared at the back of the innkeeper's head for a moment and then sighed.

"I'm not here to insult you-all. It's just that I've seen a lot of towns since I left, and never yet have I seen even one I'd like to live in. But I'm not expecting to stumble on the town of my dreams. I'm going to build it myself."

"And what'll it be like, this town of yourn?" said the man with the sideburns, throwing down a card and pretending to be still concentrating on the game.

"Like a lot of others, except that gunfights would be permitted there, and it could never be pacified – that would be written in its constitution. The only law would be one keeping lawmen out. It would be a dangerous place where everyone will finally learn his true worth. A place where you constantly have your breath taken away, sometimes because of the scenery, and sometimes because your throat's been cut. My town will be called New Babylon, and people will come from far away just to be able to say they've been there."

"It'd be a hellhole," said the man. I know some folks that likes hellholes, but they're not the kind of folks to found a town. You won't find no one to sign that constitution of yourn."

"To start with perhaps, but believe me, there's money to be made wherever people want to go. Guys of average intelligence chase after gold, but real visionaries keep a step ahead of the crowd. To be there to welcome it, and cater to its smallest needs.

The future isn't hatched from domination anymore, but from deliberate servitude."

"Nobody'll want to go to a place where there's no gold," said the innkeeper, putting an end to the conversation rather than contributing to it.

"You-all are here, nevertheless," said Bill, putting his hat on again. "Ladies and gentlemen, I take my leave and I bid you-all good night." He picked up his leather bag and his gun and went upstairs whistling.

⚹

Russian Bill slept hugging his rifle. At first light, he opened an eye and with a corner of the sheet wiped away the saliva that had run onto the butt of his Spencer. He swung his legs out of the bed and leaned over to pick up his boots. Then he saw the hem of a woman's dress projecting onto the floor. He squatted down to discover a poorly closed suitcase under the bed. There was something wrong about this room. He told himself that the previous occupants must have left in great haste, or else had never left at all.

Opening the top drawer of the bedside table, he found an ink-well and a pen. In the second drawer were a notebook and a sheet of paper that seemed to have been folded several times. He took out the piece of paper and ran his eyes over it:

~~Dodge City~~
Santa Fe
Taos
Albuquerque
Silver City
Tucson
Tubac
Prescott
Salt Lake City
Denver

He got dressed and went downstairs, finding it difficult not to leap some of the steps. He found the room arranged as it had been the evening before, but devoid of any human presence. He called the innkeeper several times until finally the man appeared at the top of the stairs. He came down leaning on the banister, looking half anxious, half irritated. The stranger informed him that things had been forgotten in the room where he had slept and asked who had been the previous occupants. The innkeeper informed him that it was normally the young woman of remarkable beauty who occupied the room.

"Pearl! Come here!" he called toward the back of the shop.

"Good morning, sir," the young woman greeted Bill as she approached.

"You mean to say that you threw this young lady out of her room to rent it to me?"

"She's not a young lady, she's an employee."

"Miss," the stranger began, turning toward the young woman, "I'd like to tell you that if I'd known that anything so outrageous had been done in my name, I'd never have accepted the room."

"You should have thought of that when I told you there was no room available."

"Excuse my frankness, sir, but I think that this young woman deserves better than to be treated like a slave in a place that – forgive me again – could be described as an appendage to New Mexico. Miss, if you are agreeable to getting your personal effects quickly together and handing in your resignation, I promise to take you away immediately."

The owner nodded, and then stared at the stranger, lifting his chin.

"You hear that, Pearl?"

But Pearl Guthrie was already climbing the stairs. She dragged her trunk along the corridor, and Bill went up to help her. From the doorway the innkeeper, arms crossed, watched his maid-of-all-work throw her suitcase into Russian Bill's wagon. Standing there breathing the cloud of dust raised by the departing wheels, he watched incredulously as these two who had never yet exchanged a word headed off side by side.

Some say they were carried away by the wind of freedom. Others say it was too sudden, too crazy, not to be proof that it had all been arranged in advance – that even the displays of boldness had been struggles against fear, and that the two rebels were merely underlings changing masters. What exactly had happened that morning? Nothing, the Reverend Aaron would have said, nothing worth getting excited about.

He saved me from hanging for no good reason, and no one does something like that. Maybe that's why I hate him.

LA POSTA

MAY 1878

The first thing you saw of La Posta when arriving by road was the church's two towers and its white stucco facade. The sun had only just set. At this hour the white of the buildings was less brilliant, and everything seemed grey, or even ochre in places where the stucco was flaking away to reveal the adobe bricks. Around the church, the retinue of square houses barely stood out against the peak of Mount Cabazon far behind. The streets were too narrow for the wagon. They abandoned it at the entrance to the town and went on, each leading a horse by the reins.

They found the hotel by chance, despite the absence of any sign indicating the establishment's name. The room that Bill took for himself was tiny and longer than it was wide, with the bed pushed up against a window that admitted very little light. There were no public rooms in the inn. The other customers ate outside with their backs to the adobe walls, like those Mexicans in their serapes that are often seen doing nothing except watch the passersby. Bill and Pearl ate sitting on the bedroom floor by the light of the oil lamp.

"How long do you think it will take before we can start out again, once we get there?" asked Pearl.

"A few weeks, maybe a month. Time enough for the property to gain value. It won't be long before people can't wait to get their hands on it. And the money will allow us to keep going till I find the perfect spot to build New Babylon."

"And if I can't find a husband in the meantime?"

"Then you'll find one in New Babylon. There'll only be fearless men there, and very few honest women. You'll have your pick.

And between here and there you'll have crossed a lot of towns off your list."

Pearl cut herself a slice of bread. Bill raised the jug of water to his lips. A shrill sound reverberated. It took a few notes for them to understand it was the blare of a trumpet. The amateur musician must have been on the roof of a house across the street. He played slow, sad melodies – Spanish tunes – until a few protesting voices reduced him to silence.

"It'll soon be a month we've been travelling like this, and I don't think I've thanked you enough," said Pearl.

"There's no need. After tomorrow, I'll be the one indebted to you."

"You know, I wasn't that badly treated in Perryville. I could have left any time. I wanted to tell you that. To be truthful."

"You shouldn't travel alone, anyway. Basically it was a good thing that your employer was inconsiderate enough to give me your room. If he hadn't, I'd have left and you'd have stayed in that hole, and we wouldn't be where we are today. Tomorrow, our real life begins."

When they finished eating, Pearl carried the empty plates to the kitchen with its arched ceiling and then went up to bed. She could hear Bill praying aloud in the other room. "Thank you, Lord, thank you!" She heard no more because the musician set to work again. In their separate rooms, Bill and Pearl soon fell asleep, lulled by the sound of the trumpet, despite the breathing difficulties and wrong notes. Long minutes later, a shot rang out. Bill woke up abruptly and sat at the bottom of his bed to see through the window what was going on, his Spencer at the ready. There was complete silence outside. No more music, no panic-stricken voices. A knock came on his door, and he got off the bed. "It's me," whispered Pearl. Bill put his rifle down across the bed and pulled a shirt on over his underwear before going to open the door.

"Did you hear that? It was very close."

He invited her in. She put the oil lamp down at her feet. He leaned over to pick up his revolver, which was lying on the ground underneath his pants.

"I think that trumpeter's a goner," he suggested.

Russian Bill had excellent hearing and was able to identify various events involving firearms by the sound. A low sound, dull and repeated, in the daytime: children trying to kill a snake. Whistling and repeated, at night: a drunk trying to shoot the moon. Two shots in quick succession followed by a silence, then a third shot: an exchange of fire between two men. A single shot followed by a silence: a lawman giving a warning by shooting at the ceiling. A single shot followed by a strangled cry: a murder.

"That's awful. How can we go to sleep after that?"

"It's none of our business," answered Bill, checking the cylinder of his revolver, which he then laid beside the rifle. They remained standing in silence, contemplating the two weapons that lay in the centre of the unmade bed like presages of war.

"Do you know how to use a gun, Pearl?"

She shook her head.

"If you find it acceptable ... We could share the same room. I'll sleep on the ground. Or we could lay the rifle between us, if you think that's proper."

Pearl accepted, making him promise never to cross the borderline of chastity represented by the gun. She also made him promise never to abandon her in a town where she didn't want to stay, and never to hurt her. In exchange, Bill admitted that he was wanted in Texas for cattle rustling, and made her promise never to betray him. Lying on their backs, with the Spencer between them, they slept side by side. They had drawn a line never to be crossed, in the way that in other places the frontiers of a prohibited neighbourhood were drawn to ensure the safety of respectable people.

A real outlaw would never have honoured such a rule, and thrown the rifle away the very first night. Or after a few days. Several times during their shared existence Pearl felt a wave of affection for Bill, to the point that she wished he would infringe their code and make a move toward her. But that would have made him a scoundrel, and then she wouldn't have desired him anymore.

Some people suggest I've no breeding for I only take my hat off when I feel like it. I can see it in their eyes, that they're saying to themselves, "That one will end up at the end of a rope. He breaks the law just to break the law." Even unconsciously, folks sometimes do that. If people only knew how many laws they obey by doing nothing.

O'DERMODY

Bill and Pearl were surprised to come upon O'Dermody so soon after skirting Mont Cabazon. The publicity spoke of the place like a virgin territory where anything was possible, though it was just a mile from a long-established Spanish village. Bill took the newspaper cutting from his pocket.

> Fortune Awaits You in O'Dermody
> The First Couple to Marry in the Town Receives
> A Free Plot of Land and a House!

Roman Catholics believed in saints, so they gave their towns saints' names, like San Pedro and Santa Barbara. They weren't bothered by the fact that this restricted them to a finite list of possibilities, since there were only so many saints and often the newly canonized bore the names of the earlier canon. The Methodists and their forebears didn't believe in saints and so named their towns Temperance, Charity, or Revelation, as if the continent had been laid out on a grid by the Almighty Himself in order to confront his Adversary at chess. Though a superstitious man, Lester O'Dermody had never been susceptible to the beauty of abstract concepts, so when he decided to found a town he chose to call it O'Dermody.

✷

The town possessed everything that La Posta lacked: a row of wooden cabins, all new and unoccupied, across from a row of stores filled with merchandise for which there were still no customers.

Bill parked the wagon in front of the first store and asked to speak to the mayor or clergyman. It so happened that the former was the founder himself, and the latter, his brother. Bill helped Pearl down from the wagon and introduced her as his fiancée. A few hours later, they were married in the presence of the eight other residents, all Mr. O'Dermody's employees.

At the eastern edge of town, under the midday sun, on a wooden dais that one day would no doubt serve as a floor, the clergyman united them in marriage. Pearl wore her cream-coloured dress and Bill, his top hat. Thanks to Lester O'Dermody's useful contacts, the bells of La Posta's Catholic church rang the moment the ceremony ended. Only their echo reached them, distant and in duplicate, from beyond the mountain. You might have thought they were ringing for someone else – as if accompanying a remembered wedding rather than the actual one. Bill and Pearl signed this first marriage certificate as Guerro and Eva Tate.

That evening, the procession approached the house awarded to the first couple to tie the knot in O'Dermody. To applause, Bill carried Pearl across the threshold in his arms. Then while everyone imagined they were enjoying their honeymoon, the newlyweds slept on a mattress on the ground, with the rifle between them. Around them, not a single piece of furniture.

Their new home was a wooden cabin constructed by folk who had no intention of ever living in it themselves. Nothing would have been easier than to cut slots in the walls so that in case of an Indian attack the occupants could point their weapons through and defend themselves from within. Through the rear window they could see only the arid, empty plain, as well as the dry dirt road along which one day thousands of pioneers would swarm.

A month later, Lester O'Dermody began to wonder why the lovebirds had not yet acquired a bed. But it was already too late. The lure of speculation had begun to make itself felt. Settlers were arriving in waves, increasingly eager to get a spade in the ground. Before O'Dermody had time to go and knock on their door, Bill and Pearl had sold their plot for an exorbitant sum and continued their journey.

When you spend your whole life in the open air, when you eat in the open, when you sleep in the open, and when the rest of the time you're on the move to reach your next bit of open air, you're no different than a savage. There's some that kill Indians on the excuse they're savages, but basically they're no different from them.

———————◆–◆–◆–———————

VALVERDE

JUNE 1878

Most likely Bill had never set foot in Russia. Instead, he had abandoned an aristocratic world whose inflexible hierarchy manifested itself in the way the ladies fluttered their fans on high balconies and the men smoked their cigars and whipped their slaves from horseback. He had exchanged this world for another, where power was displayed in the way a man listened to the wind to detect the approach of danger and played with the cylinder of his Colt – a world too vast for reputations to be trusted, in which you had to sniff the other like a dog in order to figure him out. Bill had every intention of excelling in these skills, but failed to recognize that instinct was as important as discipline.

Sometimes he felt a need to fill the silence, and then he talked about his father, who often used to say that Americans would do anything to defend their freedom, even if it meant living in constant fear: "He said that basically they had more need of fear than of freedom. My father couldn't stand Americans."

Every morning Bill practised the precision and speed of his draw, when it would have been more useful to have practised spitting. He carried with him pieces of chalk wrapped in a cotton bag that he kept in the inside pocket of his jacket, where they were less likely to get broken. He would take one out with his fingertips and go to draw a large X on a rock, varying the height from time to time. Then he would put the chalk away and take nine steps back before taking aim and firing. Next he would increase the difficulty by retreating farther, or by turning around and shooting over his shoulder or under his arm, or running sideways with little steps.

"The best kind of practice is to put your targets on a railway train and try to hit them when it starts to move," said Bill. "The problem is, that doesn't teach you to evaluate the human factor, and I still haven't found a way to practise evaluating that."

✳

One evening – it was a Sunday – they passed through the ruins of the old town of Valverde, formerly a Spanish village. Right at the entrance was the field where the most westerly battle in the entire history of the Civil War had been fought. Before that event, the inhabitants had already been forced out of Valverde by Apache and Navajo raids. Bill and Pearl camped beside the ruins of an adobe building of which only the corner of a wall with no roof remained. They lit a fire over which they cooked the black beans they had bought from a Mexican vendor in Socorro. From the rubble Bill pulled a thick plank of wood which he set up like an altar. On it, he taught Pearl to play chess. He allowed her to win this first game.

The next day the sky was cloudy, and there was a roll of thunder. One of the horses began to paw the ground with a rear hoof, digging up pieces of coloured glass that looked like fragments of church windows. Then they realized they had slept on the site of an old missionary church. "There are places not meant to be lived in," said Bill, as if to excuse some unspecified offence.

The next day they crossed the Rio Grande and entered San Marcial, where for the second time they were united by the bonds of marriage. The nascent community had nothing better than a mule to offer as a wedding gift, but it had only cost Bill and Pearl a lie.

✳

Bill and Pearl travelled from town to town on the wagon, often passed by lighter and faster riders who in a few hours covered the distance that took the couple a day. They consoled themselves by saying that they were acting like true pioneers. For people who wanted to build structures that would still be standing a century later, slowness was appropriate. "Tomorrow, we'll sleep in a town with living people," Bill would often promise, hoping to reach their destination before nightfall.

After heading south as far as they could, they turned north into Colorado. They stopped before the ruins of a mission school for Indians that the Indians had burned down. They passed through settlements that once swarmed with panners for gold and businessmen who had come to dig in search of a fortune, now become ghost towns overrun by yuccas and desert sage. Yet despite the untamed vegetation's dominion over human construction, the gold rush years had left their marks: bullet holes in walls, the earth stripped away and dynamited, excavations, and dried-up streams. Maybe it was the soil itself, weary of being sold for a song, of being exploited without being cultivated, that had cast off these men. Maybe the earth had gone bad from soaking up the blood of human conflict.

"I once tried prospecting myself," Bill admitted one day. "I was quite good at it. At Central City, I came across a nugget the size of an apple. I'd erected a shelter for myself beside all the others. From the moment I found my nugget, I seldom left it. I guarded my treasure night and day, for I expected thieves. But they never came, and I became tired of waiting. I threw the nugget in the river and left Colorado. Today, I regret that decision. With that nugget alone I already had enough to found New Babylon without needing to lift a finger. But at the time I had no objective, no latent project in mind, apart from an obscene desire to get myself killed and so earn the right to kill in return."

You couldn't care less what I did in other places, but it's reassuring to realize that if you pass the rope over the head of someone who frightens you and consign him to nothingness, you have the power to be rid of him. It's the only thing that can give you any comfort, because the one thing that never goes away is gravity.

BIG BEND

JULY 1878

In the southern part of the Dolores River valley was a ranch house converted into a restaurant. Its food was so good that travellers would go miles out of their way to eat their evening meal there – famished men who chose to fast a little longer so that they could eat the best. Unlike the canteens, this restaurant did not tolerate rowdy drunks, and the other customers took care of ejecting them. For even though they paid for the meal, men felt at home there. They spent their evenings singing and dancing. There were no women, but always some clown to mimic the delicate tread and pretty ways of the ladies, and the diners would have a ball until the proprietor went upstairs to bed. Then the revellers would go outside and sleep under the stars, or move the dining table aside and stretch out on the earthen floor.

Bill and Pearl had detoured many miles to reach this legendary spot. They arrived one evening when the restaurant was empty. What was supposed to have been a festive evening was just another solitary dinner, another missed opportunity for Pearl to meet potential fiancés and for Bill to entice future settlers to New Babylon. By the light of a cart wheel hung overhead that served as a chandelier they ate smoked trout with anchovy sauce, stuffed eggs, and dried figs. Between mouthfuls, Bill pursued his monologue.

"There's something cowardly about this way of paying a stranger to rid you of a man, only to die yourself at the hands of a stranger in the pay of some other man. It used to be that men confronted one another face-to-face. They didn't kick the bucket when they were snoring in bed," he groused, "but with guns drawn. When my father, in Russia, had to shoot someone, it took two good minutes to recharge the gun with powder between each shot. As for my great-great-great-grandfather, I imagine he didn't even own a musket, just a knife he had to shove in deep until the flesh of his wrist touched that of his victim. Now just look at me. Three seconds and it's over and done with. I'm not sure I deserve that."

The owner shut Bill up. "It's not the guns that upset me. It's damn fools like you make me sorry for gettin' up in the mornin'. Them that reads cheap novels and comes here thinkin' they've seen it all. Here, it's real life. Savin' a damsel in distress ain't enough to make you a hero. No one comes here to die, and no one wants to kill anyone, yet there's plenty that die, smart alecks like you first of all."

In such moments, Pearl occasionally imagined she was somewhere else. Sometimes she considered really marrying Bill. This daydream generally ended with Indians breaking down their door and grabbing him. She would imagine herself in black and fantasize about the pity and respect her dignified widowhood would inspire.

✯

Bill and Pearl entered Big Bend the next day, planning to marry for the third time. They had chosen their false names, they were prepared. But they came too late. A large family had arrived ahead of them and married their eldest daughter to a local man. Bill and Pearl walked together to the hotel, where they were given the room next door to the bridal suite. They lay back to back, each of them sulking. It took them some time to get to sleep because of the sounds of deflowering coming from the next room.

"We'd have gotten here in time if we hadn't taken that detour by the ranch," said Bill, while Pearl was asking herself whether all this business of false marriages wasn't itself an enormous detour.

*Now you're happy because the marshal and the others said
I deserved to hang. If you only knew how many times I've met a
marshal who gained experience as a bandit before going straight.
Sometimes I tell myself I'd rather be an outlaw than an impostor.*

———————◆—◆—◆———————

Now you're happy because the marshal and the others said I deserved to hang. If you only knew how many times I've met a marshal who gained experience as a bandit before going straight. Sometimes I tell myself I'd rather be an outlaw than an impostor.

LAKE CITY

AUGUST 1878

They had taken the trail that ran alongside San Cristobal Lake, and for a while the scenery was different. Under the wagon's wheels, the volcanic rock retained its reddish hues, but the vegetation had grown back, so they were now travelling along a corridor of pine and fir that cast a cool shadow on the trail.

They planned to spend just one night in Lake City, an incognito stopover before setting off toward their next marriage. They drove around a rocky outcrop and encountered a sign erected across the trail:

> No Firearms Allowed in Town
> All Guns to Be Turned in at Sheriff's Office
> Whoever You Are

The town was still far away, a mossy clump at the base of a mound of ochre dirt. Bill leaped down from the wagon and began to drag the horses toward the mountain. At first Pearl thought he was trying to bypass the sign, and then realized that he was steering them toward the butte.

"What on earth are you doing?" she exclaimed.

"We're not going to stop in at some hole where an honest man doesn't have the right to defend himself."

She jumped down too. "I'd really like to sleep in a real bed, like an honest woman."

"In the next village."

"What if the next one doesn't allow guns, and the next one after that as well?"

Bill gave an exasperated sigh.

"People who write that kind of rule are the kind that go around carrying six-shooters to make people notice them," he said, lifting his bag off the wagon.

"You promised."

"What can I do, Pearl? There are people holding grudges against me. I can't just wait defenceless for them to come and get me."

"But the people holding grudges against you will have to turn in their guns too."

Bill stopped and stared at her.

"The people with a grudge against me aren't the sort who obey rules written on signs," he said. "Even if they offered us the whole town on a plate, it'd make no difference to me. I've slept with a gun since I was eight. I don't even take it off to go to church. That's not going to change now."

Until then, Pearl had believed that the rifle served above all as a chasm keeping them apart. Out of respect for her. For *her* protection. "All right, you do what you like. But I'm sleeping in town tonight," she decided, holding out her hand.

Bill gave her a few coins and immediately turned away.

"Childishness!" he proclaimed.

"You think you're the adult and I'm the child? That I need you more than you need me? You're wrong. The only difference between you and me is that you're the one holding the purse strings. But without me, the purse would be empty. Who knows, maybe I could earn more, and faster."

"Wrong. The biggest difference between you and me is that I can use a gun," corrected Bill.

✻

Pearl walked for an hour under the sun, not wanting to lose her way, and finally passed beneath a rusty iron archway that marked the entrance to the town. She wiped her brow with her shawl and saw that the main street was deserted. It was a quiet hamlet, but for the barking dogs. All around, the San Juan Mountains embraced the city, dividing the street with a huge patch of shadow. On the front porches, men in rocking chairs sat in the shadow, all along one side of the street. On the other side, in full sun, the passersby shaded their eyes. She found the hotel farther on, a lone brick building, a premature eruption of permanence in a hastily constructed neighbourhood. She went upstairs to her room, drew all the curtains, and slept fully dressed, lying across the bed.

She was awakened by a ruckus. A handful of men were eating their evening meal on the ground floor. She joined them, wearing a felt hat adorned with flowers and with ribbons falling down her back. She sat at a table by herself. The men observed her in silence. "Animals," she said to herself. "Eyes to devour you, but no tongue." She would have liked one of them to come and talk to her, to display some gallantry toward her, ask about her circumstances, and offer to bring her somewhere else, to a more civilized place. Then she thought of Bill, and a wave of fatigue overwhelmed her. She went outside to walk in the wood-smoke-scented air, but the temperature fell quickly once the sun had set. She spent the evening in her room watching the street through her window: a mestizo using a broom, a peasant crossing the street with a bag of flour in his arms that he set down to scratch his pants bottom, then no one for a while, then a man emerging from the gambling den and spitting over the rail, then another talking to his mare as he fed her.

✳

The next morning, Pearl lay in bed long enough for Bill to become uneasy. She put a scarf over her hat as protection from the sun and retraced her steps of the previous evening. Now the men lounging on front porches were all on the other side of the street. The sheriff's office was in the last house before the archway. On the porch with no guardrail stood the marshal, a redheaded colossus with freckles the likes of which were only produced in Ireland.

"Where are you off to, like that?" he hailed her unceremoniously.

Pearl nodded toward the archway, not troubling to add any words to such an obvious answer.

"If I was you, I wouldn't go that way."

"What's going on out there?"

"There's a man hiding in the high rocks, near the road. He's armed, like he was goin' to take on the whole cavalry. I dunno if he's alone or if he has henchmen farther on, but if I was you I'd avoid walkin' thereabouts."

Pearl smiled, bringing her hands to her waist. "I think you're talking about my brother," she said.

The marshal seemed to be reflecting. "I kind of suspected that. The thing I don't get is why it was you slept in town but not him."

"Because he doesn't want to be parted from his guns, and I haven't got any."

The marshal lifted his hat and ran his fingers through his hair before putting it back on his head. "I hope he's your little brother, and not your big one."

"Why's that?"

"Because if I was so scared of the town that I didn't want to venture into it without a gun, I wouldn't send my little sister there all on her own."

"That's what I told him," she lied. "Can I go on now?"

"I won't keep you."

She went on, aware that the marshal was watching her. She cursed Bill, who cast a shadow over her even in his absence. Soon she drew near enough to see him standing in the middle of the road gazing in her direction, one hand shading his eyes.

"It's almost nine. I nearly left everything here to go and look for you," he confessed.

Without greeting him, she collapsed on the blanket spread close to the fire, where a few embers still glowed.

Then they headed off toward the horizon. Desert after desert. Always more marvels of nature. But still no sign of what they were seeking.

"I'd rather die than marry an outlaw or an Indian," my mother used to say. At the time all I wanted was a father. I'd have liked an Indian father, to protect me from his people.

━━━━◆◆◆━━━━

TELLURIDE

OCTOBER 1878

They arrived in Telluride along with everyone else. A month before they got there, there was nothing but grey rock and conifers.

Ahead of them, a team of mules was pulling a billiards table roped to a wagon. Piles of planks and blocks lay here and there, the embryos of projected buildings. All the fragments that would construct Telluride were there in separate pieces, a jigsaw waiting to be assembled.

They were married that very day in the tent that served as a cantina, with its canvas rustling in the October breeze. There was no clergyman, but the owner of a funeral parlour offered to officiate. Outside, amid cheers, they climbed onto the billiards table and the men threw their hats in the air as the newlyweds kissed, with a panorama of snow-capped summits as a backdrop. For a wedding gift, they received a plot that was useless for prospecting but well-situated for a place of business. Bill marked out the four corners of their scrap of land with sticks and erected the conjugal tent near the edge, next to the roughed-in main street. In the dark of night there was no street, just scattered tents lit from inside like lanterns sprouted from the ground itself.

The next day, Bill helped the other men to build a house. They pulled on the rope to raise an already assembled board-and-batten wall, grimacing with the effort, their shirts as dark with sweat as in summer, while Pearl boiled water and carried tea and coffee to the other founders of the new community. In the evening, they all shared a bottle of brandy and sang around a campfire. The only musical instrument brought along was a Jew's harp, and they laughed as they danced to the rhythm of the sizzling flames and crackling branches. One day, when evenings in the town had become noisy, the inhabitants of Telluride would recall this time when they owned nothing but had everything to gain.

That evening, the newlyweds ended up sitting on a large upturned chest. The whiskey brought a blush to Bill's cheeks and the flames made his eyes shine.

"An opponent's body offers a variety of targets, forcing the novice to choose, and therefore to make mistakes," he explained for the benefit of the other settlers. "It would all be so easy if we didn't have any choice, if life could be reduced to a single quest," he soliloquized, "a battle to be repeated for the sake of the same objective. We're made stupid by the multiplicity of our desires. It abolishes necessity and makes failure unavoidable," he went on, unaware that he was losing his audience.

Pearl was dozing. Bill offered her his shoulder to rest her head on, but she preferred to go to bed. She dragged herself to the tent, stirring up the sand as she went, invisible in the dark.

When he returned to their quarters, Bill could barely stand. It was the only time Pearl saw him drunk. He dropped onto the mattress, his arms over his head.

"How do you say 'Good night' in Russian?" she asked. Bill uttered a few indecipherable syllables. Pearl couldn't tell if it was because of his drunkenness or his unfamiliarity with the language. "Now, how do you say 'dirty liar' in Russian?" she tried next. He emitted a guttural rumble.

During the winter they resumed their journey southward. After Telluride, they were married in Alamosa – because sometimes, in the words of a drunk that Pearl had often served in Shawneetown, "You have to sin a little to reach your heaven."

I had a dream last night. There was a great cloud that dissolved into a mountain of snow. There was a boat leaving. People were throwing stones at it, whether to sink it or prevent it from escaping, I don't know. There was a man smoking a pencil and another writing with a cigar. One said, "Write down and remember." The other said, "Burn and forget."

ELIZABETHTOWN

FEBRUARY 1879

Bill and Pearl arrived in Elizabethtown in the middle of an auction sale. Fine snow was beginning to cover the surrounding hills, where trees were sparse. From his dais the auctioneer was praising the soundness and low price of an upright piano, while his assistant wiped melting snow from its keys.

In this hamlet smelling of boredom and of the burnt sage that the women scattered to drive away ghosts, Bill could spend his evenings telling his cock-and-bull stories without anyone shutting him up. "Truly, the palaces of St. Petersburg have no reason to envy the Venetian ones, apart from the climate. Even when you attend a ball in winter you have to wear your furs. It's not very elegant, but you get used to it. Once, there was an assassination attempt directly opposite me during Princess Maria Alexandrovna's birthday party. The man fell into my arms during the waltz ..."

Pearl thanked heaven for this man's presence in her life — not perfect to be sure, but playing his part to perfection. Yet it only took an implausible word or anecdote to nullify any feeling of gratitude or affection toward him. For Bill to be considered a mistake again. What had she been thinking, to run away not with the village idiot but with the idiot of every village between Denver and Yuma?

On the eve of their marriage, they walked arm in arm from one end of the street to the other. Bill, wearing his black suit, was invisible in the darkness. He tried to keep step with Pearl, and readjusted the shawl on her shoulders. In her modest bright velvet dress, she challenged the dark, like the deerskin-clad natives who call the wolves on moonlit nights. They came to a disused mine, well-hidden from view. In the light from the main street, they sat on the rocks that had been placed to block the entrance. It was here that Bill offered Pearl a bunch of flowers wrapped in newspaper and admitted to her that she was the most beautiful thing that had ever happened to him, that when he was with her he no longer needed an opponent, and that she meant more to him than anything in the world, more than his honour, more even than New Babylon. He went on with his declaration until she shed a tear. Then he asked her why she was crying, and she answered that it was because all that left her cold.

The return to the hotel was difficult, with the future bride-groom paying no further gallant attention to his fiancée, while she wiped her cheeks and lowered her reddened eyes. No compromise was possible, no negotiation between one person utterly in love and another not at all. Love me fifty per cent less and I'll love you fifty per cent more – is it a deal? No! They were condemned to wound and be wounded, and there was nothing they could do about it. If at least she had had another admirer she could have been offended by his confession: "How could you dare to take it for granted that I would prefer you? What arrogance!" But the humiliation she inflicted on Bill wasn't inspired by any rival. His defeat had been assured from the outset.

She wanted to sit down in the company of loose women and drink with them. Yes, Bill was the rejected one, yet it was she who wanted to go drinking. She felt a pang of the hurt she was causing him. She told herself there was no difference between dealing a blow and receiving it, not when each was suffering the same injustice. There was no difference between giving too much of yourself and giving too little.

Once Bill fell asleep, Pearl went to a tavern. Only men were present. With her hair in disarray as if she had just gotten out of bed and the top button of her bodice undone as if she had been running, the future bride ordered a glass of whiskey. It was not so much to drink as to test the villagers, to see if they would react to depravity or if they themselves were so depraved that they would allow the farce to run its course, giving them a tale to tell afterward.

"It's so sad to hate a person for what he is, and not for what he has done," she said to some strangers, who didn't comprehend a word.

※

The community of Elizabethtown made no claim to offer anything whatsoever to attract young couples. It restricted itself to trying to keep the ones already there.

The gambling dens had all closed their doors. The stagecoach no longer stopped in the town. There were still some shops, a pharmacy, a boarding house, and a few taverns, but not many men to help them prosper. The cattlemen thereabouts preferred to go farther off, all the way to Taos, where you could still play a game of cards without the outcome being decided in advance. The cemetery counted more permanent inhabitants than the village.

As a wedding gift, the inhabitants of Elizabethtown granted Bill and Pearl a deserted shack that must once have been worth something. The ceilings were so low that you had to stoop under the lintel to pass from one room to another. The windows were so dirty that nothing was visible through them.

One Sunday, Bill, squatting on the ground, with the Spencer to his right and his Colt to his left, had unrolled a map of New Mexico. Pearl, just returning from church, tossed aside her parasol, hat, and boots without paying any attention to where they would land.

"What a waste of time," she said.

"What, the service?"

"No, this town. There's nothing but cattlemen, all married and settled, and who think I'm married too."

"It's not a waste of time for me, Pearl."

"This shack is worthless. I don't see why we're staying here any longer."

"There'll be buyers."

"When? And why would there be?"

"If it isn't for gold, it'll be for silver, and if not for silver, it'll be for the railway, or something else."

She strode up to Bill and crossed her arms. Bent over his map, he ignored her. She went around the mattress and stood with both her feet on the map of New Mexico. Bill looked up, his jaws clenched.

"You promised not to let me rot in a town where I didn't want to stay," she said.

"I promised I'd never abandon you in a town where you didn't want to stay. It's not the same thing."

That evening, Bill wondered if she only stayed because there was no way for her to escape. With no stagecoach, she was a prisoner. Then he began to consider the idea of intentionally avoiding busy towns where transportation was available. For her part, Pearl began to think about setting the house on fire.

The guy that wrote the Bible, I never voted for him. But I know perfectly well the law's not the rules made by the guy you vote for. It's the rules of the guy that wins.

———————————◆◆◆———————————

SILVER CITY

MAY 1879

Bill and Pearl entered Silver City on their wagon, observing the fauna of village hicks all around. Another town that only welcomed you with coolness and suspicion. New signs, new rules, not to be confused with those of the previous community. The same business names as everywhere else. The same lack of originality, though everyone thought themselves unique. It wouldn't have taken much for the inhabitants to find a source of pride in the fact that the sun set in the west just where they happened to be.

Previously, this had been a part of the country where the inhabitants never asked themselves any questions. God was good, and no one doubted it. Husbands loved their wives and wives their husbands. People knew what they wanted, for there wasn't much to want. But that was before copper was found, and then silver. Before they began to dream of things God couldn't guarantee them. Before men started to hate their mothers. Now, when they said "I need supplies," it was because they'd run out of ammunition, and every day they would defy death with a shrug.

✳

Wearing a new top hat, Bill was holding the reins of the wagon in one hand and a cigar in the other. Pearl had rested the handle of her parasol on her shoulder, and was spinning it behind her. The wood of their wagon, bleached by wind and sand, was beginning to crack, following the identical process that transforms rock into dunes. Bill and Pearl travelled on with the confidence of victors. They had just left Elizabethtown with full pockets, for three weeks after their sixth marriage a developer had moved in and bought a third of the town. Bill was triumphant because he had been proven right, and Pearl was content because she had finally left the place behind her.

Like all new arrivals in Silver City, they were greeted by a charlatan with a handlebar moustache who spoke to them of expeditions and treasures that had belonged to the Spaniards until the Apache stole them. They attended a performance of *Macbeth*. Although most of the dialogue was inaudible because of the catcalls and cheers from the rest of the audience, Pearl so badly wanted her applause to be heard that she removed her gloves.

In a hotel they took a room for the week, directly above the main room of the casino, where cartridge shells were used as chips. The floor of raw wood was covered with a carpet that might once have been crimson, its Persian curlicues now almost worn away. They fell asleep lulled by laughter, the splintering of glass, and the player piano. The music covered the chirping of the crickets until dawn.

The next day, Pearl awoke to the smell of meat being smoked and the echo of chattering voices. She turned over and saw that she was alone in bed with the Spencer. She went across to the window, which overlooked the outhouses and, farther on, the backs of charcoal-blackened houses. Once she had done her hair and was dressed she tried to leave the room, but it was bolted from outside. Bill had locked it.

Time passed without her knowing how late it was getting, with hunger hollowing out its path, until her anger flared. She hurled the pillows to the other end of the room. She hammered on the door, crying "Let me out!" and spent a large part of the day stretched out on her back contemplating the ceiling laths, with the Spencer jammed against her shoulder and its barrel brushing her cheek. It must have been three o'clock when she heard the key scrape in the lock. She hurled herself at Bill to slap his face, but he caught her hand in time. "When we're in New Babylon you'll be so scared that you'll plead with me to barricade you in," he said before releasing her hand. That evening, they went to the theatre again, but she didn't clap at the end of the performance.

✳

On the second day, Bill returned with a pile of bound books. "I hope you can read," he said, setting them down at the foot of the bed.

Pearl, sitting at the window, turned her back on him. "If I wanted I could escape through this window."

"But you don't want to," concluded Bill before closing the door behind him and locking it again.

On the third day, he found the young woman in tears. He tried to console her, coming over to take her in his arms, but she pushed him away. "I've had enough," she spat at him. "Everyone thinks I'm your wife. Nobody will ever want to marry me."

On the fourth day, she was sitting on the floor, giggling.

"There now, you've got your good humour back, it seems."

She had just emptied all the rifle bullets and thrown them out the window. The gun lay in the middle of the bed as if nothing were amiss, and Pearl was enjoying the idea that it was no longer anything more than a toy. If Bill found out he would kill her, but at least he wouldn't be able to use the Spencer to do so. That night she kept watch on the rifle, praying with all her might that Bill's enemies would finally turn up to murder him.

On the fifth day, he found her reading.

"If I'm to be kept a prisoner to the end of my life, I'm going to need a lot more of these," she said, pointing to the pile of books.

✳

On the sixth day, a man driven crazy by anger entered the gambling den. He struck the tables with the butt of his hunting rifle and shouted, "Where's that bastard Redburn?"

All that could be heard was the enraged man yelling and shooting at the ceiling while chairs and tables fell or scraped on the wooden floor. The circle widened around him as the men retreated to the back of the room, overturning glasses and candles in their haste. A string of men stood with their backs to the walls, unable to retreat any farther, as if awaiting execution. One by one they succeeded in getting out, shoving one another in the back; the last one looked over his shoulder: only the proprietor remained, hiding under the bar, as the frenzied man shouted, "Redburn, you sonofabitch!"

Outside, the women kept quiet on the other side of the street. The men were laughing, except for Bill. Pearl was locked in their room upstairs, directly above where the demented man was shooting. Bill posted himself in front of their window and shouted her name several times, but she didn't answer. He was stunned for a few minutes, powerless, and then began to shout even louder. From a distance Bill and the lunatic could be heard in a canon of "Redburn," "Pearl," "Redburn," "Pearl" in turn.

The marshal finally arrived with two deputies, and the three of them were able to subdue the madman. He was still foaming at the mouth as they escorted him under curious eyes to the marshal's office across town.

Bill was the first to rush into the gambling den, even before the proprietor emerged from his hideout. He took the stairs two at a time. He would have broken down the door rather than unlock it, if he had been able. Pearl was standing in a corner of the room with her arms crossed, but looking concerned. He threw himself on her and pressed her to his chest with one hand on her nape. Together, they collapsed to the base of the wall and stayed there staring at the two bullet holes in the carpet near the bed.

On the seventh day, they left Silver City.

*I don't like women because they want to lead me away from death,
and because I think I need death to be able to live.*

NEW BABYLON

MAY 1879

Bill climbed down from the wagon and contemplated the valley with its tawny undulations at the foot of the Animas Mountains. Pearl followed him, knowing that the moment had come. He took a dozen steps in a random direction. All the trails seemed risky across the expanse devoid of landmarks. What seemed to be a human skeleton lay at his feet. All around lay other bones and body parts reduced to their most basic form, most likely the relics of an immigrants' wagon train that had become lost on its way to California.

"We'll bury these remains. If there'd been a town here, these folk would still be alive," claimed Bill. "At least they wouldn't have died like that."

Pearl remained silent, seeking a sign in the cracks of the earth rather than on Bill's face.

He surveyed the landscape, from one horizon to the other. "Here's where the cemetery will be," he declared.

One of the things Pearl could have held against him later was this planning of the cemetery before anything else. He hadn't proclaimed: "This will be the perfect place for a town!" No, he had said: "This will be the perfect place for a cemetery." Yet clear thinking was never remote from the absurdities that Bill uttered. Every town had its twin: a town for the living, and another for the dead. In each, the same family names could be found.

He took a few more steps, squatted, and took off his hat. His hair was flattened against his scalp, and the wind ruffled a few wisps above his ears. He scraped up some dry earth with his pocket knife and took a fistful of it in his right hand. He stood up, and then turned to Pearl. "Welcome to New Babylon!"

Bill had decided to adopt a place where grass had never grown, but where corpses of pioneers lay. He had considered it preferable to adopt a place where there was nothing, rather than lose everything in a place that had everything.

✳

Their camp had been set up for two days when, as solitary as the Messiah in the desert, a rider on a chestnut mule appeared in the middle of the valley. He had noticed their white tent, which was equally lost in the expanse, and had perhaps taken it for a kind of mirage.

The rider wore a wide-brimmed grey felt Stetson that cast a shadow over his face. He approached slowly, warily – a cautious man, no greenhorn, one who has experienced the disappointment of desirable expectations going unmet, as well as the sudden appearance of villains in places where nothing was expected. He stopped opposite the tent without dismounting, and cleared his throat.

"Anyone here?"

Bill was the first to emerge, his cartridge belt across his shoulder and the Spencer against his chest. "Oh oh, I'm not here to cause you any concern."

The man pushed back the brim of his hat to allow his eyes to be seen, revealing at the same time a voluminous moustache covering his upper lip. "It's a long time since I've seen anyone around here."

"You'd better get used to it," replied Bill.

"I hope so, but if I had to get used to a place, this isn't the spot I'd choose."

"So what spot *would* you choose?"

"Probably where I live already." He pointed in a northeasterly direction. "I've a ranch on the other side of the mountain."

"Do you know where there's water to be found around here?"

The man scratched his cheek. "Seems to me there's no water around here. Apart from rainwater sometimes in summer. It doesn't happen often, but it does rain a little more on this side of the mountain than on the other."

Pearl separated the tent flaps and came out, nodding to him.

"My name is Henry Sarazin. If you need anything, you're welcome to come by. It'll save you from having to travel miles to town. And my wife likes a bit of company too," he added, looking in Pearl's direction.

He pulled his hat over his brow again and stirred his mule with a click of his tongue.

Hands on hips, Pearl waited for him to leave before saying anything. "A nice man. I'm sure he's not expecting the most dangerous town in America to grow up in his back yard."

Bill passed his cartridge belt over his shoulder, went into the tent, and laid his weaponry down on the bed. "Maybe one day he'll come and ask *us* for supplies."

✳

They still had what they needed to cook a week's meals, but Pearl complained of a lack of reading material. Bill asked if she could wait a few days. She shook her head. Early next morning, he harnessed the wagon and set off for the town of Animas, thirty miles to the north.

Pearl could not have escaped, being in the middle of nowhere with no horse, but in any case it wasn't a concern anymore. She no longer wished to escape. He had decided to give her all she asked for, down to the smallest detail, even things it had not yet occurred to her to want. She was dependent on him in every respect, yet he would obey her wishes. Each day she would see New Babylon rise, plank by plank, and when the town that they dreamed of together became a reality, she would become unable to hold a grudge against him. He would be lord of the liveliest town in the New World, and she would never again consider leaving the embrace of his protecting arms.

Pearl watched Bill ready the horses, telling herself that perhaps she had been too hard on him. Then she repeated to herself that when she really married she would be a truly good wife to someone.

⁜

A week later, Bill postponed his plan to dig a well and set about building a fence instead. They had become used to drinking the water from the jugs he went to fill at the Sarazins' every five days. Then he began to erect a two-storey house, though he had never built as much as a birdhouse before. Could a man in a derby hat, in the middle of the desert, really be taken seriously as a carpenter? Pearl often wondered about this. He had to make three trips to Animas to fetch the wood and adobe bricks needed to construct a modest one-room cottage. By the time it was completed, winter was knocking at their door and the money from the sale in Elizabethtown was all gone. Then Bill announced that he was going to "make an investment," in other words, to go looking for a herd. Except that instead of setting off northward he went south, where there was absolutely nothing. Beyond this nothing was Mexico and the scattered ruins of an ancient empire, a civilization that to Pearl and Bill seemed barely more developed than that of primitive tribes.

He returned two days later with a motley herd of animals that he drove into the corral. Pearl didn't ask any questions. Bill could go to hell as long as he brought back what she needed to satisfy her belly and her mind.

In the corral, the calves and goats died before they could all be consumed. One after another they collapsed, emaciated from grazing on barely existent grass. Soon, Pearl was able to decorate the cabin with polished skulls and horns, for Bill and she were still alive, which was sufficient to prove man's superiority over the animals.

⁂

"I don't deserve you," Pearl blurted out one evening. She was reading by lamplight, surrounded by two tottering piles of books brought back from she knew not where.

Bill was busy playing with the heel that had separated from one of his boots. "What would make you deserve me?"

She didn't answer, but looked outside through the open door.

"I was an orphan, you know," he said in response to an unasked question.

Pearl looked up from her book in astonishment. "I thought you are the son of Countess what's-her-name ..."

"Yes, but I was adopted. Before that, I was an orphan. That's why I'm not perfect. When you start out on life like that, you never come to anything later, you can forget about perfection." He went on: "I don't remember anything about it. I was too young. I was removed from a chain of generations of brutes, paupers, and drunks. I was inserted into another chain, the chain of honour, from which it's just as difficult to free yourself. When I left home I told my family I was going out west, into the American territories, to be free of those chains and not live in fear anymore. They were happy for me. They told themselves that I'd be safe, at least. But they were wrong. I had no desire to lower my guard. I want never to stop living in fear. I don't know what I'd have become without it. In that way, I have to admit, I'm more American than Russian. And then, as everyone knows, there's no safety in the West."

⁂

On his return from his next trip, Bill gave Pearl a silk-covered jewel box. It contained dozens of rings, higgledy-piggledy, all different, but clearly valuable: a mosaic of gold objects with origins as varied as they were remote. The next time, he brought back a new hat for himself and a roll of lace for Pearl. The time after that, it was a little dog that she named Oliver. For, after all, there could be Apaches hiding anywhere.

MARCH 1880

Pearl was counting the logs stacked against the outside wall of the cabin when she heard Oliver yapping. As she rounded the corner of the house, she saw a cloud of dust rising in the distance. Retreating inside, she tried to hush the dog. When she looked through the window, three strangers were wandering around the cottage, and the same number of horses were pawing the ground in the corral. All three wore leather chaps with buttons down the side, and dark clothes made lighter by the dust of the trail.

She put her hand to her mouth and moved away from the window. She thought of the pistol she had hidden under her pillow the night when she had given Charles Teasdale a bed, and cursed Bill for having taught her to play chess instead of showing her how to fire a gun. Two of the strangers moved apart, and Bill appeared behind them. She went out and stared at him without responding to his greeting. His clothes seemed as dirty as those of the others, except for his brand new hat which seemed to have issued from a different world – a world in which hats were merely a statement, and never served as containers from which mules might drink.

One of the men was named Firmel. Under his straw hat he had long, greasy hair that fell down his back; his nose was so red that it seemed almost blue. His gloves had holes at the fingertips, and the nails were chewed so much that his fingers resembled toes. His entire pride seemed to reside in his pistols, valuable objects of chiselled metal with ivory handles, which he polished the way others scratch themselves.

The younger one was named Billy. Barely eighteen, he stood tall but seemed puny under his broad-brimmed beige hat. Judging by the little scarf knotted around his neck, he appeared to be a cowhand from a good family. The others often ordered him about. "Billy, do this. Billy, do that, would you?" And, tight-lipped, the young man obeyed in silence.

And then there was Sandy King, dressed like a respectable individual in a jacket buttoned over a white shirt with rolled-up sleeves. His long black moustache contrasted with a growth of beard that was scratchy just to look at. He had an agreeable expression, but calculating eyes.

It was said of Sandy King that as a child his father had forbidden him to interfere with the rabbits he was raising in the garden to sell to the magicians in the town (which was somewhere in Arkansas). His father had threatened to give him ten lashes with a whip on the soles of his feet if he disobeyed. Sandy didn't like rabbits, and liked his father even less. He then had the bright idea that it would be great fun to catch one of the little creatures and prick it with a needle. His father whipped him, as promised. The next day, Sandy picked on another rabbit. This time his father gave him thirty lashes, leaving him unable to stand on his feet. The day after that, Sandy crawled to the garden on all fours, his bloody heels turned heavenward, and proceeded to prick a third rabbit. When asked how this story ended, he would reply that it had no end.

"This is Pearl, the unfortunate recluse I saved from the clutches of an abusive employer," said Bill by way of an introduction.

"How d'you do, miss," said Sandy, doffing his hat.

He patted the neck of his horse, no doubt the fruit of one of his many thefts. Behind him, Firmel spat without looking to see where his spittle would land.

After the meal, the men began to play cards and drink. They talked about a certain Curly Bill as if he were their leader, a reminder that even bandits who broke every law owed obedience to someone. They discussed a Sheriff Whitehill, with whom they said they had a score to settle, and also some elderly man named Clanton, who was always wanting more cattle. Once, young Billy raised his voice to exclaim, "Careful what you're sayin', that's my pa you're talkin' about."

Pearl didn't know any of these people, for she knew nobody except Bill and the Sarazins.

She sat embroidering in her corner of the room. At one moment she got up and felt Sandy's eyes following her while the others waited for him to play his card. "Careful, Sandy, she's not for you, that one," said Firmel.

"I'm not used to limitin' myself to what's mine," Sandy retorted, his eyes still glued on Pearl.

Bill scratched his jaw. "Come on, Sandy, you can find better than a woman who's been married thirty times!" he said, throwing a card on the table.

Firmel uttered a raucous laugh, his shoulders shaking. Pearl turned her back to them. With jaws clenched and eyes closed, she wasn't laughing.

When night came, the guests slept on the wooden floor. As soon as the room resounded with their snores, Bill sat up in bed. "Don't worry, I know what I'm doing."

"I hope so, because I don't understand at all what you're up to," she sighed, turning away on her pillow.

"I'm founding New Babylon. That's what I'm up to."

✳

The next day, Pearl was stirring corn porridge over the fire. The others were smoking cigars or picking their teeth. Firmel picked up the Spencer that was still lying on the bed. "So, Bill, who is it needs a rifle under the sheets, you or her?" he asked, mimicking obscene acts.

Bill marched across to the jackass, snatched the gun from his hands, and with the butt dealt him a blow between the eyes. The men laughed, slapping their thighs, except for Sandy, who was content to rotate his cigar in the corner of his mouth, allowing spirals of smoke to rise before his face.

"How come he can make a joke, but not me?" whimpered Firmel, turning to look at Sandy.

"Because when Curly isn't around, I'm the boss."

"Where's it written that you're the boss? It's Pa Clanton pays us."

"It ain't written nowhere, but everyone knows. Thing is, you're too stupid to see it. Now ask the lady's pardon."

This intervention should have been reassuring for Pearl, but it wasn't.

⚹

"Do they know?" Pearl whispered in the dark.

"They know nothing. I've told them I had a hideout, a place no one knows about, somewhere you can go when you need to keep out of the way."

"You told them about New Babylon?"

"Of course not. They have to think it's a hideout for them and no one else. They think I just want to belong to the gang."

"So that's not what you want?" She couldn't see Bill, but heard him sigh.

"You know very well what I want."

"You want to found New Babylon. I understand."

⚹

On the third evening, two other men arrived: a handsome fellow called Frank, who had a moustache and goatee, and a firebrand named Ike.

The men drank non-stop. Firmel and Ike climbed on the kitchen table to dance as the others applauded. Then they went outside and howled at the moon. Sandy undressed, mounted his horse naked, and with a click of his tongue sent it trotting around the corral like a circus act. They lit a campfire, sat around it, and passed the bottle from hand to hand.

"Do you hear that, guys?" asked Ike.

"Hear what?"

"Nothin'. That's just it. There's no one to tell us to shut up. No one to complain about it bein' dangerous. Ain't it just grand to live somewhere there's no sissies givin' off?"

Pearl remained impassive, wrapped in her woolen shawl, sitting erect between young Billy and Sandy.

"Me, if I had to build a town, that's what it'd be like. It'd be a town where no one would ever complain about danger," declared Bill.

"It's easier to wipe out a town than build one," said Sandy. "Just ask the Injuns. All you've got to do is chuck a dead body down a well. The locals will take forever to figure out that the water's poisoned, and meantime they'll all have drunk gallons of it, and their horses too."

Then they all laughed, and in the middle of their hilarity Sandy announced, "Once I stop drinkin', I'll be the real boss."

"Cut out the talk, Sandy. You sound like some old kill-joy at temperance camp."

"Still, it's the truth. When I'm drunk I get in my own way. The other day again, there was this guy from Charleston I'd promised to bump off. Before the night was done I was buyin' him drinks. I fought with this other guy instead, one that's filthy rich and who I'd promised to butter up with false promises. The only reason Curly acts the boss and not me is that I'm not sober enough for my ambitions."

"There's some that drinks even less than Curly. Bill here, for example," Firmel didn't neglect to point out.

"It's true Bill spends so much time talkin' rot that he forgets to drink. Or maybe he does it on purpose. Maybe he fancies becomin' the boss too."

All eyes turned on Bill. He reddened up to his ears. He was preparing to answer when Pearl cut in. "It's me; I don't let him drink. One time in Silver City he came home blind drunk and I wouldn't let him into the bedroom."

The men took a few seconds to react. "Well fancy that," said Ike. "She's quite a shrew, your little wife."

Bill began to laugh with the others, but then he looked up at her across the fire. He knew he couldn't reproach her for this intervention without getting the answer: "I did it for New Babylon."

✳

Pearl never complained about the repeated visits of Sandy King and his gang. Had she protested even once, or given the slightest sign of exasperation, Bill would have sent them packing, more or less diplomatically. But she needed this latent grievance, this very live danger that meant the rifle would remain lying in the bed between them. What did she care if these ruffians came to her doorstep to brag and let their animals drop dung in her yard? It wasn't really her house, not the house where she intended to live for the rest of her days. But in fact Bill was impatient to be rid of them so that he could get back to practising his shooting. "No one must discover how fast I am," was his justification.

"Yet they'd have more respect for you."

"I don't need their respect. Just their confidence. The respect will come later. Maybe even not till I'm dead."

Then he set about building a stable to show that he wasn't neglecting his settler's responsibilities.

※

MARCH 1881

From whichever direction you approached it, Russian Bill and Pearl's nameless cabin dominated the centre of the Animas Valley, surrounded by wild lavender and prickly yuccas that grew level with the soil.

When the Reverend pushed on the door, it had been unoccupied for months. Sand had blown inside, covering the wooden floor, the bed, and the table with a thin layer of granules. He was content to look around from the threshold, as if entering would have disturbed the past. A few footprints were already visible in the shroud of dust. Someone had not been as discreet as the Reverend. Someone who had passed by a few days – or maybe even a few hours – before him.

Wisdom isn't worth a damn. If it was worth something, old folks would be happier than young ones, and I've never seen no old folks that make you want to grow old.

———————◆◆◆———————

SARAZIN

JUNE 1869

Ochre dirt as far as the eye can see, strewn with green clumps. A cloudless blue sky, under which each day resembles the one before. A colonial-style wooden house, painted white, with a porch all around, serving both as a pedestal for the settler and as an observatory to survey the surrounding infinity. Always a smell of warm bread. A place from where you could dream, and dream about.

The Reverend Aaron had passed by the Sarazin homestead early in his career as an itinerant preacher. Recently returned from his Mexican odyssey, he had not yet become accustomed to the idea that, on American soil, preaching is more in demand than confession. This was long before he fell silent and Mrs. Sarazin's hair turned white.

Ramona Sarazin emerged from a cloud of flour. Under the layer of white powder coating her from head to foot, she had a bronze complexion and sinewy arms and stood no more than five feet tall. She must have been of mixed blood in another life, before becoming a perfect little wife with her hair in a bun and swelling petticoats – the kind of housewife to spend her days cooking for a swarm of absent children. From the doorway, she barely sized him up before beckoning him to follow her.

The Reverend came in and Ramona returned to rolling her dough. "I was just baking a loaf, and cooking a pork roast with applesauce – just wait – the best you've ever tasted."

She looked up and noticed the Bible in the stranger's hand. She suddenly seemed to come alive. "I'm so glad, you can't imagine, Reverend. The last time a preacher stayed for dinner, I'm telling no lie, it was a good seven years gone. Henry says we just have to read the Bible ourselves, but how much of it do I understand?"

"It's not easy to read," the Reverend observed, looking around him. The ground floor was one spacious room. In the middle reigned a massive fireplace, one side used for cooking and the other for heating. Over the hearth hung rosaries, images of the Madonna, and a yellowing crucifix with the dying Christ in relief, probably carved from an animal's tusk.

"Does it bother you that we're Catholics, Reverend? Myself, I don't care whether *you* believe in the Pope or the Saints or not. But I'd understand if it upsets you. You wouldn't be the first to leave on that account. Sometimes I tell myself I'd be ready to pretend I don't believe in them so that we too might have the right to listen to the preachers from the North. But then I tell myself I can't do that to the Blessed Virgin."

"Maybe Northern folk don't believe in the saints, but they do believe in ghosts," replied the Reverend. "Their houses are less pagan, but they're haunted. Between you and me, it's the same thing."

※

DECEMBER 1879

That first winter, Bill was away for longer than usual. Four days, five days, and he still hadn't come home. On the sixth day, when panic had consumed everything and there wasn't a single floorboard that hadn't been paced up and down, nor the slightest scrap of horizon left unscrutinised, Pearl wrapped herself in a blanket and walked for hours on the mountain. On that December day, a cold rain fell and a north wind blew chill enough to freeze the bones of anyone unaccustomed to it. At first she shivered, then she began to sweat, and then to shiver again, fluctuating uncomfortably around a precarious point of equilibrium. She walked forever, all the way to the Sarazins', where she collapsed on the cow's hide they had laid as a rug in front of the fire and wept for as long as it had taken her to get there.

At one moment after the meal, she told herself that she must have died. She had taken a hot bath, from which she had emerged as if from a second womb. She had eaten the best oxtail soup and the most succulent buttered scones. She went out on the porch as if to pinch herself, to confirm that the sulphurous earth of the Chihuahuan Desert was still spread about this cozy nest. While the sun set outside, Ramona and she rocked in front of the hearth. Pearl asked her the secret of her smooth skin, judging by her hair as white as a judge's wig that she was elderly.

"The secret is I'm not as old as I look. The other secret is I gave birth to eight children who all died before they could be christened, save one – one that had time to be baptized before he drew his last breath. He was six months old when I found him stiff and cold in his cradle. My hair turned white overnight. Now I can't say his name. I'd rather he'd never had a name, like the others."

Pearl said nothing, but looked at her so sadly that Ramona waved a hand dismissively. "There's worse things than white hair," she said. "In my village, there was a girl loved a boy. She didn't even know if the boy loved her back, for she'd never asked him. Every minute she thought she'd die of it. No one realized till all her hair fell out. She wasn't even thirteen."

"I think I've lost some hair myself this last while," said Pearl. "But not for the right reason. Not for the reason I'd have liked."

"The only right reason should be old age. But sometimes you'd think it's life that ages us, instead of old age bringing us closer to death."

Pearl nodded, gazing into the fire. Three years before, when she was still confined to Shawneetown, if she had been told that one day she would die of emotion, it would have consoled her, but she knew that if she confessed it aloud she would be lost. Boredom was unseemly, like the sadism of the rich and the masochism of the young, all feelings outside the proper scheme of things. People had to put up with misfortune, not suffer from its absence.

"There are things born from the moment they're given a name, even if they've existed all along, and others that have a name but are never born," said Ramona to fill the silence.

Pearl wondered if New Babylon would exist one day – if it could be said that the town existed already, but had ceased to exist the day before.

⁂

After weeping for four days, Pearl became used to the idea that Bill was dead. Her anguish had given way to sorrow, and sorrow to the future. She was a widow. She was alone. She was free.

Every evening when the sun began to set and Ramona and she sat rocking on the porch, Henry came out and climbed the frame of the windmill. "He always says it's to grease the works, but the mill don't need that much greasing," said Ramona. "What I suspect is he climbs up there to have some peace and quiet. Earlier, it used to be before nightfall, when there was still Apaches about, to make sure there wasn't a column of smoke in the distance. Now there ain't any Apaches about here no more. When there was, he never said anything about greasing."

On the fourth evening, Henry climbed back down right away, as if he had seen something in the distance. Ramona drew herself up on the edge of her chair, shading her eyes with a hand to judge the distance despite the dying rays filtering toward them. Pearl did likewise. "There's a rider coming," shouted Henry.

The three shut themselves inside the house, the women drumming on the table with their fingernails while Henry reloaded his hunting rifle. They heard the sound of a galloping horse coming closer and closer, and then Bill's voice, distraught not to have found his wife at home. He threw himself on her and hugged her. She didn't weep until they were back in their unlit, icy cabin, where he gave her a pocket watch of chiselled gold.

"One day, we have to have the right time," he said.

"I don't think I could live through that a second time, Bill," she replied, sniffling.

From then on she insisted that Bill take her to the Sarazins' whenever he was setting off for longer than a day.

One evening, just after saying grace, Ramona asked Pearl to describe her time in Dodge City. Pearl refrained from admitting that life in Dodge City was no more dangerous than living, even for only a day every couple of months, in the company of Bill's new friends, whose existence she could not mention in front of the Sarazins.

"How lucky you've been, as a woman, to have travelled so much!" exclaimed Henry.

"If I'd been a man, I'd have been lucky! You can't imagine what it's like to be shut up all evening in a room listening to music as if you were there, yet couldn't be there. To hear girls earmarked like cattle laughing their hearts out, as if they were the ones that pitied you. To hear shots on the other side of the street and tell yourself they're just fireworks you're not allowed to watch."

She was surprised at herself for uttering these words. The barrier that separated her thoughts from her words had just given way under the pressure of something stronger than her will.

✳

AUGUST 1880

The air was chilly for a summer morning. Bill had just brought Pearl to the Sarazins'. She was sitting in one of the chairs in front of the house, at a corner of the porch. Bill was letting his horse drink. The five steps creaked one by one under his weight, then he disappeared inside. She could hear him saying his thanks, excusing himself for his delay the last time, and then Ramona praying that God grant him a safe journey, as He always did. Then she heard the door close and the dull thump of Bill's heels on the porch, followed by the metallic clink of his spurs approaching. Pearl looked into the distance at the valley as it lay inert. The desert wolves were quiet in the mountain recesses. There was only the everlasting red rock and the mesquite bushes growing at their Lilliputian pace.

Bill stood behind her, a thumb hooked in his belt and his hat in the other hand. He seemed to be waiting for some reaction, but she didn't make a move. "Goodbye, Pearl. I'll be back in six days."

She turned around as if she had been unaware of his presence until that moment. "Goodbye, Bill."

The clink of his spurs went away, and then it was the sight of him on his steed, shrinking as he approached the line beyond which everything became a mystery.

✷

Bill returned six days later, as promised. He was accompanied by Sandy, Ike, and Firmel. When the mountain came into sight, the group turned off to the right to reach the cabin at New Babylon, while Bill went straight ahead. He rode around the mountain, but pulled up his horse as soon as he saw the Sarazin homestead. There weren't any sheets to be seen on the washing line, as there usually were. Nor were the usual horses tethered around the enclosure. He passed the strap of his Spencer over his head, intending to alert his companions, as a precaution. They were all wanted men, and there was a price on Sandy's head. If Bill fired two rifle shots into the air, the Sarazins would think that a hunter was active in the hills, while the members of his group would understand the signal. Bill squeezed the trigger, but found that the gun wasn't loaded. For a moment he looked at the Spencer incredulously. He couldn't remember having used it during the past months. He loaded it and fired two shots. The sound travelled to every corner of the valley. In the distance, horses neighed. Dogs barked. Then Bill put the gun away and rode on. He had so often imagined this situation that he seemed to have experienced it already. His instinct told him to turn back, but instead of obeying the intuition he had cultivated every day with exemplary discipline, he embraced traitorous denial and trotted up to the homestead. When he dismounted, the house was immersed in total silence. He stood still, holding his horse by the bridle, and then called Pearl. No answer came. Yet through the window he could see a presence, and a moving shape. He called out to Ramona, and then to Henry. With one hand he drew his Colt, when at the same moment he heard a click behind him. "Drop it," said a voice, coming closer.

Sheriff Whitehill emerged from the house, followed by Henry Sarazin, armed and ready to shoot, while a sheriff's deputy emerged from the stable, another from behind the house, and another from the mountainside.

✳

MARCH 1881

After searching through what remained of New Babylon, the Reverend Aaron went to the neighbouring ranch to question the Sarazins. Ramona recognized him, and crossed herself. She led him toward the house by the arm, giving thanks to the Lord. He was welcomed by the yapping of a little dog. "Quiet, Oliver, quiet!" she said. Nothing had changed, and for that very reason the Reverend was glad he had come.

"Not two days ago a man came this way. I didn't let him in, not that one. He said he was looking for a preacher that didn't preach. Now I see you, I wonder if it wasn't you he was looking for."

"The Matador, no doubt," indicated the Reverend. "You've nothing to fear from him. And if he continues to keep ahead of me like that, neither do I."

During the meal he asked them about the New Babylon lovebirds. The Sarazins had had no news of Pearl Guthrie since Russian Bill's arrest. Then it was Ramona who questioned the Reverend about what God thought of the whole business, of an unmarried couple living together, of a wife betraying her husband to the authorities, of the bandits and the redskins who outdid one another in cruelty.

The Reverend took a deep breath. "And if it was you, Mrs. Sarazin. Suppose you were God. Would you allow those things?"

"No, of course not," she replied, indignantly. I'd have married those young folks once and for all, and I'd have snatched that young man from the clutches of those criminals."

"Me, yes, I'd have let things be," interjected Henry. "Let them go and steal and massacre other folks' children. That way, we'll all be equal."

Henry sniffled, pushed away his plate, and drew back on his chair. Ramona shook her head in a disagreement too deep for verbal expression.

"Amen," concluded the Reverend.

I hate prison, but not for the same reason others do. Other guys, when they're set free, go crazy with joy, even when it's the desert outside. Me, sometimes, I can't see no difference.

SANTA FE

SEPTEMBER 1880

In Santa Fe, the capital of New Mexico, there were two prisons. First there was the territorial penitentiary, the construction of which had never been completed for lack of funds, and which had been languishing for decades in a state of advanced decay. Then there was the two-centuries-old prison, which could contain no more than eight prisoners at a time – too small to meet the demand. It had been built at the time when Santa Fe was still a mere village – the most northerly village of the Spanish empire in America – and its prison was a cage in which undesirables were kept until the tools needed to rip their tongues out or their ears off could be collected.

From their cells in the old penitentiary in Santa Fe, inmates could admire the ruins of the other prison and smile at such a triumph of disorder over modernity. However, the prison guards compensated for the age of the premises by an excessive use of irons, balls, and chains. In addition, there was the fact that the territorial administration, lacking the means to pay for new jails, could not afford to feed the prisoners either.

This gave rise to a genuine polemic among the regular inmates: was it better to be shut up in a fortress where the treatment was good, or in a dungeon where the conditions were inhumane but there was a better chance of escaping?

Twice a day, Pearl Guthrie brought a meal to be delivered to the prisoner William Tattenbaum, alias Russian Bill. She had no choice. It was the only way she could be sure he would survive until his execution.

Pearl Guthrie swore on the Bible before a justice of the peace that on several occasions Bill and she had sheltered Sandy King and his gang under their roof. The judge asked her where this roof was to be found. "In the valley of the Animas Mountains," she replied. "We called the spot New Babylon."

She was unable to prove that Bill himself had broken the law, but the sums of money and gifts he brought back from his expeditions in their company suggested that he had played an active part at their side.

The only other witness heard by the judge was Harold Firmel, who depicted himself as a close friend of Bill's. He claimed that he had never seen Russian Bill riding with the Sandy King gang, that he had visited Bill's ranch several times, and that to his knowledge no one in that gang knew where it was.

"And why would this woman want to see her husband condemned?" asked the judge. Firmel shrugged.

"How would I know? The slut has been married more times than she has fingers for rings. Maybe she wanted a change."

Two days later, Bill was released without a trial. The authorities had no evidence against him, nor was he notorious or hated enough to be given a show trial.

Indeed, New Mexican justice had little interest in Russian Bill at the time. If Sheriff Whitehill had made such an effort to capture him, it was with the objective of tracking down Sandy King. Twice as many men had been posted at New Babylon as at the Sarazin ranch. Thanks to Bill's warning signal, the gang had been able to turn aside before falling into the trap.

※

A photo of Pearl in her cream dress and Bill in a top hat appeared on the front page of the newspaper:

Woman Uses Court to Be Rid of Husband

After thirty weddings, it would have been reasonable to think that Pearl Guthrie, a native of Illinois, was a satisfied woman. But no! After having had her husband, alias Russian Bill, arrested, she perjured herself on the Holy Scriptures, stating that he was a member of the infamous Sandy King gang. "A calumny!" revealed Harold Firmel, a cattleman from the Arizona Territory and an old friend of Russian Bill.

In fact, Pearl Guthrie and Russian Bill had been joined only eight times in the sacred bonds of marriage. Eight times she had kissed Bill, feigning joy before a clergyman and an assembly of strangers. Eight times, until she wearied of it. Wearied of having to act out her greatest fantasy day after day, without it ever becoming real – so weary that she would burst into tears during the ceremony, in front of all those strangers smiling to see her shed what they took to be tears of joy.

But even Pearl would have admitted that the figure of thirty marriages was no exaggeration, since each of them had entrusted themselves to the other an incalculable number of times. In Valverde, and then in Alamosa, she had stood erect against a wall while Bill practised his aim by tracing her silhouette with bullet holes. Hundreds of times she had lain down with no bodice, or any defence other than an imaginary line separating her body from his. Hundreds of times he had slept like a log, giving her the opportunity to take the Spencer and shoot him between snores. Pearl Guthrie had never married, but she was a widow. She was a widow, but her husband was still alive. And thanks to the Santa Fe daily, the *New Mexican*, the whole world knew.

✻

Bill would never discover the source of the meals that were delivered for him. "He's crazy enough to let himself die of hunger," she had explained to the guard. Pearl's only fear was that the food would never reach him, that as soon as she had turned on her heel her largesse would be diverted for the benefit of the prison staff, leaving Bill to starve.

The Sunday before his liberation, the guard handed her a letter. It was addressed to the "benefactor of the prisoner William Tattenbaum."

She returned to the boarding house where she was staying. It was a colonial-style building, its white walls stained by age and a crucifix in each room. She greeted the landlady and went up to her bedroom, which reminded her of the one in La Posta, the first she had shared with Bill.

To this day Pearl remembers the smell of roasted garlic and freshly cut onions rising from the kitchen, the braying of mules and donkeys in the street, the wagon wheels grating against the dry mud of the alleyways, the distant chimes of the church, and the cracking made by the bed when she sat on it to read the letter.

> Pearl,
>
> I know the food comes from you. I don't know why you are doing this, or for what reason you handed me over to the law, but I suspect it is now to your advantage to behave like a good wife.
>
> I can well imagine you parading up and down the streets of Santa Fe. Stolen pearls hang from your ears. In church, you pray with your hands sheathed in brocade gloves pulled from the cold arms of a victim of my final raid.
>
> You have always known I was a bandit. The only thing I ever asked of you was never to betray me.
>
> At bottom, you liked it that every night I placed the rifle down the middle of the bed between us. I have never broken any promise I made. I always kept to my own side. I should have suspected that when a woman like you covers herself with prohibitions in front of a man like me, it is for the pleasure of witnessing him transgress them.
>
> I am the prisoner, but it is you who have broken the only law we imposed on ourselves.

I would ask you not to bring anything more for me. If you are so concerned about my well-being, you will see how healthy I look on the day of my hanging.

William Tattenbaum
Son of the Countess Telfrin

⁕

APRIL 1881

The Reverend Aaron held out the newspaper cutting to the landlady.

"You're not the first to come looking for that one," she said, observing the Reverend suspiciously. "What exactly do you want with her?"

"I want to help her," replied the Reverend, displaying his Bible.

"The one that came by before you was looking for a preacher man that was asking after this girl. Looks to me like that was you. What does he want with you?"

The Reverend tapped the tips of his fingers in his jacket pocket. "He thinks he can help her too, but mostly he's hoping to help himself."

"You could never help that one anyhow," sighed the landlady. "Girls like that, they've nowhere to go. And nowhere means farther out west. That old dream of working in San Francisco, as if others hadn't thought of it first. And the girls that get to San Francisco, well I just wish them luck."

"Is that what she said, that she was leaving for San Francisco?"

"Worse. She said she was intending to go to the Mormons. That out there they're not as reluctant to marry women as they are here. Oh, I've never laughed so much in my life! And yet, you know, when I think of it now, I don't find it funny at all."

NOTEBOOK IV

The Reverend Aaron's
Four Notebooks

MOUNTAIN MEADOWS, 1842 ✤ BRADSHAW CITY, 1871

NAUVOO, 1833 ✤ MEXICO, 1864–1867

EHRENBERG, 1870–1878 ✤ CHIRICAHUA, 1880

TOMBSTONE, 1880–1881 ✤ TUCSON, 1881

GALEYVILLE, 1880–1881 ✤ SAN XAVIER DEL BAC, 1881

✤ VERMILION CLIFFS, 1881 ✤

✤

*I'm obsessed by new beginnings. Every evening, Sam would
scribble on bits of paper and then burn them. He'd say, "Son,
every time things go wrong, you just need to burn something and
you'll feel better. If you fall for a girl, write her name on a piece
of paper and keep it over your heart. And if you discover the girl
doesn't want you, burn the paper. It'll be a new beginning. There's
nothing better than watching something go up in smoke."
Fire has a life of its own. Soon, your little problem
becomes everyone's problem.*

MOUNTAIN MEADOWS

NOVEMBER 1842

The Reverend Aaron, before he became the Reverend Aaron, had a sister of marriageable age. She had never forgiven her parents for having abandoned the Mormon community in Missouri. She would repeat that it wasn't enough to pray, that you also had to try to build God's kingdom, starting over and over, leaving everything behind and building again and again in places where there was nothing. One evening, she announced that she was going to marry her Mormon sweetheart and return to the bosom of the Latter-day Saints. Her father forbade it. She answered that nothing was going to stop her now that she had heard the Call, and that in any case, she would not submit to any law except the will of the Almighty. This scene was eternally inscribed in the Reverend's memory, like a black blotch in the eyesight of a child who had stared too long at the sun: his father getting up and slapping his sister; his sister staggering, then recovering her balance, holding a hand to her reddened cheek; his sister striding up to his father and slapping him back. An irreparable act, committed in God's name. After this event the Reverend Aaron spent his life witnessing the commission of irreparable acts, most often in the name of nothing.

Other preachers will tell you that the flesh is weak. The Reverend Aaron would have told you that the soul is even weaker. Men are tormented by the sins they have committed, while others are no less haunted by those they have failed to commit. He never again saw the sister who had slapped his father. In 1857, at Mountain Meadows, some Mormons who believed they were carrying out God's orders attacked a convoy of covered wagons carrying a hundred or so innocent pioneers, including women and children. The children, who were young enough to escape being sacrificed, were taken in and then cared for by the wives of those responsible for the massacre, and fed at the same table as the family. The murderers of their parents became their parents. Somewhere, perhaps, the Reverend had a niece or nephew born of this butchery.

Logically, the Reverend Aaron should tell you to stop obeying anyone. But such a rebellion would mean obeying the Reverend. That is why he keeps silent.

I think that God Himself must have a God greater than Himself.
Otherwise, how does He choose? Why would some things be
agreeable to Him and others not? If I was Him, I'd invent a god
for myself and tell people to do what I say because, like lousy
deputies who are content to obey the sheriff's orders, it's not really
me that decides. If it's so important for Him to respect His damn
commandments, He just has to find a way for me to respect them.

———◆◆———

BRADSHAW CITY

DECEMBER 1871

The only new arrivals in Bradshaw came bearing bad tidings. The camp was perched halfway up Mount Wasson and had no town centre or main street. You had to weave your way haphazardly among the buildings to find a hotel or restaurant. New arrivals could be recognized by their way of peering around corners and searching this way and that on horseback.

First came the Reverend Aaron, who brought no news but whose inexplicable presence was interpreted as a bad omen.

Then came Joseph Seymour, a saddler from Prescott who had just killed the man who had shot his brother, who had shot the other man's son. Fine snow was falling that evening, but Seymour's horse was sweating. He went to take refuge with his brother-in-law, the town's assayer of metals, who agreed to hide him until tempers cooled. "You're going to have to find another solution, Joe," he would frequently remind him. "The prospectors are clearing out, and I'm clearing out soon too."

Then came the Matador wearing his enormous flat-crowned hat and his poncho that dragged on the inn floor. The heels of his calfskin boots printed muddy squares on the floorboards. The day after he arrived, the Matador stopped in every establishment in the town asking to speak with Joseph Seymour. Everywhere, people shrugged, but there was always some drunkard or busybody to point out to him that Joe Seymour didn't live in Bradshaw but in Prescott. "That's where I've come from," the Matador merely replied.

Leading his two horses by the reins, the Matador scaled a ravine that led higher up the mountain, and took up his position in front of a stony hillock overlooking the town. But what he did not know was that at that very moment the Reverend Aaron was also on the mountain, even higher up. The two men spent a few hours observing the swarming ant colony from their respective viewpoints. It was difficult to understand how the Matador managed to follow the spreading news while remaining out of earshot. To have drawn the conclusions he did from the comings and goings of the inhabitants he must have perceived something unusual about them, like an astrologer deciphering the starry heavens.

Just before closing time, the Matador entered the assayer's office a second time. From up on the mountain, the Reverend saw the assayer limping from his doorway. "I've been shot. I'm wounded. My leg ... Oh God, my leg," he howled between breaths. He tried to move forward, gripping the wound between his hands as a dark stain spread over his pant legs. He collapsed on the other side of the street as a crowd gathered around him. The Matador came next from the shop, pushing Joe Seymour, whose hands and feet were tied. He slung the captive over one of his horses and mounted the other. He took him like that to Prescott, where Seymour was hanged in the name of the law.

The town's metals assayer died of an infection three days later. His death was an additional spur to the exodus already under way, and by Christmas the hemorrhage was at its height.

Today, nothing remains of Bradshaw City except a few pits dug into the landscape of Mount Wasson and a few smoking chimneys, scattered like the campfires of fleeing Apache renegades.

✳

Once a year the Mexicans honoured a skeleton-woman named Santa Muerte and, drunk on good wine and pulque, held a picnic on the graves of their dead. So it wasn't surprising that in a part of the country still haunted by its colonial past, the Grim Reaper had taken on a Mexican appearance.

While in perfect control of himself in the daytime, at night the Matador became an inveterate sleepwalker. This was why he insisted on sleeping alone. He only went to bed with women larger than himself and who drank more than he. He hated beer and whiskey, but couldn't do without his cup of coffee each morning. It had to be boiling hot so that he could enjoy at his leisure feeling through the china how it cooled and be able to drink it at the precise temperature he wanted. When he undressed, he would put his clothes on a chair, never on the bed, because that was unlucky. At the laundry, he paid extra to obtain a guarantee that no one would try on his clothes. He had a weakness for gold, but avoided wearing yellow. He kept no weapons by him in bed, for he considered that if a man couldn't sleep in peace, his life wasn't worth living anyway. However, he refused to sleep in the open, because that meant keeping his clothes on, and only the dead sleep that way. He had an aversion to cattlemen because of the alcohol on their breath in the mornings, and the smell of manure and burnt flesh they gave off after branding their animals. But one might suspect that the fact that he had been a *vaquero* earlier in his life had something to do with it. He collected knives and daggers, was crazy about melons, and had a horror of the violin. He preferred to be called a murderer rather than a hired killer or bounty hunter – terms he found offensive because of their mercenary connotations. The object of all professions was to earn a living, for otherwise you would have had expressions like "shoemaker for reward," "innkeeper for tips," or "prostitute for cash."

He was superstitious, demanding, and predictable. If he stared at you, he would always end by striking you. He avoided killing his target when possible, but if there was a larger reward for a dead victim he would not hesitate to finish him off. "If I kill them all, people will think taking a life is easy," he explained one day. When he shot a victim who had put up an honourable defence, he would lay a flower across his jacket, like a special commendation for the undertaker. It was a great honour to be respected by the Matador when you were dead. In the Reverend's opinion, the Matador only exalted some of his prey for his own greater glory. After all, genuine matadors needed grandstands packed with fans to be able to massacre a bull.

When the Matador came to get his reward for a criminal he had delivered alive and was asked if he planned to attend the execution, he would shake his head.

"There you are, the only thing you're interested in is the reward. You couldn't care less about justice being done" – such was the reproach they levelled at him in Prescott.

"I'd be there if it was a garrotting or a firing squad, like in my country of origin," he would answer. "But hanging ... There's nothing more vulgar than a criminal who shits his pants after being dispatched to hell."

*Everyone's happy. You, because I'm dying. And the executioner
because he can use the rope again afterward.*

NAUVOO

APRIL 1833

The Reverend Aaron was born to parents who didn't tolerate
silence at a time when such a thing still existed. Unable to hear
God's voice, they worshipped the voices of men – of those who
called themselves prophets. Mormons, Millerites, and Christ-
adelphians in turn, the Aarons were to religion as trappers were
to the mountains: passionate, but with without any attachment.

Little Aaron had first seen the light of day in a wagon, with no
midwife or doctor to help. Inspired by the prophet of the Church
of Jesus Christ of Latter-day Saints, his family had chosen to sell
up everything and set off for Nauvoo, at the extreme edge of the
settled world. The child's first cry pierced the emptiness of the
surrounding prairie, a miracle of nature in the midst of nature.

After Nauvoo they had pursued their journey ever closer to
the Pacific, on the Oregon Trail. In this nothingness, the Reverend
Aaron very soon discovered that he didn't like to use his hands.
He was the first to sigh when the axe remained buried in the hard
wood like a pocket knife in a loaf of black bread, when the logs
were too heavy, when a wagon wheel fell off and had to be patched
up for the eighth time because they lacked the tools to make a new
one. He hated the stickiness of fish that were still flapping, the
screech of knives being sharpened, and the cracking of the skin
of his little fingers, dried out by premature wear and tear. The
only thing he liked to do was paint stones in bright colours. Like
other children he always carried these pebbles with him in case
he should be carried off by the redskins on his way home from
the shack that they called the "school." Then he could drop them
behind him so that his parents might find the way to the Indian

camp and rescue him from a life even more uncivilized than the one he was already forced to lead. However, he was never carried off by the Indians. But the paint eventually ran out.

According to the calculations of a preacher whose name does not deserve mention, the end of the world was to occur in 1843. The Reverend Aaron's parents therefore decided to sell everything they owned, leave home, and take refuge in the hills. For three months they lived in mountain caves like prehistoric humans, hunting possum and praying they would survive the bad weather. The end of the world never came. And the ten-year-old who would become the Reverend Aaron swore that he would become a preacher in his turn and pursue a career which, though not part of their plans for him, was admired by his family. This was the only way he could be allowed to retrace the same journey in reverse, heading for some large Eastern city or another to undertake prestigious studies and never return to the emptiness called the West.

Preaching gained a hold over young Aaron before he was old enough to carry out this intention. He was eleven; his father had just died. Standing before the wooden coffin, he uttered a few words that displayed not only great innocence, but also great wisdom. Everyone around him fell silent. A man patted him on the shoulder and then a woman stroked his hair. "It's really true what you said there, young man. You're quite right."

His father had died, and it fell to him to console others. Then it was a classmate who died; before the white cross he uttered new words that drew cries of pain from several women. Men's shoulders began to shake. Soon he was asked to speak even at the burials of dead folk whom he had barely known, and eventually, of complete strangers from nearby villages. As the new man of the house, he would be summoned immediately after the doctor to the bedside of the dying, to save their souls. Conducting funerals soon enabled him to earn enough to feed his family. When he was sixteen he joined the gold rush to California. There was no shortage of deaths, and each dead man was replaced by ten newcomers.

In those days, a man of God didn't need to ask himself if it was appropriate to carry a firearm. This was before the Civil War, before farmers took it into their heads to exchange the pitch-fork for a bayonet and learn to handle a Colt, which they never put down again. It was before old men became veterans, or the sons of veterans. Only a man of the cloth could have made them unlearn what they had learned during the war. But by this time even preachers were carrying revolvers.

Initially, the prospectors were generous, sure of their future wealth. As insouciantly as they paid triple the going price for their whiskey, they paid the funeral expenses of comrades they had encountered the evening before. But then the Reverend began to recognize disappointment on men's faces – the same disappointment that he had seen on his parents' faces as they awaited an end of the world that never came. The Californian Christians stopped paying for strangers' funerals. Far from his family, each miner died a solitary death; his remains would be buried the same day, with the eulogy delivered by amateurs. Then the Reverend had to turn to the living to earn his bread. He re-educated himself in the art of preaching sermons, an unenjoyable but profitable activity. Men who lacked any sort of entertainment weren't averse to hearing someone occasionally tell them what they should think. From camp to camp he pro-claimed his conception of a God about whom he preferred not to think. Before delivering his sermons he would rehearse them, sighing. His sweaty palms moistened the pages of his script. He would tremble and strike his brow. He would enter a tavern and climb onto the gaming tables to attract the drinkers' attention. He would utter his homily like a bad actor speaking his lines. Peanuts, dice, or glasses would be thrown at him. It was thankless work, but there would have been no merit in leading people to the light if they were headed for it anyway. His sermons were meant for those who didn't listen.

Sometimes he reread his scripts and told himself that if a preacher had come along and spouted the same words in his presence, he would have laughed at him. He would have told him he was expressing the obvious. That his sermons were a waste of time, for he could have thought them up himself. Sometimes he would look down at the good folk absorbing the maxims he uttered and despise them for being so easily satisfied, for failing to see that he was an imposter. Spontaneous, spectacular conversions left him cold. Usually, he had left a camp before the benefits of his presence manifested themselves.

The Reverend Aaron was not lacking in talent. It was simply not in his true interest for sinners to cross the barrier to spiritual redemption. The more sermons he wrote, the less he wanted them to be heard. Effortlessly, he slipped into silence.

Then the country was plunged into war. The wounded accumulated in tents by the thousand, awaiting an amputation, in ecstasy at having killed for the first time. It was mass production of the dead, who were flung into common graves without anyone knowing their names or their stories; it was the same speech repeated ad infinitum for each nameless soldier, as if by an automaton guarding the gates of Paradise.

There would have been lots of work for the Reverend Aaron during the Civil War, but he preferred to escape to Mexico.

I think it's the ring that isn't right for me. The truth is that my most memorable fights were all spontaneous. I fight better when there are no boundaries. When it's life or death.

MEXICO

MAY 1864

Anyone who had never attended a bullfight had no right to claim to know what beauty was. With its brightly coloured house-fronts, its perfectly symmetrical streets, and its luxuriant, arching exotic plants and flowers, Mexico City possessed a heart-rending splendour. But such majesty was worthless, for the more you looked at it, the less you saw it. True beauty resided in something about to disappear. So, in a sandy octagon even more arid than the natural desert, the killing of an animal was played out each Sunday before a crowd that tried to relive the emotion of the initial experience.

For every fountain there must have been thousands of naked children playing in the mud with pigs. For every cathedral there were beggars covered with sores and native women who exchanged their babies like dolls in order to attract charity. For every aqueduct there were tumbledown bridges that people crossed at their peril. For every señorita with shoulders bared there were bloodthirsty bandits – mercenaries who pinned their enemies' ears to the walls for decoration. Everything that made Mexico detestable was actually just a sacrifice for the sake of ultimate beauty, to which the Mexicans dedicated their every possession.

✳

A bullfight could be compared to a bolero in three acts: the trial, the sentence, and the execution. In the first act, the bravery of the bull was evaluated. Capes were flourished all around the arena – colourful banners calling for bloodshed the way a white flag calls for peace. Mounted on a horse protected by metal plates and armed, like Don Quixote, with a medieval-looking lance, the picador prepared to spear the animal. How ferociously would the bull, the warrior of the animal kingdom, attack the horse and perform his enraged duty?

Then came the second act. In it, the *banderillero* did his best to humiliate the bull by planting in his shoulders some barbs festooned with multi-coloured, feathery strips that drooped on his flanks and mingled with the rivulets of blood. A brave bull would never flinch at its condemnation. No *banderillero* would be able to make him look foolish. For him, this was war, not a celebration.

Once the arena was emptied of the supporting cast, it seemed to close in even more around the solitary animal performer. The final act, which belonged to the *matador*, would open amid a ceremonial silence. Attired in shards of reflective glass, armed with a red cape and rapier, the matador seemed to belong to a different race of men, one that venerated elegance and cultivated pride as a personal discipline, one that had vanished so long ago that one had to wonder if it had ever existed.

The executioner, light-footed in his ballerina slippers, initiated a waltz with his adversary the bull, who would follow the pattern until the sword pierced his heart. As he collapsed, the animal would kick up the sand around him, conferring a halo of golden dust on his killer as the latter removed his hat and bowed to acknowledge the joyous clamour. It wasn't rare to see tears trace furrows in the dirt covering the matador's cheeks. The crowd – the poor languishing in the sunny section of the arena as well as the wealthy surrounding the Emperor and the numerous French expatriates in the shaded seats – had abandoned all restraint.

The Reverend Aaron refused to pay more than three reals to attend a spectacle he didn't understand, so he sat in the sun among the less well-off. He reached his fifth bullfight before he had a revelation, due no doubt to a sunstroke that affected his mind. It occurred to him that the matador was the closest thing there was to a god. And, though he hadn't tired of his work as a minister of religion, he dreamed of a splendid funeral in honour of this demigod, and the words of an imaginary eulogy formed in his head. Maybe his chosen profession might have been right for him if only the dead had lived a life worth speaking of, he told himself.

After a disturbed night he awoke cured of his sunstroke, but not of his fascination.

✳

The two most celebrated matadors of the day were Bernardo Gaviño Rueda, the founder of the Mexico City bullfighting school, and Vicente Aguilar, the only one of his apprentices to rival him. The first wore a silver and blue *traje de luces*, the second a red and gold one. They feigned mutual respect, while secretly detesting one another. The Reverend Aaron had settled his choice on Aguilar for, unlike the master, the pupil had not yet had time to add his legacy to the annals of bullfighting.

The Reverend, who was earning his living as a scrivener at the time, knocked on his door, hoping to be hired to ghostwrite his memoirs. "Señor Aguilar knows how to write," his servant replied before showing the Reverend the door. He was more successful in passing himself off as a priest of Irish origin – something he had almost become despite his ignorance of Catholic doctrine.

"When I was on tour, I saw men like you preaching," said Aguilar, looking him up and down. "You gringo priests are so dramatic. For the faithful you become like matadors of prayer, ready to slay the devil for your audience of believers."

So the Reverend Aaron became *Padre* Aaron and discovered the most delicious of all rituals – confession. Every Wednesday he was summoned to the Matador's rooms. The little square chamber in which he was received was furnished with two armchairs and a prayer stool surrounded with lanterns. The walls were covered with white stucco and decorated with holy pictures, crucifixes, and rosaries. These gestures the Matador made toward Christ were possibly intended to win him pardon for the arrogance he displayed in every other regard, especially his tendency to keep his confessor waiting for more than an hour.

He would kiss his hand before speaking to him, but reminded him frequently who was the servant and who the master.

The Reverend didn't hold this against him, for whenever the Matador was speaking to God through him he would admit his pettiness and his greatness in a single breath. He expressed pride at having surpassed his master, and shame at his lack of success in Spain. He confessed that he wanted to die in the bullring before anyone surpassed him.

Christians do not fear death. But, Aguilar wondered uneasily, was it proper for a Christian to imagine it? He was one of those for whom neither life nor money had any value. The only thing that mattered was to have a name and pass it on to offspring who, in turn, would risk their life and money without qualm. His name would be remembered differently in the memories of Mexicans, but how? How could he reach posterity through an art which, even after the most dangerous and brilliant of performances, left no trace other than a few streaks of blood in the dust? This was why he had to turn back to the Lord, to ask for forgiveness, concentrate on divine salvation, on the truth, and possibly find himself a wife and found a line of little toreadors. But the Matador knew that any marriage of his would have been a lie. He would never have been able to feel love for a human being as he did for the vanquished bull.

"The *corrida* is a spectacle, of course. You are in the middle of the arena; every eye is riveted on you. But it's also the ultimate way to escape the judgment of others," he would say. "No matter what they think, whether they applaud or whistle you, it's the bull that decides. That's what I love in the confrontation: it sweeps away shame and pride. It's not a spectacle, it's an animal that wants to kill you. It thumbs its nose at social niceties, at established rules, at the Mass, at confession, at penitence."

"I often see women helping old ladies out of charity, and then laughing at them behind their backs. I see young boys torturing stray dogs, and I'm given a hundred Hail Marys as penance for hoping they get bitten. I repent, Father, believe me. But I'm all the more outraged by other people's lack of remorse.

"The world is evil, but the bells continue to ring. So there you have it. If you want to mock from up on your dais, go ahead. I'll make your job easier. Except you won't laugh for long. No one jokes with death.

"I live for that animal that wants to kill me. Each time, I think I'm going to die. But then he's the one who dies."

Every evening, after returning to his lodgings, Father Aaron the confessor wrote down everything that Aguilar had confided in him, for no words could be nobler. He collected more than three years of daily confessions with the intention of publishing them the day after the famous matador's death. All the *aficionados* in the capital city would fight to get a copy. During bullfights he would find himself almost wishing for the long-awaited death, yet he could hardly breathe, as if he too were below in the bullring.

One day he asked Aguilar if he had ever been afraid of death, or if he had been born that way, unfazed by the idea of his mortality.

"Fear exists, but with experience it is transformed into excitement," the Matador admitted. Then he added, "I risk my life, but what does it matter? Everyone has to die. It's not a question of avoiding death, but of choosing your arena."

✳

DECEMBER 1867

As long as he was earning his living as a bullfighter, Vicente Aguilar had despised the gun. He said it was a device that revealed nothing about the person handling it, that there was no beauty in being able to kill from a distance, and that because of this invention, women and children could become killers and his art would be reduced to a cultural relic. Maybe he was right to abhor this thing that, in a world where most men are alone, could make every lone individual into an army.

In 1867, after Emperor Maximilian I of Mexico was assassinated in Querétaro, bullfighting was forbidden by the president of Mexico. Weary of listening to the lamentations of the idol now confronted with bitter reality, the Reverend Aaron used the excuse that the Civil War had ended to declare it was time for him to return home, even though no such place existed.

As for Señor Aguilar, he experienced the worst years of his life. Deprived of work, he gradually lost all his money. Now that practising his art had become a crime, he saw every chance of a glorious death also fading away. So he sold all his remaining possessions, and set off northward. He purchased that detested object, a gun, and became the Matador, a bounty hunter.

My mother was no whore. I'd have known.
That's all I have to say.

EHRENBERG

JULY 1870

The first time the Reverend Aaron set foot in Ehrenberg, he ensured his welcome by treating the regulars in the saloon to a round of drinks. He was just starting out, and told himself he'd never be able to do anything with people if he condemned the thing they loved best in the world.

Ehrenberg was still just a modest port, grafted where the Colorado River, running serenely in its channel, cleft the red earth of the plain. A shelter built of round logs with a thatched roof welcomed prospectors into its single room, where a towel was used a hundred times before being washed. In summer, it was impossible to sleep there, because so much humidity clung to the skin. Some had built rafts on which to spend summer nights on the water and replace suffocation with sleep.

A few of the inhabitants who accommodated themselves perfectly to the codes of Christianity accused the Reverend of hypocrisy. Others, minor miscreants, watched him in action and accused him of betrayal, since basically, like others, he was preaching the path of righteousness. He answered that they were the hypocrites, for in the end they always admitted their belief in God even if they had no respect for Him.

꙳

SEPTEMBER 1878

The second time the Reverend came to Ehrenberg he was on the track of a certain Brett Nelson, a criminal who accumulated offences of considerable variety and gravity – ranging from polygamy to massacres of innocents and even cannibalism – the way others collected scalps. He had attracted the Reverend's attention by his accent, which combined vulgarity and traces of the old continent. Nelson was an outlaw Australia had washed its hands of, despite being a nation populated mostly by the scum of another. The Reverend had followed him to the bathhouse, where he had won him over by chatting to him as if he didn't know who he was dealing with.

Among murderers of women, some invoked a noble motive: it was to eliminate temptation, to ensure the triumph of morality, or to repair an offence to their honour. And then there were those who, like Nelson, admitted candidly: "I just wanted to kill one." They would be found with bloodstained coats and a harried look, as if caught sitting on the chamber pot.

The Reverend didn't like Ehrenberg, less because of its inhabitants than its topography. He preferred the echo of rocky sierras and dizzy precipices to the flatness of the plains. Wherever there was high ground, he always found a way to scale the heights to reach a point overlooking the town and providing an unusual vista over the Creation. He would sit down on a rock, take a hard-boiled egg from his bag, and shell it as he contemplated the spectacle of humanity in miniature. He observed the people strolling in the streets. The women especially. It was for women that laws had been conceived, and it was mostly men who broke them. He saw respectable women running in every direction to escape the danger of the street whenever its shadow loomed. And then there were the dissolute women who didn't run, whose bruises already hurt when they smiled. Later, when he went back down into the town, he would walk with his hands behind his back, greeting his flock with the assurance of a man who understands everything.

The Reverend had no high point from which to observe life in Ehrenberg. One evening, he went to the public baths, expecting to find Nelson performing his weekly ablutions there. His fingertips were starting to wrinkle and Nelson still hadn't showed up. Instead, it was the Matador who installed himself in the next tub, naked beneath an enormous hat whose diameter was almost as wide as the bath.

"*Padre*," he said, tipping his hat.

The Reverend observed him through the steam, rubbing his thumb against his index finger. "Dead or alive?" he asked.

"Who do you mean?"

"Brett Nelson."

The Matador pressed his lips together. That was his way of smiling. Nothing really amused him, but he could recognize when someone was trying to amuse him. "It's been a long time since I gave up confession," he answered.

"It can't be easy every day, to kill in the dark, with no spectators to applaud."

The Matador raised his two dripping arms from the water and laid them on each side of the bath. "You can think what you like about me. But you're mistaken, just like you were mistaken back then."

"I can't deny it. I thought you were a torero for the beauty of it and the fame. In fact, you were just a butcher."

"There's not so much difference between you and me, *padre*."

"I don't kill people."

"Maybe so, but to do his job a good assassin must take a greater interest in his victims' life than in their death."

"And if I took an interest in yours, like before?"

The Matador slipped down in the water until it covered his shoulders and his face vanished beneath the brim of his hat. "I'd tell you again that I've no interest in confessing."

The next morning, the Australian's corpse was spotted floating in the Colorado River. Since the deceased had no real friends in Ehrenberg and the only spiritual director available was the Reverend Aaron, no effort was made to recover the body.

I watched Sam, who spent a lot of time practising his signature, and I told myself that class had nothing to do with your work or your wealth. Having class meant having a nice signature. I wanted to be like him, so I soon learned to read and write. One day I came home, and there was Sam taking a nap. I came across some scribbles he hadn't yet thrown in the fire. I asked my mother why Sam signed Leonard Pope when his name was Sam Ambrose. My mother couldn't read. "You're sure that's what's written there? And there, is it the same?" Leonard Pope's name was well-known. He'd been a member of a gang of robbers who were wanted in four states. My mother didn't wait till Sam woke up. She tied his hands to the bed. By the time he understood what was going on, she had tied his feet too. She sent me to get the marshal. I didn't understand nothing. They hanged Sam the next day.

———◆—◆—◆———

CHIRICAHUA

JANUARY 1880

Russian Bill had been trotting all day long along the slopes of the Chiricahua Mountains. It was well into night, and he first found the gang's encampment by the light of their fire. In the distance, he could hear shots fired at irregular intervals, followed by the neighing of the horses who, unlike to their masters, never grew accustomed to the sound of shooting.

The men were gathered in a circle around a bonfire in the centre of the valley. Among them were four prostitutes from Galeyville, two of whom were laughing, as limp as rag dolls, one who seemed to be pouting as she stared at the fire, and another who gnawed on a chicken thigh while shaking her skirts and waltzing around to music only she could hear. Now and again the men aimed at the heavens and shot in the air for no apparent reason. They spat in the fire and drank from the bottles, which they then tossed over their shoulders. Russian Bill had to duck one. He was standing outside the circle of light when he asked if he could join them. They were too drunk to refuse. He ate their food, drank their water and whiskey, listened to their stories, and then intervened in the conversations as if he had always been one of them.

"I had a shoulder wound," he recounted to anyone who wanted to listen. "Never mind," I told myself. "I went in, I tore down the drawing-room curtains, wrapped myself in them like in a Roman toga, and then returned to the fight with a sabre in each hand. As I remember, I must have killed about thirty Turks that day alone, but I was in no shape to go and take their pulses. And after a massacre, who can tell a dead Turk from one who's sleeping?"

The next morning, when they raised their heads from their saddles, Russian Bill was stretched out among them.

The sun had been up for two hours when Curly Bill announced it was time to get going. The women were left behind, surrounded by a wasteland of empty bottles. Around the still-smouldering ashes, they pleaded for the men to come back, but they had already left and could be seen gradually shrinking in the distance.

At the back of the column, only Russian Bill turned around in the saddle to cast concerned glances at the temptresses in distress.

"Don't worry," said the rider in front. "They'll still be alive when we get back."

Two days later they returned with a stream of steers and goats stolen from the haciendas of Mexican ranchers. The empty bottles were still lying where they had been thrown, but the women were gone.

※

It was in the heart of the Chiricahua Mountains that the offshoot of the Apaches known by the same name was born, assembling the most warlike Indians of the Southwest, pillagers by tradition and cruel by principle – ones that even the other Indians dreamed of seeing exterminated.

At the foot of these mountains there were also gathered white men that other white men considered pests. They were the sons of disappointed miners, raised amid the bitterness of failure to strike it rich, of losing the war, and finally of never being able to achieve anything anywhere. They had come to the San Simon Valley to avenge the humiliation of their fathers and the opportunities that were lost forever. Some hoped to grow rich by rustling cattle, others to achieve fame by catching the rustlers. When they weren't busy being tracked by the locals, the two groups chased each other and fought in order to enjoy the illusion of some kind of victory.

Choosing hurriedly, the Reverend Aaron had decided that the two most interesting outlaws in the region were Curly Bill

Brocius and Sandy King. He couldn't make up his mind between them. That was before Russian Bill disturbed the lay of the land.

✳

The abandoned whores had been rescued by another gang of cattle dealers on their way to Galeyville. Although one of them couldn't stop sobbing, they weren't allowed an afternoon off. The Reverend Aaron took advantage of this to question each in turn.

"Curly Bill, you'd better never gainsay him. Sandy King, that guy doesn't know what he wants."

"There was Bill the bastard and Bill the Russian. Bill the Russian, now he was a gentleman. He'd never have left us there in the desert," said another, wiping her nose.

"There was a wooden box the likes of which I've never seen, then he took out a white piece. Said it was a queen. Said they're all the same but all different too, and he said that that one looked like me, I swear that's the truth. I asked him why he played that game instead of entertainin' himself the same way as everyone else, and he said it was because too often they hadn't let him. Before, they didn't even let him throw snowballs. That's why he plays chess. Anyways, that's what he told me."

"He's crazy," commented another. "Smooth guys like him, they always want strange things, things that ain't human at all. I tell you, Reverend, guys that respects women like me, they're hiding stuff. You shouldn't trust them."

You go into a whorehouse, and your money lets you pick a girl; she does whatever you want. You're in control, but it's all make-believe. There's middle-class folks from Chicago that come this way, who say they've gone looking for adventure. But actually they're able to go back East any time. What I tell them is, when the day comes that they've no more power over their lives, then they'll see what life's really like.

TOMBSTONE

OCTOBER 1881

In the very heart of the San Pedro Valley, there was a town all too appropriately named. You had to see the chandeliers with eight lamps hanging from the tavern ceilings and lighting the walls painted with murals. You had to feel the polished rosewood of the bars, so dark and silky that between the round marks left by the glasses you could admire your own reflection in it. You had to see the men in three-piece suits and derby hats as they felt for their pocket watches while discussing astronomy. Outside was scrubland and Geronimo's Apaches, but inside the sons of chimney sweeps took themselves for budding politicians, and prostitutes took themselves for actresses. Tombstone was the future, they said. They weren't far wrong: everything always ends with a tombstone.

In Tombstone, there was a real theatre with a red curtain that rose on real actors and opera singers. There were benches screwed to the floor and balconies along the sides for folks who came to be seen as much as to see. For, yes, it was good to be seen in a place where people flaunted themselves. It wasn't '49 anymore. The reign of gold had given way to the rule of silver, a mineral that could only be extracted from the rock thanks to capital investment. Not just anyone could go mining in Tombstone. The rush of poor men had been succeeded by the parade of the wealthy. Mother Nature's lottery, which bestowed treasures on whoever happened to turn over the soil in the right place, was over.

Whiffs of hostility would re-emerge now and again, when rumours of Apache attacks were rife in the streets, or when rustlers turned up in their leather chaps, smelling of horse sweat, to defend their entitlement to disorder and despise others' fortunes while squandering their own.

The Reverend Aaron was in Tombstone until October 1881, just before the events that made the town famous – the bloody gunfight between a gang of cowboys and a group of lawmen, followed by an interminable feud, like a confrontation of mirrors that perpetually reflect a murder from one to the other.

Does the Reverend regret not having remained to witness this outcome? Not in the least, he would answer. The only part of such a scene worth remembering was the cloud of sulphurous smoke surrounding the lifeless figures lying in the dust. Once people began shooting at one another there was nothing more to tell.

✺

DECEMBER 1880

The Reverend Aaron travelled to Tombstone after the execution of the two false murderers of Charles Teasdale. He spent his days shut up in his room in the boarding house, where he had overspent his credit but which was run by a lazy fellow who feared the wrath of God. Maybe he viewed having a preacher as a non-paying lodger as a kind of investment.

One evening, the Reverend could no longer bear the sight of the floor littered with balls of paper and the permanently unmade bed. He went to the Oriental, a gambling den where it was possible to ruin yourself in respectable company. He was sitting alone at a table in the back of the room, jammed in between faro games, when Russian Bill's head, surmounted by a hat of brushed felt, stood out above all the others. Standing on a chair, the way the Reverend used to do, he cleared his throat.

"Oyez, oyez!" he proclaimed in a ceremonial tone of voice, holding a bottle of whiskey over his heart as his other hand flailed in the air like a drunken actor's. "I am enormously happy to be able to announce that I am back in Tombstone, this time for good.

I have no house anymore, and no wife. They nearly hanged me but, by God, I'm alive. I'm buying a round for everyone, even for cheaters."

The Reverend had picked up his books as soon as the first words were uttered, and was threading his way between the tables toward the exit.

"Even for you, Reverend," added Bill, pointing at him with the cork from his bottle. The Reverend put on his hat, continuing in the direction of the door.

"Come on now, when for once there's a chance of loosening your tongue. Maybe that's just what you need: to take a good swill, like everyone else."

The Reverend turned around and spoke, contrary to all expectations. "I'm sorry, Mr. Tattenbaum, but right now everyone knows that you're not as drunk as you're trying to pretend."

A few cowboys from Bill's gang burst out laughing, while the other gamblers exchanged glances.

"And you, Reverend, it's no use your going about everywhere carrying your Bible; everyone knows you're not a real preacher."

The proprietor scratched his chin and pulled his earlobe, a code telling his croupiers to be on their guard, even though the tension involved the two most inoffensive people in Tombstone.

"So, if I were a real clergyman, you'd let me leave in peace?"

"I don't know about that, but I know that if I'd died in Santa Fe, there'd have been heaps of people to bury me. But you, no one wants to kill you because you can't hold anything against a guy that never says anything and never does anything. But there'd be no one to mourn you either."

"So you want me to be like you and lie instead of keeping quiet? Let me tell you, Mr. Tattenbaum, you go on and on about your exploits, but you're probably the most tiresome person I've ever met. I truly hope that once you're dead, and the many friends you have to bury you are dead too, you'll sink into an oblivion equal to the excessive attention you'll have captured in your lifetime."

The Reverend left, and the swing doors clashed behind him. He had always tried to respect tiresome people. Among all sins, dullness had to be the most forgivable. But that evening, he had had enough. Henceforth he would be unremitting in his contempt, like a disillusioned young saloon girl who had made every effort to avoid being dragged into the business, or an animal that defecates wherever it likes to avenge being domesticated.

✳

The next afternoon the Reverend sought refuge in the Golden Eagle bar, where he mistakenly thought no one would bother him. The doctors, lawyers, and wealthy businessmen who met there already had their church and their minister. These were gentlemen who carried neither bowie knives nor revolvers, but walked using canes with carved or gold-plated handles. Governed by the laws of good society, in which speculation and corruption were the only acceptable crimes, the Golden Eagle was renowned for its quiet atmosphere.

Russian Bill, whom no one expected to see there, made a discreet entry. With his white high-crowned hat and his close-fitting jacket, it has to be admitted that the mythomaniac had been able to give himself the appearance of the gentleman he professed to be. He scrutinized the customers, skirted the obstacles as he approached the Reverend, and then set his chessboard down on the table in front of him. He threw an arm over the back of his chair and stared at the preacher without saying a word.

"I have to admit that you surprise me, Mr. Tattenbaum."

Bill lit a cigar and waved the match, with a gratified air. "I knew you'd be first to speak."

"I haven't taken a vow of silence. I've never even said I intended to say nothing. That's the advantage of silence: you can make it say what you want."

Bill began to place the pieces on the chessboard.

"I don't play," the Reverend interjected.

"I know. You don't need to play," said Bill, with a sweeping gesture, "because all this is a game for you already."

"The buffoon does have a certain flair," reflected the Reverend. He remembered the times he had told himself that people everywhere were just a source of amusement. That the whole thing was an entertainment, even when he was wounded and spending his days howling with pain and humiliation. That all these pioneers were libertines chained to their liberty, while he was a missionary who had chosen servitude. "The same for you too, I suppose," he said. "If things don't go the way you like, you can just return to the Russia of your birth, or to the refined society of the East Coast, where obviously you'll fit in better. You can leave whenever you want. The West is a theatre; you're well-placed to know that."

Bill gazed absently over the Reverend's shoulder. His cigar burned away in his hand, the smoke escaping like lost time.

"You were nobody in the East, so you need the West," the Reverend continued. "You need that kind of people – cowpunchers, rustlers, criminals."

"And you need people like me. People who surprise you." He pointed at the chessboard. "Let me surprise you, Reverend."

⁂

Russian Bill had his own box in the Bird Cage Theatre in Tombstone, where he attended performances in his tallest hat, beneath which he wore the serious expression of a music lover. On evenings when the moon was full, he would go backstage while the dancers were changing and sing them ballads praising their grace and virtue. For several weeks, he ended the night in the company of Forrestine and Valentine, two dancers originally from Storyville, whose accent evoked the marshes. He spoke to them in French, a language that all well-educated Russians mastered better than English. One night, he promised both of them his eternal love, before picking his way between the rows of the main auditorium and then going outside, where the sun was already beginning to appear.

After a few hours' rest, Bill set off to rejoin Sandy King and the Clanton gang for a fresh raid across the frontier. He returned several days later, with his pockets full and a beard growing on his cheeks. He first went to the laundry, and then to the barber to have him trim him a moustache worthy of the name. Next, wearing an impeccable suit, he went to the Golden Eagle, where the Reverend Aaron was waiting for him to play chess.

From the opening, the Reverend had given up all hope of victory, and Bill had given up all hope of holding his tongue. If they had had to wager, the respectable citizens around would have put their money on the Reverend, who seemed absorbed by the game while Bill chatted interminably and barely looked at his pieces before making his moves. Soliloquizing seemed to require his attention no more than blinking.

"I'm not accustomed to this climate. In Russia, there were walls of snow reaching to the sky. In some winters, even aristocrats like me became victims of the cold. If I was unlucky enough to be out hunting and got caught in a storm, I had to make my own trail through the snow. It was like threading your way through a labyrinth with only a single path. It seems tough, but for a Russian it's the way of life. And then, at times like that, you've no choice to make. That's the good part about surviving," he reflected.

As the Reverend improved from game to game, their contests lasted longer. Toward the end, Bill became less verbose. Enveloped by the hubbub of the other customers, the intervals of silence were prolonged, and the playful pretence of their tête-à-tête crumbled. The two men were united in a confrontation to the death that was playing out beyond the chessboard. In the end, Bill would always find something to break the tension. When they became dazed by fatigue, he would fall back on his innermost thoughts, drawing on a poetic register that never failed to distract the Reverend.

"There's nothing like a cool wind to bring tears to your eyes, not only because it makes you blink, but because it wafts in the air like a gift, a deliverance, even if it never lasts and the heat always returns, and if it's not tomorrow, it'll be next year," he once confided.

"There's nothing more pleasurable in the world than stretching out between some red rocks just before sunset, feeling the dying heat of its rays and shedding a few tears on your own fate," he confessed in another moment.

"The sound of her feet, bare on a parquet floor. An almost inaudible, muffled sound. When I heard the floor creak, but not the sound of her heels, I knew she was barefoot."

Stripped to the quick by constant upending of the sandglass, like meteors shattering in their attempt to plough the sky too deeply, Bill's words would be reaching rock bottom by the time the bar emptied.

"I'm fed up with not being able to fight. They treat me like a woman. So I have to forgo my anger, like women do, by weeping in the dark of the theatre or in the solitude of the herd. If they only knew how little fear I feel. I swear to you, one of these days I'll force one of them to come to blows with me."

"I should have kept at it from the first, until I killed someone or someone killed me. It was the same with Pearl. I should have married her from the outset. She'd have refused, but I should have seduced her. Or beaten her. Done what was needed for her to stay."

"That whore from nowhere, I should have abandoned her in Perryville."

"They take me for Sandy King's lackey. But you'll see. It'll end in a gunfight. One big sonofabitch gunfight. I know already who'll win. Often I wonder what I did to God that He heaped so many qualities on me and so few on others."

⁂

The longest of their games lasted into the early hours. Only Bill and the Reverend would be left, each dozing in turn while the other thought out his next move. They had to wriggle their jaws and open their eyes wide to dispel the impression that they had been sitting there from time immemorial.

"At West Point, we played in secret," Bill let drop. "I used to win all the time. It was almost boring. The real challenge was not to get caught by the officers."

The Reverend looked up at him. "Did you say West Point? Like the military academy?"

Bill was holding an ebony rook between two fingers and spinning it on the table like a top. In a barely audible voice, and without ever lifting his eyes from the chess piece, he told in a single outpouring that he was the son of a rich tobacco grower of Russian origin who had made so many enemies in Virginia City that he had decided to send his only son to the military academy.

"They'll try to kill us, all of us, or at least your father," my mother told me when I was eight. "He'll be dead, we'll be dead, but not you. They're not expecting you to be so well-prepared. You can't stay here; you've got to escape. You'll have to run as fast as you can and take a stagecoach out of town. You mustn't take the train, you mustn't even go near the station, for that's the first place they'll look. You have to buy a horse and saddle; you must leave immediately and ride without stopping. You mustn't rest before you reach the desert. You'll make your way from town to town, you'll sleep in people's houses. Most often on the hard ground. You'll spend nights in the open, in makeshift tents, when it's wet and windy. You'll sleep in the houses of people who are poor, halfwits, or depraved. You'll work with your hands, you'll be exhausted, confused, and ruined, but you'll have an easy mind, for you'll be far from here. You'll stay there till you're a man. Then, when you're grown up and formidable, you'll come back and avenge us. One day they'll get you, perhaps. But before then you'll have had a lot of children who'll be able to avenge you in turn, and one day they'll have children to avenge them, and so on."

He paused, and set down the castle among the other pieces he had taken. "All I wanted was to learn how to react if they came to murder me, but I'd known for a long time no one would come. So I did like everyone else, and once I graduated, I became an engineer." He sighed. "I didn't want to be an engineer. In Ohio, I was appointed head inspector. I was supposed to inspect the bridge over the Ashtabula River."

The Reverend nodded. The tragedy was still fresh in people's memories. The bridge had collapsed a few days after Christmas and a train full of passengers had plunged into the river. "You didn't exactly kill those people."

As if he heard fingers snapping, Russian Bill straightened up and began speaking aloud again, adopting his usual aristocratic tone. "Well, we won't go over that. I don't know what more I can say for you to take me seriously," he said, moving his bishop into an open space.

✳

The Reverend was awoken at midday the following day by some shots fired in the street. He had slept all morning without removing his clothes or boots. He went over to the window and drew back the curtain. Russian Bill was advancing meekly as the marshal disarmed him and shoved him in the back. The Reverend was no longer sure what had occurred the previous evening. Had he lost as usual, or had he won his first chess game? Had Bill revealed where he came from, or had the preacher imagined the whole story in a dream, dozing between moves?

He went to the marshal's office and asked who Bill had shot at. "No one," answered the marshal.

From a drawer, the marshal took the portable chessboard. The Reverend opened it on the desk. It was peppered with bullet holes, one in the dead centre of each square. "You arrested him for that?"

"For carrying and using a firearm within the town limits, which is against the rules. Even if you and your little gang don't give a damn about the rules," he shouted in the direction of the cell.

Bill was sitting on the cot with a coarse blanket over his shoulders and his hands clasped between his thighs. "It's the rules that don't give a damn about us," he retorted.

The Reverend went over to the cell and gripped one of the bars. He pushed back the left-hand tail of his coat and brought his hand to his belt. "So, Mr. Tattenbaum, which of us two was victorious last night? My memory fails me."

Bill shrugged.

"If you tell me, I'll pay your fine."

"You'll have to consult your Bible. Everything worth knowing is in it, apparently."

"So that's what the Bible represents for you?"

Bill shook his unkempt head, he who always had his hair parted so carefully. The Reverend wondered if this time he hadn't gotten drunk for good.

"I'm not going to start unburdening myself all over again. The Bible means no more to me than it does to you."

"Have I ever told you what it means to me?"

"No, but I know."

"So you're one of those people who think they know what's in a book without having read it?"

"I don't need to read the Scriptures to know they disapprove of everything I do, Reverend. I've broken my oath on them often enough."

"God doesn't bother to whisper things to you that you know already. He's God. He knows what you know and what you don't know."

"Some things should be neither known nor seen."

The Reverend pushed up the brim of his hat with his index finger. "Well, given your bitterness, I'd say you lost yesterday."

"Yes, I lost. But only on the chessboard."

"Oh, there's nothing more important than the game, Mr. Tattenbaum. I imagine you agree with me about that."

He turned his back on him and went to lay several banknotes on the desk of the marshal, who took the bunch of keys from their hook and freed Bill immediately. The two men went down the office steps side by side.

"When will we play our next game? Surely you'll find another chessboard."

Bill held his hat against his chest. "I'm leaving Tombstone for good, Reverend. I'm heading back to New Mexico. Sandy King and me, we're going to try to settle down somewhere decent. A quiet spot. Maybe I'll even find myself a new wife, who knows."

The Reverend chewed his quid of tobacco without saying any-thing, and then sniffed. "If I had let you win, would you have stayed?"

Bill pursed his lips, gazing into the distance. "It's not losing I'm bitter about. It's that after all those hours I've spent confiding my thoughts to you, you've never written a word about me. Though I should have suspected it. You did warn me, after all."

Bill doffed his hat, and turned on his heels. The Reverend watched him leave with a knot of panic in his throat – probably the kind of sudden paralysis felt by a scout who has tracked some renegade Apache for several hours and notices that the tracks in the sand peter out just as he is hemmed into a narrow pass – a man whose heart stops beating for a moment as he slowly raises his head toward the walls that tower above him, knowing that he has fallen into the trap his enemies have devised with such ease.

✳

The Reverend Aaron rushed to his room and threw the contents of his bag on the bed. His bible had been replaced by a real Bible, and his collections of sermons by actual collections of sermons. He had indeed slept during the game. He returned to the mar-shal's office, but the marshal had left. He searched Allen Street up and down, and found the marshal feeding a stray dog in front of the entrance to a nameless dive overlooking a cross street. He set one foot on the uppermost step and rested a hand on his knee. "I regret having paid that fine," he said.

The marshal, standing in the Reverend's shadow, stroked the dog between the ears and raised his head. "There's no refund for fines."

"I shouldn't have allowed you to let him go free, because now I have to ask you to arrest him again."

The marshal waved a hand in the air. "They've left town, him and Sandy King. Off to cause trouble somewhere else, I suppose. They're no longer in my jurisdiction. You'd best speak to the sheriff."

The Reverend walked to the sheriff's office, jostling the passersby as he went, yet offering no excuse. He found the sheriff surrounded by businessmen, sipping whiskey by the stove. They all began to laugh when he described his request. "Come on, Reverend, you can't be serious!"

"My whole life is in those books."

The sheriff stared at him without budging, arms crossed, while the amber liquid in his glass distorted the outline of the star pinned to his chest.

"You know how much a mule costs, Reverend? And a horse? And a whole herd of cattle like some that gets rustled these days? And a man's life, because there's some lose theirs? I'm not about to tire out my men runnin' after the only book you can be sure of buyin' anywhere. There's even been Bibles seen on the Indian reservations."

"What about my collections of sermons, that I wrote myself? You can't find them anywhere."

"I didn't know you wrote sermons. That was for another town, I reckon."

The men laughed even more uproariously. The Reverend stared at each in turn, then put his hat back on his head.

"Don't you worry about that there Russian," said the sheriff, seeing the preacher make for the door. "He's forbidden to set foot in New Mexico. They'll arrest him before he's had time to abuse your Testaments."

All my life I've convinced myself that I wanted to die in the ring because that seems more respectable. Now that I think about it, I'd rather be hanged, just to have the right to speak. That way, I wouldn't have written so much righteous crap for nothing.

TUCSON

JANUARY 1881

In Tucson, the Mexican men dressed like Americans, and the Americans married Mexican women. It was simpler that way. The women never complained that the town was too Spanish, or about the constant dirt on the floor – the inevitable part of living on a floor of beaten earth. They didn't insist that wood-frame brick houses be built for them the way American women did, so they suffocated in summer and froze in winter.

The Reverend entered Tucson and went along Meyer Street, where the blocks of adobe buildings succeeded one another in a straight line all the way to the sunset. Close to one edge of town stood a gabled house surrounded by a flower garden and wooden fence, as if the most perfect little American home had been transported thousands of miles and set down where it would be most incongruous. However, this was no family home, but a brothel owned by a woman who was reputed to be an expert on feet.

The Reverend went in and waited for the mistress of the house to welcome him. He stood bare-headed, holding his hat behind his back.

"Reverend!" she exclaimed, waving a fan before her bosom and stowing it in her cleavage as she advanced toward him. She bowed with her bottom rising up, and then brought her eyeglass closer to her face to study the preacher's feet.

"Those aren't your boots, Reverend. They're too big for you. Either you're a thief or you have a knack for getting yourself into the kind of scrape that ruins your footwear."

"Neither is the case, my dear lady. Instead, I'm an eccentric who dreams of having large feet."

The foot expert despised the impurities carried in by customers coming and going. They would enter with muddy boots, leaving long ochre tracks on the floor that she strove to keep immaculate. They threw the ancient green banknotes that stained their fingers down anywhere. They left the girls covered in filth – they who devoted hours to painting their faces, maintaining the softness of their skin and the fragrance of their pores. They entered a world of crystal vases and demolished everything in brawls that turned into battles and then riots.

"Would the Matador happen to be around these parts at present?" inquired the Reverend.

The first time the Matador had gone there, the lady hadn't liked his boots. Too noisy, smelling of wild animal, in addition to which their owner's sighs sounded like the gusting wind feared by shepherds. She had palmed off her least desirable girl on him but, contrary to all expectation, he had liked her. "He's been paying a visit to Shannon every evening for the past week," she informed him.

The Reverend gave her a dollar and then crossed the street to sit in the cantina opposite, at a table facing the rectangular opening that served as a door.

The Matador entered the brothel toward six o'clock and re-emerged shortly before seven. The Reverend stood with his back against the adjacent building, one foot flat against the wall. The Matador stopped as soon as he saw him.

"*Padre*," he answered, partly in greeting and partly as an observation.

The Reverend bowed his head. The Matador pushed his hat back and placed his hands on his waist beneath his jacket.

"I have a mission for you."

"A priest who asks for my services!" said the Matador, surprised.

"An easy mission. My Bible and sermons have been stolen. I know by whom and I know where. I'm coming to you because I don't want the guilty party to be mistreated and because I have no money to pay with."

"And why do you think I would do it for free?"

"Because they're holy books."

The Matador's moustache expanded in a smile, displaying a pair of widely spaced teeth. "They'll always be that, even in the hands of the thief."

"I don't think I could find another bounty hunter who would accept this job for the sake of God."

"For the sake of God ... You'd have better luck convincing me by speaking of our past friendship, *padre*. Find me fifty dollars and I'll get you back your books."

The Reverend waited a few days before paying another visit to the Matador. He found him in a cantina, smoking his pipe. He laid a purse on the table. The Mexican sat up.

"His name is William Tattenbaum, but everyone calls him Russian Bill. You'll find him around Charleston or Galeyville. He wears Texan spurs and calfskin boots. He spins the most tedious stories, like all cowboys, except that his aren't about cowboys. On the other hand, the insults he throws at others are completely genuine. You'd take him for a good-for-nothing, but he's more cunning than he appears."

"Usually, when people talk so much, it's to hide the fact that they don't know how to defend themselves in other ways," said the Matador. He looked up at the Reverend. "Does he know how to defend himself, this Russian?"

The Reverend sighed. "Honestly, I have no idea."

"What inspired him to steal your books?"

The Reverend shrugged. "One of my sermons. He didn't like it."

"One of your sermons! I'd like to hear it someday. Just to see if there are things I can learn by listening to someone who has listened to me for so long."

※

The Reverend knew that his plan had failed when the foot expert didn't ask to look at his shoes. Behind her fan, her face remained deadpan, her jaw locked in a hypocritical smile. "The Matador came by yesterday," she indicated. She handed him a cigarette paper which he unrolled, observing the lady, who was looking elsewhere. It read:

> Padre, since they are such sacred objects, I wanted to deliver your books into your own hands. In the name of our shared affection for high places, I will meet you at the top of the hill east of San Xavier del Bac.

The Reverend stuffed the note in his jacket pocket. "Is Shannon available this morning?"

The lady shook her head, bringing a hand to her lower back.

"Is there another girl I could question?"

"I'm sorry, all my girls are busy this morning."

The Reverend nodded, more to indicate his understanding of the situation than his approval. He settled his hat on his head. "Tell me, madam, what disappoints you most, that I am not a real minister or that you haven't been able to work it out from my boots?"

She brought back her smile, as if it were mechanical. "Goodbye, Mr. Aaron."

I dunno why he saved me, that preacher.
He knew I'd end up being hanged sooner or later.
He told me so himself.

GALEYVILLE

OCTOBER 1880

Galeyville was headquarters for the San Simon Valley's rustlers, a place where bandits could sleep on their backs, legs wide apart, snoring blithely – one of the rare places where they were not asked to part with their guns on entering town, yet the only one where they never needed them.

No signs identified the stores. Everyone knew where to find tobacco and flour, and where to greet the simpleton who was posted on an overturned railroad wagon alongside the trail to keep watch. No one knew where this wagon had come from nor, like the stones for the Egyptian pyramids or Stonehenge, how it had been pulled so far. The lookout was supposed to ring a bell when a stranger approached, in which case all the men would come out onto the street carrying their guns and yapping like dogs. "A town guarded so fiercely shouldn't have much need of the Lord," the Reverend Aaron had said to himself the only time he had ventured into it.

He had noticed, just before the village came into sight, that black scarves had been rolled around the branches of paloverde, in contrast with the trees' yellow flowers. They were probably a signal to inform wanted men that the authorities had a representative in town. Sitting at the back of the dining room, he had tasted the best turkey galantine in all Arizona, even though he suspected the cooks had spat in it.

FEBRUARY 1881

In Galeyville, the various dens of vice were so profitable that prostitutes earned a margin seldom encountered in the trade. They alone provided a living for the dressmaker and the pharmacist. During their breaks, they paraded in the streets as proud as great ladies under their custom-made hats. Rarely did one encounter whores who suffered so little from depression.

One day, one of the girls put a bullet in her head with a client's Colt, which brought the atmosphere back down to a more normal level. To raise their army's morale, the brothel owner organized a splendid ball during which the girls could flaunt themselves while keeping their clothes on for the entire evening. He knew that they loved their dresses with a passion equal to that with which customers ripped them. There was no chandelier on the ceiling, only lamps on the tables, all of which were pushed back along the walls to create a dance floor. Nor was there an orchestra, just an amateur fiddler who spat on the ground between tunes. Lit from below, the women gave the impression that their features were even more drawn than usual, despite the excess of rouge on their cheeks. The men who turned up didn't know how to dance and merely tried to grope the girls with no consideration of the setting. The few passable dancers, most of them already drunk, barely managed to whirl the girls around before heaving them over their shoulders and lifting their skirts to smack their bottoms.

Russian Bill made his way between the abused ones who slapped their partners and those who sulked in disappointment. "This isn't a ball, it's a battlefield," he complained, going off to obtain a glass of champagne that he downed in one gulp. He approached a lonely damsel whose breasts were still inside her bodice, and dragged her to the centre of the floor. He led her in a waltz, and then taught her every step of the mazurka, ignoring the inappropriate tempo of the music. Soon it was the men who were sulking on their chairs while all the girls copied the steps called out by Bill as they turned around an imaginary partner in the half darkness. One of the girls stood at the top of the stairs, too wonderstruck to step down. It was the most beautiful thing she had seen in her life. A real ball.

The Matador was in the room too, as several girls were able to testify later. Hidden in the shadow of an unlit corner, he rolled himself one cigarillo after another, deaf to the appeal of the waltz.

✳

No witness exists to the encounter that took place between Russian Bill and the Matador in Galeyville that evening. Perhaps the Matador's elegance attracted Bill's attention as he whirled with one of the girls. After all, his appearance and manners were described in the Reverend's notebooks. Perhaps Bill had slipped behind the door of his own hotel room, awaiting the arrival of his assassin. He probably thanked heaven that, seeing the door handle turn, he was able to stick his gun in the intruder's back, definitively reversing their roles.

"How is it you were expecting me?" the astonished Matador is said to have asked.

"I've been awaiting this moment forever," Bill is supposed to have answered. Perhaps he mocked the Matador by throwing the books at him one at a time with a repeated flip of his wrist, the way a horseshoe is thrown at the target. "Here's what you're looking for."

"How do you know who I am?" asked the astonished Matador.

"It's all written in there," Bill is said to have answered.

Perhaps, after an attempt at mutual assassination, the two men returned to the tavern together and drank to their shared resentment toward the Reverend.

In any case, it seems that after this brief sojourn in Galeyville, Russian Bill developed a sense of invincibility that dispensed him from his legendary need for prudence, while the Matador nourished a smouldering desire to avenge himself on his former spiritual adviser, a desire similar to what had motivated many of those who hired him.

If I've got to die, I'd rather be killed.
Let it give pleasure to at least one person.

———————————◆———————————

SAN XAVIER DEL BAC

FEBRUARY 1881

San Xavier del Bac was an old Spanish mission a few miles from Tucson. Its two white bell towers and its roofline decorated with arabesques were lashed by whirling sand and its garden was overgrown with wild cacti. Inside, bats had roosted in the nave under the opaque gaze of saintly statues. Abandoned though it was, the colonial majesty of the building, standing solitary in the immensity of the Sonora Desert, was enough to induce travellers to make the sign of the cross.

The Reverend slowed his horse and remained turning it in a circle for a long moment, as if to deaden the shock of this preternatural vision. Then he trotted off toward the butte of rocks and bushes that accompanied the church on its right, like a twin building. At its summit, a fire was burning, the yellow flames standing out against the azure sky. He hitched his horse to the mission's low wall and scaled the hill. The Matador was nowhere to be seen. The Reverend approached the brazier and squatted on his heels. His eyes were stinging, but between blinks he saw, in the heart of the embers, the charred binding of a book and pages with their edges scorched like the extremities of an ancient parchment. He let himself fall backward, spat in the fire, and rested his chin on his knees. He remained like that until nightfall. He could have escaped, but he knew the Matador too well to believe it would have been of any use.

The Reverend never heard him approach. One moment there was no one, but then the Matador appeared on the other side of the fire, his face glowing red and his dark clothes blending into the darkness. He pushed back his hat until it fell down his back, held by a cord knotted at his neck. "A magnificent spot, isn't it?"

The Reverend looked over his shoulder. The white church reflected the moonbeams, like a lighthouse for lost souls. "You're going to kill me, I suppose?"

The two men stared at the fire to avoid looking at each other. "Why did you come if you thought I wanted to kill you?" asked the Matador.

"I didn't know till I saw my books in the fire."

"So what did you think then?"

"I suspected you would open them. I thought it would renew your penchant for confession." The Reverend tore up a tuft of dry grass and threw it in the fire. "You've already killed a priest before me?"

The Matador didn't reply.

"If you must kill me, do it quickly."

"I don't want you dead."

"What do I know about it?" replied the Reverend shaking his head.

"I only kill when there's no other solution."

"So you say."

"You're talking as if I'm the liar here," pointed out the Matador without raising his voice.

The Reverend shook his head again. "So I'm a liar. What of it? You're all obsessed by the truth. The truth means nothing to me. What interests me is authenticity. Yours, for instance, in the days when I was your confessor. You thirsted after glory – a feeling you couldn't invent. The man who confided in me back then would have given anything to become a legend."

"The man who confided in you was already a legend."

The Reverend nodded his agreement. "But you weren't able to remain one. I could turn you into a killer who was once a great bullfighter. I don't understand why you'd rather remain a bounty hunter who's a nobody."

For a long moment, only the crackling of the fire could be heard.

"It's all the same to me if the people here know or don't know what I once was. I've nothing more to gain from that profession. But back there ... I won't allow anyone to tarnish the perception of what I was where I came from. Vicente Aguilar was the greatest matador in his country. I won't allow you to turn him into the bullfighter who became a hired killer. You can either write nothing and live in peace, or write and have me on your tail."

The Matador said no more.

"All right," said the Reverend. He stood up, donned his hat, turned his back to the flames, and went back down the hill in the dark, feeling the steep ground with a foot. He showed no haste to get out of the Mexican's sight, though the man could easily have shot him in the back.

✳

The next day the Reverend went to the general store to replace his destroyed notebooks. The clerk handed him a bundle of four, tied together with string underneath which a purple cactus flower had been stuck, as if it were a gift. Or as if the notebooks were the Matador's successful target.

"It's been paid for," the storekeeper informed him, "courtesy of a man who didn't want to give his name. He said you'd know."

The Reverend detached the flower and brought it to the foot expert. "Please tell the Matador he can offer it to a different victim. I've no intention of writing a word about him."

Three weeks later, the Tucson newspapers reported the deaths of Russian Bill and Sandy King in New Mexico. The Reverend headed for the railway station and bought a single ticket to Lordsburg.

"It's been paid for you already," said the ticket agent, handing it to him. The Reverend refused it and insisted on paying his fare. In Lordsburg, he got off the train and then went to the livestock wagon to recover his horse. He led it by the bridle to the main street and hitched it to the first rail he came to. He then walked to the stagecoach depot, where he reserved a seat on the next coach to Shakespeare, two miles away. The scenario he feared was not repeated. The agent pointed to the fare quite normally, without glancing at him.

"Too expensive," lied the Reverend, suppressing a smile with difficulty, and then turned away.

So the Matador had decided to leave him in peace, at least outside Tucson – unless he had guessed from the outset that the Reverend had no intention of going to Shakespeare by stagecoach when he could simply ride.

I've sowed trouble and I've reaped it. I got what I wanted. Maybe all nightmares are basically secret desires, and all desires become nightmares when they've been fulfilled.

VERMILION CLIFFS

MAY 1881

Of all the Mormons who had taken part in the Mountain Meadows massacre in '57 only one was condemned for murder. Become the scapegoat of the Church of Jesus Christ of the Latter-day Saints, John Doyle Lee had taken refuge in the irrigable zones of Vermilion Cliffs. At the confluence of the Paria and Colorado rivers he built and operated a system of ferries that allowed Mormon families arriving from Utah to cross toward the south. For those who had never known anything but the fertile plains and grassy green valleys like those cherished by the English tradition, an environment as dramatic as that of Vermilion Cliffs was inconceivable.

The story is told that one of John D. Lee's wives, when she laid eyes on the land of their exile for the first time, exclaimed, "Oh, what an isolated ravine!" It couldn't be called a desert, for water ran through it, muddy meanders and crystalline torrents sometimes side by side in the same bed. She was referring to the orange cliffs carved out as if by a knife, at the foot of which you felt you were at the gates of a Moorish castle: bare coral rock, as smooth as if polished by a sculptor, and rust-coloured earth that seemed spat from a dragon's belly. It was as if God had kept a corner of the world where He could let off steam, far from human sight.

Most of the inhabitants you encountered in these parts tried to discourage you from travelling unaccompanied. The Indians claimed that this was sacred land, the Mormons advised that outlaw bands hid in the canyons, while the outlaws warned that the region was infested with Mormons and Indians.

The Reverend Aaron crossed the Colorado River with his horse at Lee's Ferry. Armed with a pilgrim's staff, he led his horse from one dwelling to another: cabins of round logs and houses of reddish stone that melted into the background of the vermilion rocks, hillocks, and mountains, all of the same hue. He knocked at the door of each home. A woman with children would answer, but rarely a man. He introduced himself as a Mormon from Missouri looking for a sister he hadn't seen for forty years. He said he supposed that she had changed her name, but that he didn't know whom she had married, or if she was still alive. In this way, he was able to obtain lodging and look over all the young women. He claimed to be searching for the features of a possible niece, though he was really hoping to recognize Russian Bill's widow, whose picture had accompanied an item in the *Santa Fe New Mexican*.

Sometimes he followed the honeymoon trail, a road rutted by the wagon wheels of young Mormon couples heading for Utah to be properly married. Since he had changed his identity and was no longer pretending to be a preacher, he had found no trace of the Matador travelling ahead of him. At one juncture, he almost managed to believe that he really was searching for his sister, now an elderly woman, who had slapped their father and run away from home.

✳

Each of the two women lived with her children in a cabin of her own, but they would end their evenings on one or the other's porch, exchanging the day's gossip. They wore identical bonnets tied at the neck by a broad ribbon, one of them apple green and the other lavender. You would have thought them sisters, dressed by the same matron from the Great Beyond. These women, who shared a husband, had detested each other in the past, but since their man had found himself a third wife they had been drawn together by their shared hatred of the intruder.

The Reverend was grooming his horse in front of the house when he heard them talking about a Mexican with a broad hat and studded pants who had been roaming thereabouts looking for a preacher who was himself looking for a girl who was said to have been married thirty times.

"I know him," put in the Reverend.

"Which one?" inquired the woman in the green bonnet.

"Both."

The women exchanged a glance.

"The first is a bounty hunter. The second is the Reverend Aaron," said the Reverend.

"Are they dangerous? What do they want with us Mormons?" asked the second woman.

The Reverend shook his head. "Whether you're a Jew, Negro, or Mormon, for them those are just generalizations. Those people have specific targets."

"So why here? Why among us?" asked the woman in the lavender bonnet.

"Because, my poor lady, they no longer know where to look."

The two women seemed satisfied and said nothing for a while.

"They can't be very religious, then," concluded the lady in the green bonnet. "Anyone who has already found God always knows where to look. They must deserve their fate."

"What did that pastor do, that there's a price on his head?" asked the other.

"He didn't do anything. They just want to punish him for being who he is."

If he'd been in the presence of anyone else, the Reverend would have had to explain himself. But the two women said nothing.

※

That night, the Reverend couldn't sleep.

Instead of proving the Matador right, he could have turned his horse around to disprove the Matador's predictions. But the less he slept the more convinced he became that his killer would be ahead of him in everything, and everywhere. There was no possible escape, since his movements weren't being tracked but anticipated.

Long after his hosts were in bed and the other lamps extinguished, he continued filling entire notebooks, describing the fear that dwelt in him in every detail. The less he slept, the more he wrote, and the more he wrote, the less he wanted to sleep.

How did the Matador go about catching his prey? It was impossible to ask his victims, for they all ended up dead, whether by his hand or by the hand of the law. And then the questions became revelations. This was how a victim of the Matador felt. He would only have to consult himself.

By embodying his adversary, he came to resemble him. As his spiritual director, the Reverend had confronted the sinful Matador with divine justice. As a traitor and a liar, he was dragged down to the sinner's level, while the Matador was elevated to the rank of executioner. The more he pursued the Reverend to prevent him from bestowing immortality on him, the more the Reverend would make him immortal. No matter where the Reverend went, the notebooks would be filled, and he would be punished by the other.

Then, as dawn appeared, his fear would evaporate. In any case, his path was shared with outlaws, Mormons, and Indians.

✳

He first heard the sound of galloping hooves far behind him: it was an echo of urgency, a rhythm evoking the cavalry, war. It could only be a pursuer's personalized gallop, addressed to the pursued.

The Reverend first thought of Indians, showing that in daylight he didn't instinctively believe in the Matador's threat. But life is always serious, even when it mocks us. The faster the predator approaches, the more the certainty of being his prey is confirmed, and the less time remains before the capture – fatality growing exponentially. First, a moment of disbelief. Then, when the bubble of denial bursts, it is already too late. The assailant has arrived.

He received the blow on the back of his head, strong enough to knock him off his horse but not to make him lose consciousness.

Falling on his face, he tried to get up, but the Matador was sitting astride him, binding his feet. He pulled the Reverend's left arm behind his back and set a foot on it, in a victorious pose. The Reverend panted and moaned, but didn't cry out.

Then the Matador drew his sabre and chopped off his right hand.

Just before he felt the pain and lost consciousness, the Reverend heard a cry – his own, as if it had escaped without his consent.

EPILOGUE

Memoirs of a Writer Who Has Lost His Hands

SHAKESPEARE, 1881

OMAHA, 1883

"Poor child," she'd say to me. *"You think you're going somewhere. The desert is everywhere. The desert is just repetition."*

SHAKESPEARE

MARCH 1881

There were no trees around Shakespeare. No trees to burn, no trees from which to hang anyone who had to be hanged. That is why Sandy King and Russian Bill were executed in the dining room of the Grant house, which served as a stagecoach station. People say that King had a dispute with a store owner whom he had shot in the finger. Russian Bill apparently tried to flee the town on a stolen horse, before being caught by the vigilance committee. This kind of event could happen so fast.

The two men were hanged from one of the ceiling beams. Rumour has it that seeing the hour of their death approach, they had exchanged roles. Apparently Sandy King began to implore the citizens so insistently that he had to ask for a glass of water to sooth his throat after begging so much for his life. Russian Bill, in the meantime, kept silent.

Was he thinking of Pearl Guthrie's bare feet on the wooden floor? Or of the sunset shining on the flanks of the Animas Mountains? The Reverend Aaron was haunted by this question all through the meal he ate in the Grant house. The dining room was rectangular, with the tables pushed end to end to make one long table, like for the banquets held a thousand leagues from there. There were no chairs, just makeshift benches on which travellers could sit packed together on very busy days.

He was alone in the room. In his ears, the sound of his chewing and the clink of the cutlery against the tinplate dishes seemed amplified. He had given up writing about Charles Teasdale, then he had been obliged to give up the Matador. But, he decided, banging his mug down unceremoniously on the table like a fist, that he wouldn't give up writing about Russian Bill. But to do so he had to find his widow.

✴

The folks in Shakespeare recall that, the day after the execution, when the travellers who disembarked from the stagecoach entered the room, they were confronted with the feet of the two hanged men, and after the bodies were taken down by the employees of the house, their appetites did not recover as quickly as usual. They say that in Tombstone, people were shocked to learn of the death of someone as harmless and entertaining as Russian Bill.

Some swear that a few months after his death, a letter from Countess Telfrin arrived from Russia, asking for news of her son Vilgem – a story reported in certain Eastern newspapers, though the citizens of Tombstone did not grant it any credit. Indeed, neither Pearl nor the Reverend believed it either.

Many stories are still told about Russian Bill, but no one ever mentions the hundred-odd people he was said to have killed.

✴

AUGUST 1881

The second and last time the Reverend Aaron visited Shakespeare, he was accompanied by Pearl Guthrie. He had agreed to help her escape from the Peachtree, and she had agreed to become his nurse and personal secretary. He had told her that he was a preacher and needed her assistance to set his sermons down on paper. For the first time, he wasn't lying. When people saw them together, they asked if they were man and wife. The Reverend would answer, "If you were a pretty young woman like her, would you be willing to marry a cripple like me?"

Pearl had insisted on visiting Russian Bill's grave, which had been dug alongside that of Sandy King. The cemetery was at the end of the main street, on a hillside between the town and the mine. The Reverend stood some way behind her. That day, there was no wind to cover the sound of her sobs. She laid a cactus flower before the gravestone for, after all, cacti were just roses without the arsenal of seduction. All around were scattered clumps of sagebrush and prickly pear among the rocks. The Reverend contemplated the landscape, the way its colour changed with distance and with the density of the bush, its strata – taupe here, beige there, now taupe again – and the cloudless sky. How sad to lie here, he told himself, so far from his ancestors and surrounded by a vegetation that grows on no other continent. "He'd have wanted to be buried in New Babylon, I'm sure of that," pronounced Pearl. "The town has never existed, but a place that has never existed can't die."

In the guise of a prayer, she admitted that she now knew why God had refused her the only thing she had always asked of Him. All the time, she had thought she was sacrificing what was of most value by getting rid of the gold nugget, but she was mistaken. It wasn't her most precious possession. She untied the cord that closed a cloth bag and took out the box containing the last thoughts of Charles Teasdale. "Say what you like, but it's thanks to that fool that I'm here. When I think about it, I'd have wanted him to behave like Bill. And I'd have liked Bill to be a little more like him."

She sniffed, and then passed the box to the Reverend. "You're a man of God. Accept this offering."

The Reverend Aaron asked me to set down my last words on paper. That's a luxury reserved for folk who die in their beds with a mother, sister, or loving daughter at their side. I'm not one of those. When I die, it will be sudden, surrounded by my enemies and honest citizens looking forward to it – to seeing me die. I have no other last words, and no one to say them to.

OMAHA

APRIL 1883

In Albuquerque, New Mexico, the Reverend Aaron dictated to Pearl Guthrie a sermon addressed to seekers after gold who refused to confront the truth and continued to believe that riches awaited them beneath their feet. "God won't make a nugget appear by magic just because you prayed to Him the night before," he declared.

They went to the middle of the main street. The Reverend climbed on a stool, ready to preach to the crowd. He drew a breath, then shook his head and climbed down again. "I'm not ready. Not yet."

In the mornings, the Reverend, who would awake in the semi-darkness of their hotel room, had to wait for Pearl to emerge from her sleep to pull on his socks for him. Then, with the passing days, she started to get up before he did. He would find her sitting by the window, holding a closed book. The next morning, she was no longer in the room when he awoke. She was walking in the leaden dawn with her parasol over one shoulder, treading the dust of roads that led her nowhere. Then, as in every other town, the Reverend could see that it was time to pack up and leave. It was she who gave the signal, but he who announced their next destination – the next parched village to survey in his search for exceptional men.

※

In Kyle, Texas, he composed a homily reproaching those who came to settle in the West in order to flee the authorities, their enemies, or their problems, whatever they might be. "Your ghosts will follow you wherever you go," he declared. This time, the

Reverend did not even trouble to climb onto his stool. He looked at the passersby and shrugged. "These people all look respectable to me. It's not the right audience for that kind of sermon."

Pearl never complained about these evasions, but now and again the Reverend made it a point to reassure her. "Soon, my dear. We'll find you a husband soon."

✳

In Omaha, Nebraska, he composed a sermon criticizing the young who sought adventure or fame and had gone there believing that you only had to find yourself in a dangerous place to be a hero: "You were nothing back there, and you'll come to nothing here," he said. "You had the impression that your life was unwilling to begin, so you're about to continue disrupting your lives with new departures, hoping to convince yourself that the future holds something better than what you're leaving behind."

They were walking along Seventeenth Street when they came to a telegraph pole bearing a grotesque poster advertising an upcoming show. It depicted a man with an enormous white moustache, a champion's hat, and wearing a buckskin jacket with a fringe. This was Buffalo Bill Cody, famous from one end of the continent to the other and across the Atlantic, the hero of countless cheap novels. Before a public thirsting for characters larger than nature, Buffalo Bill would act his own part, embody his own myth.

"I give up," said the Reverend.

✳

The streaks of ink that stain the pages of this manuscript were made by Pearl Guthrie's tears, which she tried to contain as she set down on paper the words the Reverend dictated to her. He could order her to write whatever he wanted, but he could not force her to talk. No one will ever know if she wept because of the things she had never been able to experience, or for Russian Bill, or because she had ended up as companion to a cripple. No one will ever know at what moment everything became lost to her.

Those who choose to see divine intervention in this story are free to do so. The ways of the Lord are inscrutable, especially when they leave an author of adventure novels who claimed to be a preacher no option but to become that preacher. The Reverend Aaron would have believed this, but the author of these lines never will be entirely the Reverend Aaron. There never will be any sermon.

W. Donald Wilson

W. Donald Wilson holds a degree in modern languages from Trinity College, Dublin, where he also completed a Ph.D. in French literature. He has taught at universities in the West Indies and United Kingdom, and at the University of Waterloo. In 2011 and 2013, two of Wilson's translations were longlisted for the Best Translated Book Award in the United States. In 2013, he was a finalist for the French-American Foundation translation prize.

Dominique Scali

Born in Montreal in 1984, Dominique Scali is an author and journalist who is nostalgic for bygone eras she can experience only through research and in her imagination. The original French novel, *À la recherche de New Babylon* (La Peuplade, 2015), was published to wide acclaim and won the First Novel Award at the twenty-ninth Festival du premier roman, held in Chambéry, France. It was also a finalist for the Grand Prix du livre de Montréal (2015), the Governor General's Literary Award (2015), and the Prix des libraires du Québec (2016).